To Have His Cake (and Eat It Too)

Mr. Darcy's Tale

P O Dixon

To Have His Cake (and Eat it Too) ~ Mr. Darcy's Tale

Third Edition ~ August 2011

ISBN: 1453704760
EAN-13: 9781453704769

In dedication to my greatest inspiration...
you know who you are,
and to those of you whose views
helped to shape this tale.

...And a special thanks to Gayle

Contents

Fitzwilliam Darcy had the best of intentions towards Miss Elizabeth Bennet.

His sense of duty to his family prohibited him from offering her marriage.

His love for her prohibited him from attempting to make her his mistress.

What then, is a man of means supposed to do when he realises he cannot live without the only woman he will ever love?

~ Chapter 1 ~
Under His Protection

Darcy sat high upon his magnificent stallion, surveying his environs. What an unlikely turn of events that he should find himself in such a place. *I am a long way from Grosvenor Square.* It could not be helped. Even the slightest of chances to make up for his neglect warranted his being there that morning.

Would that I could go back in time a few months.

~ ~ ~

It had all begun at Netherfield Park, an estate in Hertfordshire and the temporary residence of his friend Charles Bingley. Over the years, Darcy had perfected the art of evading eager young women and their scheming mamas—their primary aim in life being to marry wealthy husbands. However, throughout the course of a few weeks, he had observed what he surmised as the makings of a rather predictable fate for his unsuspecting friend. Darcy had not wished to see his friend entrapped by such a scheme.

He had persuaded Bingley to leave Hertfordshire the day after the Netherfield ball. In so doing, he had prevented him from making a terrible mistake in offering for Miss Jane Bennet, an angelic beauty from the neighbouring estate of Longbourn.

Darcy's intentions had been genuine, or so he had believed. He had acted in service of a friend—at least in part. In his heart, Darcy had known he acted to protect himself; for he had believed himself in great danger of falling in love with Jane's beautiful and enchanting younger sister, Elizabeth.

Darcy had found the Bennet family, with the notable exceptions of Jane and Elizabeth, vulgar and uncouth. They had no fortune, no connections, in short, nothing to recommend themselves. All that aside, he had not believed Jane returned Bingley's affections. He had not wanted his young friend to commit to such a union.

Upon his return to town, Darcy had quickly resumed his rakish behaviour, frequenting a well-established brothel known as *Madam Adele's*, and the like, with his cousin and partner in crime, Colonel Richard Fitzwilliam, in tow.

Bingley had married a young woman of the *ton* within three months of departing Hertfordshire. While he had loved Jane in his own way, it had not been enough to overcome the pressure to marry well from his conniving sisters, Miss Caroline Bingley and Mrs. Louisa Hurst, as well as his best friend.

While on his annual trip to Kent, with his cousin Richard, to visit their aunt, Lady Catherine de Bourgh, Darcy had heard of the untimely demise of his nemesis, George Wickham. His aunt had spoken at length of the scandalous connection with the Bennets. Darcy had abruptly returned to London and hired an investigator to find out the Bennet family's fate.

He learnt that Wickham, who had briefly served as a lieutenant in the army, had run off with the youngest Bennet, Miss Lydia, and had deserted his commission. Mr. Bennet had tracked them down in a seedy part of London. Wickham had killed the elderly man under the guise of self-defence, but only after Lydia had thrown herself between her father and her dear Wickham, leaving the poor girl accidentally shot and killed by her own father. Weeks later, an enraged father had killed George Wickham. The tragic death of Mr. Bennet, a perfect stranger, had given him courage to avenge his own daughter, whom the unscrupulous Lt. Wickham compromised and jilted just months earlier.

Mr. Bennet's widow had realised her worst nightmare, the loss of her beloved home—entailed to the male line of the family. Mr. Collins, a cousin who had thus inherited the Longbourn estate, had allowed the Bennet women four weeks to leave their lifelong home. Penniless, the women had been subject to the mercy of their remaining relatives to take them in.

~ ~ ~

The private investigator had assured Darcy that SHE would be there. She came to that very park and walked that exact path every morning, barring adverse weather. The sun rising across the horizon promised a beautiful day. Darcy waited.

When at last he spotted her headed towards him from a distance, he quickly dismounted. He secured his great stallion, Maximus, and began walking towards her. Elizabeth was terribly distracted. She stood directly in front of him when she looked up, sensing she was about to collide with someone.

The dispirited look in her eyes took Darcy aback. Though still very beautiful, her eyes lacked the amazing spark that had captured his heart months ago in Hertfordshire. He bowed deeply before her and uttered, "Miss Elizabeth."

What a total surprise to see Darcy, of all people, standing directly before her. She almost forgot to curtsey. "Mr. Darcy!" she exclaimed. "What are you doing here?"

"I came to see you. I had to see you," Darcy quickly replied, more nervous now that she was standing before him.

Elizabeth's mind grappled with the thought of his being there. Genuinely puzzled, she asked, "Whatever for?"

"Please pardon me, Miss Elizabeth. I recently learned of your family's misfortunes. I came here to offer my condolences."

"Thank you, sir," she started out, "I appreciate your thoughtful sentiments more than you know."

"May I walk with you, please? There is a matter I wish to discuss with you."

In light of the impropriety of his request, Elizabeth protested, "I hardly think that would be proper, sir."

"Please allow me this," Darcy implored. Reluctantly, Elizabeth gave her silent consent and began walking with him. Darcy considered what he might say with some deliberation. Elizabeth waited and wondered in silence.

"First, how are you and the rest of your family? I pray you are well."

"Indeed—very well, in light of the circumstances," she replied. Her curiosity begged, "Sir, how did you know to find me here?"

"I confess, I hired a private investigator to learn the facts, once I heard of your family's misfortunes. I cannot help thinking that it is my fault."

"Your fault? Whatever do you mean? Surely, you are not responsible for my younger sister's actions."

"I, more than anyone else, knew what Wickham was capable of, yet I shared that knowledge with no one in Hertfordshire. I left you and your family completely exposed to that villain."

"Mr. Darcy, as much as it pains me to say this, all that knew Mr. Wickham, admired him, while you, however, were not at all liked by anyone. Please pardon me sir, but who would have believed you? Especially given everything you did in bringing about his circumstances."

"There is no telling what falsehoods he may have spread against me. The point is that everyone believed him because I did nothing to refute his allegations. Though I had the proof, I chose not to use it because I was more concerned with my life and that of my family, with no consideration at all for yours. For that, I am very sorry. I would like to make amends."

"There is nothing to be done. The past months have been very hard, indeed, but we have moved beyond that, and have begun to move forward."

"How so, if I might ask? What has become of your family?"

"Well, as I am sure you already know, my family no longer resides at Longbourn. It is now the home of my cousin, Mr. Collins, and my dear friend Charlotte. Mama, Mary, and Kitty are living in Meryton with my Uncle and Aunt Phillips."

"And Miss Bennet?"

"Jane has accepted employment as a governess in Scotland, caring for two small children," she admitted, as her entire demeanour changed to one of sombre and deep regret.

Darcy observed her discomfort. It saddened him to see her thus. "I am truly sorry to hear that, Miss Elizabeth. What are your plans? Do you intend to stay here in town?"

"Actually, I am seeking a position as a governess, as well," Elizabeth quickly responded with an air of enthusiasm she did not truly possess. "I do not wish to burden my uncle and aunt. Like Jane, I intend to use my earnings to help support our family in Meryton," she concluded in a slightly subdued tone.

"I understand your wish to help support your family. However, your willingness to work as a governess is of great concern to me. While I know nothing of Miss Bennet's situation, I know enough to understand that working as a governess is not always ideal."

In her frequent letters with Jane, Elizabeth was acutely aware of her sister's situation. While Jane had not experienced physical harm, her situation was tenuous. Elizabeth knew he was right and suspected he may have sensed her unease. She covered by saying, "If Jane is willing to make the sacrifice for our family, then surely I can do no less."

"What if you do not have to? Miss Elizabeth, I have always admired your wit, your intelligence, and your kindness. I would like to offer you the position as a companion to my sister, Georgiana." Up until that moment, Darcy had never considered such a scheme. It suddenly seemed the perfect remedy.

Elizabeth immediately thought back to Wickham's harsh description of Miss Darcy. Although she hated him, he was her only source of reference on Miss Darcy, other than Caroline Bingley. Elizabeth responded, "I doubt she would look upon me favourably, based upon all I have heard."

"You have yet to meet her to judge for yourself. I dare say you will find her a dear sweet young lady, greatly in need of female companionship."

"Are you offering to employ me as her governess?"

"No, of course not. She is far too old for that. In fact, she recently celebrated her eighteenth birthday. She is coming out this Season. You would be her companion."

"What does that entail?"

"You would come to live with Georgiana and me. You would accompany her wherever she goes during the Season, and you would simply spend time with her. I know she would benefit greatly in having someone like you in her life, especially now, when she is coming out. She is so lacking in confidence. She is dreading the upcoming Season. As an older brother, there is little I can do to help ease her concerns. Her current companion, Mrs. Annesley, is advancing in years. She is not what Georgiana needs most at this time in her life. Besides, Mrs. Annesley has advised me of her plans to retire at the end of the Season. The timing is perfect."

"But I would have to move into your home, Mr. Darcy. Have you forgotten that we do not get along very well? You barely tolerate me, and I do not like you."

"Please tell me what you really think, Miss Elizabeth," Darcy said, barely suppressing his amusement by her impertinence.

"You know it is true. Why, during our last dance at the Netherfield ball, we argued during the entire set."

"I recall it as our first dance, and yes, I do remember our rather heated discussion; but I have always admired you for your courage and willingness to stand up for your convictions. You do not have to decide this moment. I wish for you to meet Georgiana first, and then make your decision."

"Do you intend to bring her here to Cheapside to meet me?"

"I would like to send my carriage to bring you to my home. Shall we say this afternoon?"

After giving the matter some thought, Elizabeth responded, "I will agree to meet Miss Darcy this afternoon; however, I cannot promise you anything more. Besides, I am certain she will not approve of me."

"I have mentioned you to Georgiana several times in my letters from Hertfordshire. I know she looks forward to meeting you. Why do you insist she will not like you?"

"Though it pains me to say this, Mr. Wickham told me that she is arrogant and aloof, much like you."

"Miss Elizabeth, please allow me to explain the history of Wickham's dealings with my family. It will help you better understand Georgiana and me, as well as Wickham's motivations." Darcy led Elizabeth to a nearby park bench to sit as he recounted his family's painful history with Wickham. He discussed how Wickham was a favourite of his father's, so much so that his father placed him on a near equal footing with Darcy. He told her the painful truth behind Wickham's lies that Darcy had denied the living bequeathed to him by the late Mr. Darcy. The truth was that Wickham had refused to take orders and had demanded the value of the living instead. Having wasted the entire sum of three thousand pounds, settled upon him in lieu of the living, Wickham returned to Pemberley and attempted to persuade Georgiana to elope, only to abandon her once he learnt he would never receive a penny of her inheritance of thirty thousand pounds.

Elizabeth was a mixture of emotions by the end of Darcy's account. She was deeply saddened for Georgiana and embarrassed by her own bias against Darcy due to her belief in Wickham's lies. His willingness to share such intimate details of his life struck her emotionally. His revelation proved to lift a heavy burden from her heart, and she became far less inclined to think badly of the Darcys.

"Thank you for sharing your story with me. Poor Miss Darcy."

"That is why I feel responsible for what Wickham did to your family."

"I do not hold you responsible."

"Thank you for that, but allow me to make it up to you still. Meet Georgiana and consider accepting the companion position. It will be an advantageous proposition for everyone. You will be able to help your family while retaining your respectability as a gentlewoman, Georgiana will thrive under your influence, and I will be happy knowing you are safe and under my protection."

~ ~ ~

Elizabeth allowed Darcy to escort her back to the Gardiners' home, though he declined her invitation to come inside to meet her aunt. She thought about all that had happened during her morning walk. She eagerly shared all but the personal details of the Darcys' dealings with Wickham with her aunt. With no hope of obtaining work as a governess any time soon, and having been with the Gardiners for months, Elizabeth knew there would be unenviable consequences should she accept Mr. Darcy's offer of employment. *What choice do I have? I have determined to embark upon a life in servitude. Either I accept the offer before me as Miss Darcy's companion where I surely will be required to attend balls, private dinners, and the like whilst in mourning, or I continue to pray that a situation as a governess soon presents itself.* She knew full well that society might frown upon either of the two choices; but at least she would have the means to aid in support of her mother and younger sisters and make them less of a burden to the Philipses. *In the end, it is the financial support of my family that matters most.*

Elizabeth soon secretly began to wish things would go to her advantage that afternoon. Although she was reluctant to let her guard down completely with Darcy, she admired his behaviour as well as his openness with her. Of course, he was just as haughty and arrogant as she remembered him from their days together in Hertfordshire, but she would not let that affect her decision. Though he would be her employer, and she would be living in his home, subject to his authority, she would be spending the bulk of her time with Miss Darcy. Elizabeth doubted she would see much of Darcy at all, except during meals, if then. As she continued to mull over his offer, she could not help but ponder his words…*that she would be under his protection*... and wonder what he meant.

~ ~ ~

Elizabeth stood at the window, looking up and down the street. Everything remained the same as the last time she had done so, just ten minutes earlier. Returning to her seat, she resumed where she left off in her book. *This is not helping. Why in Heaven am I this nervous?*

Of course, she knew the answer. She had thought of little else since her chance encounter with Mr. Darcy. *Chance encounter.* Elizabeth considered the meeting barely warranted such an account. *He planned it. The proud Mr. Darcy! Mr. Darcy, who looks at me only to find fault, went out of his way to meet me to offer to make amends for what could hardly be his fault. What is he about?*

Elizabeth's curiosity could hardly be contained by the time of her arrival at Darcy's grand town house. Not only did he send an impressive landau to bring her to his home, but he also sent a lady's maid to accompany her, as well.

The open and inviting air of his home defied Elizabeth's expectations. She had thought surely the proud man lived in a cold and forbidding house that fit his haughty and disagreeable nature. *This makes two surprises in a single day.* She only imagined what might be next.

The austere butler, as proud in appearance as his master, promptly escorted her to an elegant room. There, she espied Darcy standing before a pianoforte, listening as a lovely young lady played a beautiful sonata.

The butler formally announced, "Miss Elizabeth Bennet." His resounding voice captured the Darcys' attention. The young lady immediately stopped playing and hurried to Elizabeth, such was her enthusiasm. Darcy had spoken of little else the whole morning other than Elizabeth's pending arrival. Georgiana had looked forward to the meeting with sheer delight, such was her eagerness to meet the woman who so had impressed her brother.

She stated excitedly, "Miss Elizabeth!" Darcy quickly abandoned his spot to join his sister in receiving their guest.

Darcy bowed. Then, he graced Elizabeth with the most beautiful smile, marking the first time she could recall seeing him thus. "Miss Elizabeth, please meet my sister, Miss Georgiana. Welcome to our home."

Elizabeth curtseyed. "Thank you very much. It is nice to meet you, Miss Darcy. I have heard so much about you."

Georgiana returned the curtsey. "And my brother has told me so much about you. It is a pleasure finally to meet you. Please, call me Georgiana."

"Very well, but then you must call me Elizabeth."

"Elizabeth, will you join me in a duet? My brother says you play very well."

Elizabeth laughed. "I would be happy to accompany you, but prepare yourself for disappointment. You see, I play rather poorly, and I never take time to practise."

"Oh, but my brother never lies. He always tells the truth," Georgiana said as she glanced up at her now embarrassed brother.

Darcy interjected, "I said 'quite well.'"

"Well then, quite well is not *quite* very well," Elizabeth teasingly responded. "Come, Georgiana, what would you like to play?"

Darcy remained with the young ladies for a quarter of an hour before excusing himself to work in his study. He wanted to allow them to become better acquainted in privacy. He promised to join them for dinner.

Elizabeth and Georgiana continued to play for a short time before venturing to the drawing room to have tea. Outside the music room, Georgiana reverted into a shy and timid young woman. Elizabeth sought to regain some of the exuberance she had witnessed earlier by regaling Georgiana with tales of her family and friends back in Hertfordshire. Elizabeth found Georgiana not at all like her brother. The young woman appeared exceedingly agreeable, even if a bit shy. A perfectly charming creature indeed. Elizabeth wondered at how easily persuaded she had been to think badly of Georgiana only a few months earlier. Soon, the two engaged in a bout of laughter and earnest conversation, much to Darcy's surprise and delight, upon his return to escort them to dinner.

Mrs. Annesley joined the three of them. Once again, Elizabeth witnessed a reversion in Georgiana's conduct to timidity and shyness. Elizabeth was not sure if the change was due to Mr. Darcy's presence or Mrs. Annesley's. She viewed it as a challenge to find out. She clearly sensed that Georgiana was profoundly in need of younger female companionship. Aside from the time Georgiana had spent away at boarding school several years earlier, she had spent her entire life without the company of females of her own age.

After dinner, Darcy remained in the drawing room with the ladies for a while before inviting Elizabeth into his study for a private interview. In deference to Elizabeth and for the sake of propriety, he left the door opened. He invited Elizabeth to take a seat at his desk; he did likewise.

"I do not mean to pressure you into a decision, but please tell me what you think? Is the position as Georgiana's companion one you will consider?"

"I like her very much. I have decided that if the two of you want me, I would like to give it a try."

"Excellent. When can you begin?"

"As soon as you would like, I think. However, what consideration will be given to Mrs. Annesley? Will she be agreeable to sharing her responsibilities?"

"Please do not worry about that. While Mrs. Annesley remains with us, I expect her to continue as before, as much for your benefit as for Georgiana's. She has years of experience navigating the *ton*, and you will learn from her. We already have discussed her new responsibilities, and she has agreed that it is for the best."

"When shall I begin?"

"You must name the date. If left to Georgiana or me, it would be today."

"As I will be leaving my uncle and aunt's home to live here, it will take a couple of days to pack my belongings and say goodbye."

"I will arrange to have your belongings packed and delivered. You need only to say when."

"Oh no, I cannot allow you to go to so much trouble on my behalf. Surely, you do not go to such lengths for all your employees."

"I take my responsibilities very seriously. You will find that I am a very generous employer. Besides, as Georgiana's companion, you should expect many indulgences. Georgiana will insist, and I never deny her anything that I have the power to bestow."

~~~

As she rode along in the elegant landau for the third time in as many days, the happenings on the street barely warranted her notice. Deeply engrossed in her thoughts, Elizabeth pondered her odd turn of fortune.
~~~

The life she was now embarking upon represented a complete diversion from the life she had envisioned for herself. For as long as she could remember, Jane and she had shared a romantic dream to meet one day and fall in love with their own versions of Prince Charming and live happily ever after. Thus, her refusal to marry her odious cousin, Mr. Collins. Not that she had refused him solely on the grounds that she did not love him —*the man was an idiot!* Elizabeth knew if she had it to do all again, her choice would remain the same. An odd turn of fortune—indeed. That *idiot* now inhabited her beloved childhood home.

She felt most unfortunate in having to embark upon a life of servitude. Oddly enough, at the same time, she felt somewhat fortunate in having escaped a life of servitude in the home of strangers—beholden to people wholly foreign to her. She reckoned if she must make her own way in life, what better way than to spend all her time in the company of the delightful Miss Darcy. The two young women bonded immediately. Elizabeth's fondness for Georgiana easily outweighed her discomfort with Mr. Darcy.

Mr. Darcy. Elizabeth recalled how he had behaved during the earliest days of their acquaintance. His unguarded comment to his friend Charles Bingley that she was not handsome enough to tempt him, might just as well be stamped upon his forehead. However, it was the way he always had stared at her at Netherfield Park, that bothered her most. Back then, she was Miss Elizabeth Bennet of Longbourn—the brightest jewel in the country. *Those days are long past—never to return.* Merely thinking of that time in her life brought tears to her eyes. Tears that refused to shed. Elizabeth rarely thought about those matters long enough for that. She quickly focused her attention upon the rich colours that surrounded her, the carriage's velvet window shades and lush cushions—the elegance that now typified her life.

She smiled. *It could be worse. I might be Mrs. Collins.*

Georgiana enthusiastically escorted Elizabeth to her apartment. She cajoled Darcy into allowing Elizabeth to reside in the family wing, in a large apartment directly across the hall from her own, and just down the hall from his. His acquiescence thereby set Elizabeth apart from everyone else in his service, including Mrs. Annesley.

In keeping with his pledge to deny Georgiana nothing, Darcy agreed to the scheme. He weakly protested to her on the spectre of impropriety, but not enough to persuade her to change her mind. How could he tell his young sister how he truly felt about Elizabeth? That he found her more desirable than any other woman of his acquaintance, and he wanted nothing more than to have her share his bed each night for the rest of his life. He could never admit that to anyone. Besides, it was not as if he ever planned to act upon his desire. He admired Elizabeth too much to do anything that would compromise her. He would never possess her physically, except in his dreams. What stirring dreams they were!

Aside from residing in the family wing, Elizabeth was delighted to learn that she had been assigned her own lady's maid, Hannah. Having shared a single maid with all her sisters while growing up, Elizabeth could not have been more pleased.

It surprised Elizabeth to see all her belongings already put away, so quickly upon her arrival. As Georgiana opened the doors to Elizabeth's wardrobe, both observed how few gowns she owned and how ill prepared she was for her new life. Even though in the latter period of mourning, her clothing was hardly befitting that of the companion to Miss Darcy during her coming out Season.

Georgiana said, "Fitzwilliam scheduled an appointment with my modiste Madame Lanchester to prepare new gowns for you to wear for my coming out this Season. In the meantime, you can select from among my wardrobe. We are about the same size, and your maid may make any adjustments."

"Both your brother and you are far too generous. I am quite certain that I can get by with what I already have until I can afford to buy my own things."

"Oh, but you cannot. You must understand how important perceptions are amongst the *ton*. I expect you to accompany me everywhere. You undoubtedly must personify your part. I insist."

"But Georgiana, I do not wish to burden your brother or you."

"Elizabeth, you could never be a burden to either of us. Fitzwilliam scarcely cares what I spend at the modiste. Come to see for yourself," she urged as she pulled Elizabeth across the hall into her apartment and opened the doors to her closets to reveal her wardrobe. Elizabeth beheld the most expansive selection of beautiful gowns she had ever seen in her entire life. Georgiana explained that most of them were new. When Elizabeth declined Georgiana's invitation to choose from among the collection, Georgiana pulled her forward and began selecting ones that suited Elizabeth's mourning state. It pleased Elizabeth to see that they had similar preferences, understated and tasteful. Once satisfied with their selections, the two young women and Elizabeth's maid commenced adjusting the gowns so that Elizabeth could wear one to dinner.

Darcy had remained long enough to greet Elizabeth upon her arrival, before he made himself scarce for the rest of the day. It seemed he had failed to consider the ramifications of having the woman he loved, but could never have, living in his home and sleeping just down the hall from him, night after night. Just the night before, the erotic dreams he first experienced at Netherfield during Elizabeth's short visit to nurse her sister Jane to health, revisited him with a passion. His pristine sheets bore unmistakable evidence of his restlessness, and she had not even yet moved in.

Darcy had risen early that morning and gone out for fencing practice. He had needed to work off his abundance of pent-up energy before Elizabeth's arrival. Once Georgiana and Elizabeth had parted his company to get Elizabeth settled into her apartment, Darcy had given in to his aching need and had gone to see Antoinette, a beautiful French courtesan, who had only arrived at Madam Adele's establishment a week of so after his return from Hertfordshire. Having amazingly beautiful eyes, she bore a striking resemblance to Elizabeth.

~~~

Though unquestionably of age, Antoinette had been an innocent when introduced to Darcy. Darcy had to possess her. He had worshipped her body, as he imagined he would have done with the woman of his dreams. Once he had taken her, no other courtesan would do. He had made arrangements with the proprietor to have her serve him exclusively, with no concern for the costs.

Darcy initially had visited the establishment when his own father, the late Mr. George Darcy, had taken him there at the young age of eighteen, along with his cousin Richard. In his youth and inexperience, Darcy had been reluctant to engage in such activities. Richard had encouraged the endeavour. As an older cousin, Richard had wielded a certain amount of influence over Darcy back then. Over the years, Richard and Darcy had continued to frequent the establishment; the former relying heavily on the latter's generosity to finance his indulgence. Be-
~~~

fore meeting Antoinette, Darcy generally had preferred at least three other courtesans; it had not bothered him at all that they were also favourites of Richard. Much to Richard's chagrin, no one else, not even him, had been allowed to patronise Antoinette.

Darcy had spent the whole day with Antoinette in an unrelenting effort to quench his desire for the one woman he could never have. Upon returning home, he heard the pleasing sounds of laughter spilling from the music room. Georgiana and Elizabeth took turns enjoying the pianoforte. With each possessing such widely varying talent, the two young women delighted in entertaining one another with playful renditions of their favourite works. Darcy quickly escaped upstairs to his apartment to call for a bath and refresh himself before joining his sister and her companions for dinner.

He immediately noticed how Elizabeth looked. She never had appeared more attractive to him. She wore a well-chosen lavender gown with black trim, and Hannah had arranged her hair, especially. Darcy also noticed the incredible spark in her fine eyes that had captured his heart while in Hertfordshire, returned once more. He fought the urge to stare at her, as had been his wont in Hertfordshire, finding it was all but impossible. Darcy struggled not to show any notable regard for Elizabeth. He focused his attentions upon Georgiana; otherwise, he said little to anyone. His most telling comment to Elizabeth was to remark on how lovely she looked. He then immediately paid the same compliment to Georgiana.

After dinner, he remained with the ladies long enough to enjoy the duet that Georgiana and Elizabeth had practised during the day. He then quickly excused himself, citing his intention to go to his club. Of course, he had no intention of going to White's. Instead, he went back to visit the enticing Antoinette.

~~~

Elizabeth stood outside the closed door of Darcy's study. Her light taps gone unanswered, so she applied slightly more force. Darcy was relaxing in a comfortable chair, in front of the fireplace, daydreaming of her. It had taken a few moments before he realised there was someone at his door. When he finally opened the door, it startled him to find the object of his dreams standing before him. She never had sought him out before, despite having resided in his home for over a week.

"Miss Elizabeth, I am sorry I took as long to respond. You knocked so quietly, I barely heard you."

"Sir, I do not wish to disturb you, but there is a matter I wish to discuss with you. I can return later."

"No, please, come in. You are welcome to seek me out at any time," he said, as he stepped aside to allow her to enter the room. Leaving the door open for the sake of propriety, he admired her from behind as he followed her towards his desk and offered her a seat. He settled into the chair behind the desk.

"What would you like to discuss, Miss Elizabeth? I trust you are happy here."

"Yes, I am very happy. Georgiana is such a delight."

"I am glad to hear that."

"Pardon me sir, but are you certain this arrangement suits you? I know we are not exactly friends, but other than dinner, we rarely see you. I hope I am not the cause of your frequent absences from your home."

"No, not at all," he lied, "I simply want to give you two a chance to bond without hindrance from me."

"And we have sir. As you know, tomorrow is my day off. I plan to visit my relatives in Cheapside. Georgiana has asked if she might go with me," she stated tentatively.
~~~

"Miss Elizabeth, of course you are welcome to visit your relatives at any time, and not just on your days off, as long as you take the Darcy carriage and are properly escorted by your maid. Georgiana, however, is not allowed to accompany you to Cheapside."

Her temper rising, but attempting to remain cordial, Elizabeth responded, "I thank you for the offer of your carriage. If you insist, I will do as you ask, but please tell me why Georgiana may not accompany me, especially under the conditions you recommend for me?"

"I do insist that you are properly escorted always, regardless if it is a walk in the park, a trip to shop, or a visit to Cheapside. However, I decide where Georgiana goes and what she does. I am not in the habit of explaining my decisions to anyone."

"So, it is proper for Georgiana to associate with me, but not with my relatives?"

"Miss Elizabeth, you are a gentleman's daughter. In that sense, you and Georgiana are equals. In addition, I admire and respect you, and I see what a positive influence you are for Georgiana. However, my sister has never socialised with tradesmen. Unless I decide otherwise, she never will."

Elizabeth defiantly asked, "And what about the Bingleys; their father earned his fortune in trade, did he not?"

"Again, I am not in the habit of explaining my decisions, especially as regards the care of Georgiana. Is there anything else that you wish to discuss?" Darcy asked tersely, clearly signalling his intention to close that particular line of conversation.

Angered by his condescension and what she supposed as his attempt to dismiss her, she replied, "No, Sir!" Elizabeth wanted to escape his presence immediately. Darcy had other ideas.

"I have a matter to discuss. Georgiana and you have yet to visit the modiste. Is there a particular reason for this delay?"

"Surely, you must know I have no intention of abusing your generosity. Georgiana has given me over ten new gowns already, and while you may have a problem saying no to her, I have no such affliction."

Shocked by her remark, Darcy demanded, "This is MY wish as much as it is Georgiana's. It is very important you do not fight me on this, Miss Elizabeth. In under a month, the Season begins, and Georgiana will be coming out. A whirlwind of activities will ensue, and there is little time left to prepare. I have gone to considerable lengths to reschedule the two of you with Madame Lanchester in two days hence. She already knows what I expect, and I insist upon your full cooperation. Do I have it?"

"Yes, Sir!"

"Thank you, Miss Elizabeth."

"Is that all, Sir?"

"Yes…for now," Darcy uttered, as Elizabeth rose from her chair, inwardly fuming on account of his heavy-handed treatment. She retreated without another word. As she silently stormed out of his study, Darcy called out, "Good day, Miss Elizabeth."

Darcy was simply unable to stand as she quitted the room. He felt the danger of his strong desire for her. It had been months, since she or anyone else, for that matter, challenged him so. He found her impertinence unfathomable, given their respective roles as employer and employee. At the same time, he found her intoxicating. It delighted him to see she had not lost her fiery passion, despite her many setbacks. He wished she had slammed the door as she stormed out, at the very least. That way, he could address his pressing need without leaving his seat.

Darcy thought that since Elizabeth brought his frequent absences to his attention, she might actually look upon his company with favour. He resolved to spend more time at home, less time at his club, and far less time in Antoinette's company.

~ *Chapter 2* ~
An Uncanny Resemblance

Darcy eagerly awaited Georgiana's coming out, perhaps even more so than she. There were many places he wanted to take Elizabeth and things he wanted to show her. However, until Georgiana was officially out, the entertainment options for the three of them were few.

Darcy accompanied Georgiana and Elizabeth to the modiste as planned. For the sake of decorum, he did not stay. He gave Madame Lanchester detailed instructions on what he expected. With Georgiana's coming out, Darcy thought it likely that she might be obliged to wear up to five or six outfits a day. While he did not expect Elizabeth's wardrobe to be as extensive nor as elegant as Georgiana's, he knew she would need far more than the gowns she had received from his sister. Little did he know or even care of women's fashions. However, he knew that perception was everything amongst the *ton.* He did not want Elizabeth disparaged as she had been in Hertfordshire, by the Caroline Bingleys of society.

That evening, Darcy had the pleasure of escorting Georgiana and Elizabeth to Matlock House. Lady Matlock was anxious to complete the final preparations for Georgiana's coming out ball, as well as her presentation at court. She had only arrived in London the day before from her country home in Matlock. Though this was their first meeting, she felt she knew Elizabeth already, based upon Georgiana's letters. It did not take long for Lady Matlock to discern the changes in Georgiana. She appeared more composed and self-assured. Her Ladyship attributed the improvements to Elizabeth's influence.

Lady Matlock epitomised elegance and social grace. Her standing and reputation amongst the *ton* was impeccable. She was as intolerable of those outside her circle as was Darcy. She barely tolerated the Bingleys. She often berated Darcy on his association with the young man and especially his sisters. Darcy was no more forthcoming with his aunt than he was with anyone else in explaining his friendship. As regarded Elizabeth, Lady Matlock decided she would accept her as more than Georgiana's paid companion, but as Georgiana's friend. Lady Matlock suspected the two young women would probably be inseparable over the coming months, and she would give her support of Elizabeth amongst the *ton*, to the extent it was necessary.

Lady Matlock, affectionately addressed as Lady Ellen by those closest to her, loved that Darcy entrusted to her the undertaking of Georgiana's coming out. She had been like a mother to Darcy and Georgiana over the years following the death of their mother. She cared for them as much as she cared for her own two sons, Lord Robert and Richard. It seemed her highest priority up to that point had been to promote a suitable match for Darcy from amongst the most eligible and beautiful young ladies of the *ton*. After four years with no success, she was determined that this year would be the one to see a new mistress at Pemberley.

While it was widely known throughout the family that her sister-in-law Lady Catherine de Bourgh and her late sister-in-law and Darcy's mother, Lady Anne Darcy, desired a match between Darcy and Catherine's daughter Anne, Lady Matlock did not support that notion. Neither did her husband, the Earl of Matlock. To their way of thinking, Anne was a poor choice for Darcy. If they had their way, a union between the two would never come about. Luckily, Darcy gave no indication he would honour his late mother's wish that he and his cousin marry. On the other hand, he gave Lady Catherine no cause to believe he would not.

Lady Matlock hosted a dinner party that evening, to which she invited the Ruperts, along with their beautiful nineteen-year-old daughter, Miss Theresa, in keeping with her intention to promote a match between Darcy and a fair lady of the *ton*. She was a stunning young lady beaming with grace and charm, who, like so many others in the highest circle, had her heart set on one eligible man, Mr. Fitzwilliam Darcy of Pemberley.

Theresa's coming out had been during the previous Season. Although she had many aspiring suitors, she spurned all advances. She longed to capture the one man who sought most not to be captured. With her eye on the prize, she decided it best to bide her time. Though they were of the same sphere, she had yet to find herself in the path of the incomparable Mr. Darcy. Other than events hosted by Lord and Lady Matlock, he rarely attended social gatherings.

Moreover, for any lady to stand a chance of garnering his notice, she must be in his esteemed aunt's favour. If Lady Matlock approved of the young lady, she would make every attempt to promote a match with Mr. Darcy. During Theresa's first Season, she was not among Lady Matlock's choices. Steadfastly, Theresa had endeavoured to gain favour with her Ladyship over the past months. Her efforts appeared to have paid off; hence, the inclusion of her family at dinner that night.

Familiar with his aunt's tactics, and not at all averse to playing along for the sake of appeasing her, Darcy heaped considerable charm and attention upon Miss Theresa. That night, he had a second purpose in "wooing" her. He meant to see if he could cause Elizabeth to become jealous. As conflicted as he was over his motive, he wished to find out if she held him in any special regard.

Prior to the Ruperts' arrival, Darcy had become incensed with the amount of attention his cousin Richard had lavished upon Elizabeth. He was silently outraged that Elizabeth had seemed to enjoy it.

Richard was enamoured of Elizabeth's charms from the moment of their introduction. He found it unbelievable that Darcy had engaged such a beautiful young woman as Georgiana's companion. Her uncanny resemblance to Darcy's favourite courtesan did not go unnoticed by Richard either, and he began to suspect Darcy's motives. *No wonder I have not received an invitation to Darcy House over the past weeks.* Richard wondered if Darcy might be lusting after Georgiana's companion and using Antoinette as a substitute to satisfy his carnal desires. He decided to test the waters by flirting with Elizabeth whilst observing Darcy closely to see how he reacted.

Initially, Elizabeth was impressed with Richard, but she soon became leery of his attentions, so much so that her distress was apparent to Lady Matlock. Elizabeth's intention was to make a favourable impression on her hosts, and here Richard was with his incessant attentions. Lady Matlock took pity on Elizabeth. She told her to overlook her charming son, and to consider him harmless. Her comments eased Elizabeth's unrest considerably. The last thing she needed was to have anyone imagine she was aspiring to a match beyond her sphere.

Elizabeth always had been strong-willed and independent. As ever before, her courage always rose at any attempt to intimidate her. However, she had gained an altogether different perspective over the past months. She no longer thought and behaved the same as in Hertfordshire. The truth of Mr. Wickham had affected her sensibilities; she had thought he was the best of men when they first had met.

The suddenness of her family's change in circumstances also had affected her profoundly. She now was responsible to help support her family. She would forever be a gentleman's daughter, with all due respect, and she would always comport herself as such, but she had witnessed her family thrown out into the hedgerows, destitute. While she would have cared not how society viewed her, as Miss Elizabeth Bennet of Longbourn, the scandal brought upon her family's honour through her late sister's actions loomed considerably.

Meanwhile, Darcy was accomplishing both of his aims. Though he escorted Georgiana to the dining room, he sat with Miss Theresa. He spoke with her, almost exclusively, throughout the meal. After dinner, he sat with her and offered to turn the pages, as she exhibited on the pianoforte. Elizabeth was exceedingly puzzled to see Darcy engaging with a woman in such a fashion. He was charming, attentive and not at all disagreeable. Elizabeth had heard that he could be pleasing when he chose, and particularly among those who were his equals in consequence, but she never had expected to see him behave thus. She became oblivious to Richard and his attentions as she focused upon Darcy. Darcy could discern the effect of his efforts to woo Miss Theresa. Lady Matlock was ecstatic and filled with hope, and Elizabeth seemed a bit jealous. If not jealous, she was certainly affected.

Richard was baffled. Granted, though he was used to Darcy's exhibiting such behaviour during his mother's matchmaking dinners, he had never observed Darcy carry it to that degree. He knew Darcy was about as interested in Miss Theresa as he was in any other woman he had wooed during his mother's dinners, but there was something different about this night. The last straw was added when Darcy stood to accompany the Ruperts to their carriage at the end of the evening, and offered Miss Theresa his arm. That was a first! Richard quickly abandoned his seat beside Elizabeth and joined the departing guests.

As soon as the carriage had driven off, and they had returned inside the house, Richard cornered Darcy and demanded an explanation. "What was that all about?"

"What do you mean?" Darcy asked as he smugly brushed invisible lint from his sleeve.

"You were all over Miss Theresa! Why, she is not even your type."

"I was simply performing for Lady Ellen, as always. You know that," he replied with a smirk.

"Well, she was not the only one who noticed you. Miss Elizabeth was clearly distracted. Were you trying to make her jealous?"

"Why would you suggest such a thing? And speaking of Miss Elizabeth, she is off-limits to you."

"Who are you to dictate?"

"She is under my protection. She is not to be toyed with by the likes of you."

"Under your protection, you say. Pray, is she quite safe from the likes of you?" Richard hurled the insult back at Darcy. More than just cousins, the two men were as close as brothers, as well as the closest of friends. In essentials, they were cut from the same cloth, although somehow, one always thought of the other as the worse of the two.

Darcy declared, "She certainly is. Miss Elizabeth is a gentleman's daughter. Still, she has no fortune and no connections, nothing to tempt *you*. And unlike you, I know not to offer false hope and raise expectations in penniless young women."

"You are one to talk. Merely bringing her into your life, your intimate circle, and your home, is likely to raise her expectations."

"Nonsense."

"As for her safety in your home, tell me you have not noticed her striking resemblance to your latest courtesan."

Darcy chose to ignore his cousin's assertion. Rather, he declared, "Miss Elizabeth is perfectly safe with me. I assure you. Just make certain you do not cross any lines with her." With that, Darcy walked away from his cousin and returned to the drawing room to gather Georgiana and Elizabeth for their departure.

~~~

Darcy had ambivalent feelings about his discovery that Elizabeth was not indifferent towards him. He was in love with her after all, but it was destined to be an unrequited love. Darcy was ever aware of his duty to his family, to Pemberley, and to his legacy. He further resolved that though he could not share his life with Elizabeth as his wife, he certainly would not dishonour his love for her by offering to make her his mistress. However, as Georgiana's companion, he would share his life and his home with her. That would be enough for the time being. He knew he was selfish and self-centred, but it did not matter. His greatest fear was that Elizabeth would meet and fall in love with someone else. He did not wish to think about it at that time, but rather deal with it when and if that day ever came.

Elizabeth was particularly troubled by her reaction to Darcy's display. What had happened to the arrogant, haughty, and disdainful man she had so despised in Hertfordshire? This Mr. Darcy was charming, handsome, and desirable. She was well on her way to finding him even less repulsive, perhaps
~~~

even somewhat attractive. She knew nothing beneficial would come from an attraction to her employer. She also knew not to concern herself ever much. Despite his newly exhibited charms, he was still Mr. Darcy, arrogant and self-absorbed.

Very few words passed between the occupants of the Darcy carriage on the way home from Matlock House that night.

~~~

Elizabeth arose long before sunrise the following morning. She longed for her solitary rambles, as was her habit in Hertfordshire. That morning in particular, she desperately needed her freedom. She had awakened abruptly from a dream of Darcy a couple of hours earlier, and she had been unable to return to sleep. In her dream, Darcy was charming, amiable, and considerably attentive; but instead of devoting his efforts towards Miss Theresa, he lavished all his attentions on her.

Elizabeth dressed quickly, hoping to escape the house before anyone else stirred. Hyde Park was a short distance away. She was sure she could enjoy a short stroll and return undetected. She almost ran into Darcy on her way out the door.

"I say, are you going somewhere, Miss Elizabeth?"

"Yes, I need a walk in the fresh morning air. I am on my way to Hyde Park," she replied, as a matter of fact without a hint of remorse at being caught leaving.

"At this hour? Unescorted, I must add. It simply is not proper," Darcy condescended.

"Sir, you are hardly one to talk about propriety," she sharply retorted, observing his clothes as the very same as the night before.

"I... well... I seem to have lost track of time... my club," Darcy fumbled for a reasonable explanation. While it was true
~~~

that Darcy had begun the evening at his club, that was not where he had come from. Elizabeth did not need to know that.

After giving him a look of disbelief, Elizabeth said, "No disrespect intended; I simply need to go out for a few moments of solitude."

"You thought to go out at this hour of the morning without an escort, Miss Elizabeth?"

"Going out with an escort hardly allows for solitude."

"I said you are to be accompanied always when outside my home."

"I will NOT be dictated to!" she insisted as she balled her tiny fist and stamped her dainty foot.

Resisting the urge to chuckle at the petite young woman on the verge of a tantrum, Darcy said, "Yes, you WILL be. You, young lady, will do as I say. Wait for me in my study. I will escort you myself."

A short time later, Darcy returned to join Elizabeth. He was freshly bathed, clean-shaven, and dressed in more casual attire. He appeared so youthful and innocent that Elizabeth almost forgot how riled she was over his heavy-handed treatment.

As they walked along in silence, Elizabeth continued to fume. She refused the offer of his arm and gave her best effort to outpacing his long strides. Darcy slowed his pace considerably to let her walk comfortably ahead of him and enjoy a leisurely stroll. *What a woman!* Darcy thought. Amid the quieting blend of crisp air and peaceful, early morning sounds, her ire gradually melted away. She relaxed her pace and allowed him to walk beside her. She glanced up to study his striking profile as they walked along, and she allowed herself consciously to consider that he was an extraordinarily handsome man.

She finally ended their silence. "Sir, I do not mean to challenge you, but why do you always insist upon having things your way?"

Here, Darcy considered his words carefully. "As master of Pemberley, I am responsible for hundreds of people. I have been my own master for many years. I find it easier to follow my own counsel than to rely upon the opinion of others. I know you are fiercely independent, but you will accustom yourself to it."

"What makes you think I want to do that?" she asked defiantly.

"Miss Elizabeth, I admire you very much. Georgiana is as happy as I ever recall having you here, and so am I. I want you to be happy, as well. You are under my protection. I am responsible for your safety, and I take my responsibility very seriously. I could not forgive myself if something happened to you while you were out and about in London on your own."

"Mr. Darcy, I am all grown up. I can take care of myself."

"I think not. This is not Meryton, Miss Elizabeth. Believe me when I say that London, even Grosvenor Square, can be a perilous place for a gentlewoman. Please trust me and do as I ask."

"You mean, do as you say," she challenged.

"Of course, is that not what I said?"

Endeavouring to turn the tables on her smug escort, Elizabeth asked, "Might I ask, do you often stay out all night... at your club?"

Darcy could not believe she had the audacity to ask him such a question. He silently chastised himself for his carelessness; he never had expected Elizabeth or Georgiana to be awake at that hour. He had forgotten Elizabeth was such an early riser. Though caught, he was not about to discuss his late-night activities with her. He simply replied, "No. Any other questions?"

"Yes, what does one do all night in a club?" she implored. She could not resist baiting him.

"A gentleman might do any number of things in his club all night."

"Come now, Mr. Darcy. You must attempt to be more forthcoming than that."

"For Heaven's sake, Miss Elizabeth, as a man of eight and twenty, this is hardly a proper conversation to have with a young lady."

"Please humour me," she urged.

"Only if you promise never again to attempt to leave our home unescorted." Darcy reckoned he might as well get some reward for the uncomfortable discourse.

"I promise. Now tell me at once, for I am a very curious creature," she persisted.

"Gambling... high-stakes. It is not unusual for games to last all night."

"So Mr. Darcy, is that what you were doing... high-stakes gambling?" she probed further.

"That is enough questions, young lady."

Impulsively linking her delicate hands through Darcy's accommodating arm, prompting him quickly to cover them with his own, she asked, "Then, what shall we talk about? We must have some conversation. I am so enjoying this early morning stroll in the park."

"Far be it from me to suspend any pleasure of yours. Since we are not in a ballroom, what say you we discuss books? I trust you are taking full advantage of the library in Darcy House," he said, recalling how she had refused to discuss the topic of books during their dance at the Netherfield ball.

"Truly, I am. Still, I imagine it is nothing to the library at Pemberley."

"You are quite right. I cannot wait to show it to you."

"I can hardly wait to see it. When will that be?" she asked enthusiastically.

"Once the Season ends—we will spend the summertime at Pemberley. I trust that meets with your approval, madam."

"Far be it from me to question any decision of yours, Mr. Darcy," she mocked, giving rise to Darcy to laugh aloud.

"Wonderful," he cheerfully expressed, "and when we are at Pemberley, I give you leave to walk as far as your legs will carry you, unescorted."

"I shall hold you to that."

The conversation quickly turned to books of philosophy. Darcy guided Elizabeth to a spot where they could enjoy the sunrise as they chatted amiably. They were so engrossed in their conversation that it continued as they returned home and well into breakfast, when Georgiana and Mrs. Annesley joined them.

~ *Chapter 3* ~
None of the Benefits

Over the next couple of weeks, a plethora of activities ensued in preparation for Georgiana's coming out ball and her presentation at court. Georgiana and Elizabeth spent most days with Lady Matlock, either at Matlock House or Darcy House.

Lady Matlock's fondness for Elizabeth grew more each day, as she continued to observe the astounding transformations in Georgiana. Lady Matlock often spoke to Georgiana about her obligations to the family as regarded the upcoming Season. More than anything, she encouraged Georgiana to enjoy the Season and all that it had to offer. She counselled her against suffering any pressure to make a match. There was plenty of time for that.

Darcy, on the other hand, was a different matter. Her Ladyship was determined that he should make a match soon, that very Season if she had any control over the matter. Lady Matlock had grown weary of Darcy's blithe bachelor behaviour. She bore her son Richard's conduct far better than she did Darcy's. Being a second son, Richard did not bear the same responsibilities as Darcy.

It was also essential that Richard marry extremely well. He needed to wed a woman with her own fortune, and a sizeable one at that, if he had any hope of maintaining the style of living to which he was accustomed. Lady Matlock did not promote matchmaking schemes for him. Heaven forbid that she be perceived as mercenary.

Lady Matlock was well aware that both men had reputations as rakes, though no evidence existed to support such notoriety. She was pleased no rumours of mistresses, allegations of adulterous behaviour, or compromising of innocent young women were connected with either of them. Lord Matlock would not have tolerated such recklessness. It was distressing enough that his eldest son and heir was known to keep a mistress. Lord Matlock did not want Darcy and Richard to follow Lord Robert's example. He suffered serious anguish over the knowledge of their patronage of the brothel. To that day, he blamed the late Mr. Darcy for his role in introducing the young men to such a place. Despite its widely held practice and acceptance as appropriate conduct for gentlemen of their circle, he firmly believed that if Darcy and Richard were not such long-standing patrons, they both might have chosen a wife from among the eligible women of the *ton* years ago.

Every time her Ladyship attempted a matchmaking scheme for Darcy, she found the initial introduction gratifying. The greater the young woman's beauty, the more he would seem to fancy her. The last dinner with Miss Theresa Rupert left Lady Matlock hopeful that she might be the one. Lady Matlock made sure to invite the Ruperts to the dinner party to celebrate Georgiana's presentation at court.

~~~

The day of Georgiana's presentation was in a word—*perfect*. Lady Matlock was entirely pleased. The dinner party did not go as she had planned. Her Ladyship was disheartened as she witnessed Darcy's aloofness towards Miss Theresa. He acted as if
~~~

he had never met the young lady before. He greeted her kindly, but as an indifferent acquaintance. He remained no more cordial to her than if she were a stranger.

Elizabeth watched the callous scene playing out before her eyes. She was far from amused. She hardly believed the level of indifference Darcy demonstrated towards Miss Theresa. She could not help but be concerned for the young lady as she witnessed Darcy's neglect and inattention to Miss Theresa's charms. She felt a pang of sympathy. She was so bothered, she even remarked upon it to Georgiana.

"I wonder what your brother is about this evening. He behaves as though he does not know Miss Theresa."

"Oh, Fitzwilliam—that is his way. He never looks at any woman more than once. He says he does not want to raise their expectations," she commented nonchalantly.

"I find it incredible that anyone can go from one extreme to the next in but a matter of weeks," Elizabeth said.

"You will see," Georgiana replied.

Elizabeth was not at all pleased with Georgiana's casual remarks about her beloved brother. To top it off, Darcy was being distant with her, not at all as he behaved when the two of them were alone. They often spent hours discussing books, art, and even politics. Elizabeth began to wonder if she would ever meet the true Mr. Darcy, that intriguing man of whom she only caught fleeting glimpses.

Richard expected Darcy to behave as he did towards Miss Theresa. Over the years, the two of them had perfected that game. His role that night was to focus his attentions upon Miss Theresa… *to lend a shoulder for her to cry on, metaphorically speaking*... to ease the sting of Darcy's rejection. The two men believed that was the best way to encourage the lady to abandon her pursuit. Lady Matlock recognised this pattern in their behaviour towards young women. She was appalled.

Lady Matlock viewed Darcy and Richard to be as thick as thieves. After the death of Lady Anne, the two began to spend almost all their time together before Richard went off to school. Apart from each other, they were not inclined towards mischief; when they were together, there was no telling what the two would get into. As a loving mother, she doted on the two of them. Though, she could not decide which of the two was the worse influence upon the other—Darcy with his vast wealth and willingness to finance their escapades, or Richard with his devil-may-care attitude and zest for life. She often chided them on their callous behaviour. In the end, they always suggested she should stop playing matchmaker. That would never do. She was determined to see Darcy marry well. She persisted in her matchmaking schemes. Darcy and Richard continued to play the game.

As Theresa sat in her family's carriage upon their departure from Matlock House, she silently recollected the events of the evening. Exasperated, but far from put off, she reckoned that if Darcy thought he could trifle with her in one instance and dismiss her in the next, then he had much to learn about her strength of determination. It was merely a vexatious setback, for the Season had just begun. Besides, she was still in Lady Matlock's favour and would continue to be put in the path of the elusive Mr. Darcy.

~~~

As beautiful as Georgiana appeared the night of her coming out ball, Darcy thought Elizabeth was even more so. Of course, it was Georgiana's night. Darcy wished it to be one of her most memorable.

Darcy, Georgiana, and all of their Fitzwilliam relations stood together in the receiving line to greet their guests. A large
~~~

number was expected to attend, including the Bingleys, to Lady Matlock's dismay. That Bingley had married a young lady of the *ton* did little to recommend him to her Ladyship; he still had those two sisters, Caroline and Louisa, and his hapless brother-in-law, Mr. Hurst.

Bingley's party arrived amongst the first guests. Once inside the ballroom, Charles noticed Elizabeth and soon approached her.

"Miss Elizabeth," he said as he bowed.

"Mr. Bingley," she responded as she curtseyed.

"Allow me to introduce my wife, Lady Grace." Both women curtseyed as Bingley continued, "Lady Grace, Miss Elizabeth and I met when we both resided in Hertfordshire." Turning his attention towards Elizabeth, he continued, "It has been so long since I last saw you. Not since November, I think. You look very well. Darcy told me of your dear father and youngest sister. Please accept my condolences."

"Thank you for your sentiments, Mr. Bingley." Changing the subject she said, "It is so nice to see you again and to meet your lovely wife. I see that your sister Miss Bingley is here as well."

"Indeed, she is here. Even now, where I go, so too my dear sister goes," Charles remarked absent-mindedly. He immediately coloured, having had time to consider the implications of his words. Of course, he loved his younger sister despite his greatest wish that she would follow his example and marry. What Charles wanted most was to inquire of Elizabeth's sister, Miss Bennet. How could he do so and maintain propriety?

After a few moments, Bingley and his bride focused their attentions upon the arriving guests. Elizabeth quietly observed Lady Grace. She had a warm and pleasing countenance, although nothing about her compared to Jane's beauty. Lady Grace appeared to give justice to her name; she was graceful, pleasant, and kind. Elizabeth wondered how she fared with her new sisters.

Although titled, Lady Grace's family was severely lacking in funds when Bingley and she married. Her eldest brother, upon inheriting the family's grand estate, quickly gambled away all but their homes, including Lady Grace's dowry. The family needed money. After three Seasons, she had not received an offer of marriage. Caroline Bingley was ecstatic when she learned of the family's situation. She surmised that a marriage between her brother and Lady Grace would suit both families. The Bingleys would gain highly sought connections, and the family of Lady Grace would receive much-needed funds. Caroline did all she could in encouraging the union.

Elizabeth also detected a change in Bingley. He was amiable as ever, but he lacked the jovial attitude that had defined him while in Hertfordshire. She wondered how she could have been so wrong about him; even Jane had said he was not as affected as Elizabeth professed him to be. Elizabeth had been convinced of his affections for Jane. Then he had abruptly left Hertfordshire and married another woman shortly afterwards. She recalled his once saying, *"Whatever I do is done in a hurry; and, therefore, if I should resolve to quit Netherfield, I should probably be off in five minutes."* She had thought him to be joking! Often she wondered if her family's fall from grace might have been the reason behind his decision not to return for Jane. Elizabeth recalled when she had written to tell Jane of Bingley's nuptials. It had been the hardest letter to compose that she ever had written.

The sounds of the orchestra signalling the start of the first set interrupted her reverie. Darcy opened the ball with Georgiana. He danced the second set with Lady Matlock, and the third set with his cousin's wife, Lady Elise. Once having fulfilled his obligation to dance with all of his female relations, he sought to spend a portion of the evening in Elizabeth's company. She welcomed his approach with a warm smile.

"You are much in demand, sir. I confess that I find it a bit of a surprise that you would take a break from the festivities to sit with me."

"I am sorry I have neglected you this evening," he offered in jest, smiling at her temerity.

"Oh, do not worry about me. It is Georgiana's night."

"Yes, thank you for being here for her tonight. She possesses great confidence and self-assuredness. I owe it all to you."

"You are too kind, sir."

"No, I am quite serious. I do not know what we might do without you, and, by the way, I will always worry about you."

"Perhaps Georgiana will meet and fall in love with her future husband tonight. We would find out soon enough how you would manage."

"Heaven forbid! I hope for at least two Seasons before I have to see her go."

"I thought you hated society and looked forward to retiring to Pemberley."

"Why is it that you think I hate society?"

"Mr. Darcy, I am aware of Lady Matlock's intentions for you. Why, every single woman here seems enamoured of you," she teased, waxing poetic.

"Not *every* single woman, I fear," he whispered in her ear, after leaning forward subtly, sending involuntary chills throughout her body.

Though his intimacy caught her entirely off guard, she quickly recovered, "Name one."

"Never mind that. Tell me, are you enjoying yourself this evening? I have observed more than a few gentlemen admiring you."

"Yes, I am. Everything is incredibly beautiful. Georgiana is amazing."

"She is stunning, and so are you. I shall be quite busy turning gentlemen callers away."

"Turning away callers for Georgiana?"

"For the both of you."

"Why would you do that?"

"I am not looking forward to losing either of you," he confessed, further confounding Elizabeth. Darcy remained by her side for the rest of the set, albeit in silence. Darcy was pleased with the awareness that she was not entirely immune to his charms. Elizabeth knew not what to think.

A short while afterwards, Darcy escorted Elizabeth to Georgiana. She was standing with Lady Matlock, Mrs. Rupert, and Miss Theresa.

Lady Matlock said, "Dear Fitzwilliam, here is our Miss Theresa. I trust you are available for the next set?"

"Yes, of course, Madam. Mrs. Rupert, Miss Theresa," he bowed and offered his arm to the young woman. "Miss Theresa, may I have the next set?"

"It will be my great pleasure, Mr. Darcy." The slightly aggrieved female did her best to make a convincing show. The fact of the matter was that she had her heart set upon dancing the supper set with him. That way she would have been sure to have his undivided attention for a large part of the evening. Alas, she would have to wait until supper to engage him, for he voiced not a word to her during the entire set.

A scrumptious supper was served at midnight. Elizabeth was surprised to be seated on one side of Darcy, with Georgiana seated on the other. Lord and Lady Matlock were seated at the table also, along with Miss Theresa. It appeared her Ladyship had not given up. It slightly vexed her seeing Elizabeth seated next to Darcy. Having directed Darcy's housekeeper on the seating arrangements, Lady Matlock placed Miss Theresa at Darcy's side. She certainly did not place Elizabeth at their table. Nevertheless, there was nothing to be done about it. Unbeknownst to Lady Matlock, Darcy also had spoken to his housekeeper about the seating arrangements.

Fortunately, the table setting was conducive to interaction among everyone. Lady Matlock endeavoured to direct Darcy's attentions towards Miss Theresa throughout the meal by engaging the young lady in conversation about her many accomplishments. Elizabeth reflected on how Miss Theresa seemed to meet all of Darcy's prerequisites of being a truly accomplished woman, including the improvement of her mind by extensive reading. Despite his aunt's best efforts, Darcy would not be tempted. Unless Miss Theresa asked him a direct question, he did not speak to her. When he chose to respond, his answers were terse.

As before, it astounded Elizabeth to see Darcy exhibiting such indifference to the uncommonly beautiful and polished Miss Theresa. Even she was impressed by her list of accomplishments and thought it no wonder Lady Matlock was so eager for Darcy to court the young woman. Exasperated by Darcy's behaviour, Elizabeth decided to challenge each of his curt responses to Miss Theresa; even if it meant confessing to opinions that were not her own. What a challenge it would be, Elizabeth considered. Miss Theresa barely acknowledged her. She was as dismissive of Elizabeth as she was solicitous of Georgiana.

Seeking once again to gain his attention, Miss Theresa said, "Mr. Darcy, Lady Matlock tells me you recently acquired a first edition of *The Mask of Anarchy*. The author, Shelley [1],is one of my favourites; I would love to see it."

---

1 References to the poet and his works are included for entertainment purposes only. No historical accuracy is intended.

"Indeed, it is a treasure," Darcy replied. Elizabeth slightly creased her right eyebrow. She thought to herself, *What sort of answer is that? She asked to see it!*

"I am especially interested in his thoughts on the role of government," Miss Theresa continued.

After a few moments, when it became clear that Darcy did not intend to respond, Elizabeth said, "I find his views prophetic. It causes me to wonder if he is clairvoyant."

Darcy nearly choked on his wine. Elizabeth and he had just debated that topic earlier in the week. Elizabeth argued the author's views were archaic. The fact that she was so clever and extremely adept at arguing opinions that were not always her own was an immense source of pleasure to him. He could not resist her taunt. He responded, "There are some who would argue that his views are antiquated."

Elizabeth feigned astonishment. "Who would argue such an opinion? What say you, Miss Theresa?"

"I beg your pardon, Miss?" Theresa asked, pretending not to know Elizabeth's name, whilst pondering why Georgiana's companion sat at their table, next to Mr. Darcy no less.

"Elizabeth," she replied, pretending unawareness of the deliberate snub. "I asked if you agree with Mr. Darcy that Shelley's views are antiquated." Darcy shot Elizabeth a look that read, ***Stop it, young lady!***

Finally, Miss Theresa responded, "Mr. Darcy, if you believe that, you and I should best discuss another subject."

Darcy looked at the young woman as if she had grown a third eye. Refusing to take the bait, he resumed speaking with Georgiana.

After a long moment of awkward silence, Lady Matlock persisted. "Miss Theresa, what is the name of the poem you mentioned last week?"

"*Laon and Cythna*, your Ladyship."

"Yes, of course. Fitzwilliam, I believe you are an authority on that topic, as well."

"Is that true, Mr. Darcy? It is rare to meet someone who shares my passion for the Ottoman Empire. I would love to discuss it with you."

Darcy ignored Miss Theresa, so Elizabeth intervened again. "Mr. Darcy, I recall having heard you mention that you met the author while at Cambridge. I am sure Miss Theresa would be interested in hearing of your experience."

"I doubt that Miss Theresa would find it interesting, Miss Elizabeth."

"On the contrary, Mr. Darcy, I find anything you say enlightening."

Darcy briefly glanced at Miss Theresa, and then returned his attentions to Georgiana. Elizabeth decided to give up. Darcy was determined to ignore Miss Theresa, and there was nothing to be done for it.

After supper, the ballroom festivities resumed. Elizabeth resolved to enjoy the rest of the night and not give another thought to Darcy's rude behaviour towards Miss Theresa.

Later, the Bingley sisters joined Elizabeth and Georgiana, thus providing the first opportunity for Elizabeth and Caroline to interact since their last meeting at Netherfield. Elizabeth easily surmised that Caroline disliked her as much as ever before.

"Miss Elizabeth, my brother Charles tells me you are residing here at Darcy House, as Miss Darcy's companion. I had no idea," she condescended.

"Yes, it is true. We have been together for over a month."

"I trust you are enjoying your *place*... pardon me, your position," she derided, in a caustic manner, reminiscent of her conduct in Hertfordshire.

Georgiana responded, "Of course, she is. Having Elizabeth here with my brother and me is the best thing to have ever happened to us."

"My dear Miss Darcy, did you just say, your brother?" Caroline bristled, wondering what Georgiana was insinuating. While she had not failed to notice Darcy's admiration of Elizabeth when they were all at Netherfield, she thought surely he had gotten over his infatuation now that they were back amongst society, at least she hoped he had.

"Yes, Elizabeth is very important to both of us."

"How nice for you," Caroline retorted. At that moment, Darcy joined the group and requested the next dance with Caroline. As Darcy escorted her to the dance floor, she turned back towards Elizabeth and smirked.

Elizabeth was surprised to see that Caroline was as possessive and solicitous of Darcy as ever she was in Hertfordshire. Now knowing what she did of how he behaved in society, it dawned upon her that Darcy treated Caroline only slightly better than he treated Miss Theresa. Elizabeth perceived Caroline as even more preposterous than before. After so many years, Caroline still had no idea of Darcy's indifference towards her.

The last guests departed in the wee hours of the morning. Georgiana was alert and vibrant during the entire night, no small feat considering it was her initial coming out in society. Indeed the night was quite memorable. She was so excited to discuss everything that she dragged Elizabeth into her apartment to talk.

Georgiana went on and on about the guests at her coming out ball. Some she already knew through her family acquaintances, but there were many in attendance she had never met. She expressed her utter delight over the prospects for the upcoming Season, particularly her pleasure for her aunt's encouragement to enjoy herself. Georgiana intended to do just that. She was overjoyed that Elizabeth would be there by her side every step of the way. If she could change anything about the evening, it would certainly be the inclusion of one particular guest.

"I must apologise for subjecting you to Miss Bingley. She was absolutely dreadful."

"You must not apologise for Caroline's behaviour. I am afraid she simply does not like me. She never has, and I doubt she ever will."

"Had I known, I would have insisted that she not be invited."

"That would have meant that her brother Charles might not have attended."

"I imagine you have a point. I like Mr. Bingley very much. He is very kind, nothing at all like his sister. His wife seems very pleasant."

"Indeed," Elizabeth remarked. "She seems too good to be true. She brings to mind my own dear sister Jane."

"Elizabeth, if only Miss Bennet could have been here tonight. I know how much you miss her. I wish to know everything about her."

Elizabeth reflected upon the irony of Georgiana's remarks. Indeed, how different her life might be if Jane and she were still together. Instead of discussing such matters with Georgiana, she shared an account of their stay at Netherfield while Jane was convalescing, without getting into details of Mr. Darcy's disagreeable comportment. The two young friends talked until dawn.

~~~

Darcy rose early that morning, as was his habit. He breakfasted
~~~

alone and then went out to train with his fencing master. Upon his return, he was surprised to find that neither Elizabeth nor Georgiana was about, especially given the lateness of the hour. He sought out Mrs. Annesley to inquire of his sister, but she too was nowhere to be found. Darcy decided to go to Georgiana's apartment to check on her. He knocked. Upon receiving no response, he entered. Darcy was surprised at what he found. The two people he loved most in the world were asleep upon Georgiana's bed. Darcy quickly exited the room. He never expected to find Elizabeth there. Recovering from the vision of Elizabeth sleeping peacefully, her dark hair spread all over the pillow, he thought she was even more beautiful in her sleep than he ever had imagined.

No callers were received that day. He let them rest.

Much later in the afternoon, Darcy summoned Elizabeth to his study. He desperately needed to see her, to spend some time alone with her, and he devised the perfect excuse.

Elizabeth softly knocked at his opened door and walked over to his desk. She curtseyed and stood before him, "You wished to see me, sir."

"Yes, please have a seat," he said as he stood to help her in her chair. He then walked over to close the door. Elizabeth thought to herself, *He never closes the door when we are alone in his study.* Darcy returned to his seat behind the desk.

"I want to discuss last night. I am not pleased with your behaviour at supper."

"My behaviour?"

"Yes, you were baiting me deliberately on the subject of Shelley."

"Sir, pardon my saying, but sometimes you are so obtuse. I feel it is YOUR behaviour that reflects poorly."

"In what regard?"

"In the way you treat Miss Theresa. At first, you overwhelm her with your charms. Then, the next time you see her, you behave as if she does not exist. Are those the acts of a gentleman?"

"You do not understand what it is like for me to be sought out constantly by every mama with a single daughter."

"Poor Mr. Darcy," Elizabeth chided.

"What would you have me do, Miss Elizabeth? I have asked my aunt to stop her matchmaking schemes. She will not listen. It has become a game."

"Perhaps it is a game to you and your chum, Colonel Fitzwilliam. I assure you, it is not a game to the young lady. It is cruel and adolescent. Better that you should remain arrogant and taciturn from the start, than to engage the young lady's hopes."

"Miss Elizabeth, I will not have this conversation with you."

"You asked me here to discuss my behaviour at supper. I am only telling you how I feel."

"Yes, what was I thinking?" he bemoaned as he massaged his raised eyebrow. Darcy expected Elizabeth to challenge him, but he certainly had not planned for her to berate him.

"Fine, if you do not want me to bait you, as you say, then stop being so ridiculous! Your aunt likely will continue her matchmaking attempts, but that does not stop you from playing your malicious games." With that she left the room.

Though amazed at Elizabeth's audacity in criticising his behaviour, Darcy knew she was right. While it never bothered him before what others thought of his callousness, he did not want Elizabeth to think badly of him. He promised himself that he would no longer play such games, ever again.

Upon deeper consideration of all that Elizabeth said, Darcy pondered his circumstances. *All of the chastisement of a wife with none of the benefits...*

~ Chapter 4 ~
No Such Promise

As the Season steadily progressed, Darcy's possessive attitude with respect to Elizabeth became increasingly evident when she started to attract the attention of other men. Although Darcy strongly believed he could not have Elizabeth, he certainly did not intend that anyone else might. His constant fear was that another man would recognise her worth and steal her away from him. He knew he was being selfish and absurd. Still, he worried ceaselessly.

By and by, Elizabeth discovered that a potential suitor had appealed to Darcy, asking if he might court her. Without speaking with Elizabeth first, Darcy had flatly told the gentleman that Elizabeth was not interested. Matthew Clennan was a handsome man, kind and amiable, and at least twelve years her senior. In appearance, he might easily be taken as a more mature likeness of Darcy himself. He owned a modest estate in Devonshire. He had called on the Darcys on several occasions and had always been engaging. Elizabeth had soon suspected he fancied her. Though she had liked him very much, she had not been attracted to him. As she was not the sort of female to torment a respectable man, she had sought not to encourage him into thinking they might be anything more than acquaintances.

Upon learning of Darcy's interference, Elizabeth was so angry that she stormed into his study and demanded an explanation. Darcy confirmed her accusations that indeed, he had spoken with the gentleman on her behalf. Elizabeth was livid.

"How dare you? You owe me an apology and your promise not to interfere in my affairs again!"

"I owe you an apology?" Darcy echoed, thinking he had done her a great service. "Whatever for, might I ask? I watched Mr. Clennan and you carefully, and was persuaded you were not interested. Was I mistaken, Miss Elizabeth? Are you favourably inclined towards Mr. Clennan?"

"No, I am not. That is not the point. The point is that I decide, NOT you."

"Miss Elizabeth, you are a young maiden, living in my home, and under my protection. It is honourable and expected that would-be suitors speak with me of their intentions towards both Georgiana and you."

"I am NOT your younger sister!"

"Clearly," Darcy uttered, exasperated at having to account for his actions. First of all, Georgiana would never question him; but most importantly, he was in love with Elizabeth and spent nearly every waking hour thinking of her, not to mention his nights.

"Mr. Darcy, I cannot prevent anyone from coming to you to speak of their intentions, but do not presume to speak for me. I am nearly one and twenty. I speak for myself," she insisted, now directly before his desk, tightly clutching her small fists at her side. Elizabeth stood her ground. "I demand an apology and your promise to desist!"

Darcy loved to see Elizabeth lose her temper thus. Deciding to provoke her even more, he raised himself from his chair. Leaning forward with his hands resting on the desk, he said, "I do not apologise, and I will make no such promise."

"Insufferable man!" she furiously shouted, as she spun around upon her heals and stormed from the study, slamming the door on her way out.

Elizabeth was upset. She wanted desperately to rush out of the house, unescorted, for a long, solitary walk and a much-needed breath of fresh air. However, the last thing she desired was another confrontation with Darcy. Instead, she raced upstairs to the privacy of her apartment. She needed to think. *Why must he be so controlling, overbearing, and stubborn?* In truth, Elizabeth was disinterested in Mr. Clennan, as well as any of the other gentlemen she had met over the past weeks. Inexplicably, every man she met, she compared to Darcy. Whereas the gentlemen were amiable, sensible, and always did their best to flatter her ego, their discourses failed to stir the same passion she felt when she carried on conversations with Darcy. Though she was certain she was unaffected by him, she was sure that she desired passion in a relationship. Still, Darcy's interference infuriated her. *It is understandable that he should make such decisions for Georgiana, but why is he interfering in my felicity and chances for happiness?* she asked herself.

Soft knocks on the door abruptly halted Elizabeth's reflections. Georgiana spoke quietly outside the door. "Elizabeth, may I come in?" Elizabeth collected herself and invited her friend inside. Georgiana hastily approached Elizabeth and warmly embraced her. "Elizabeth, are you terribly annoyed with Fitzwilliam? I overheard you when you left his study. He has remained closed off in there, and you have been tucked away in here, ever since."

"I am sorry, Georgiana. Your brother and I have never gotten along very well."

"Please have patience with Fitzwilliam. He greatly admires you. He only wants what is best for you, for all of us. I could not bear it if a misunderstanding between you two results in your leaving us."

"Georgiana, you must not worry about that. I will be here for you until you march down the aisle, as long as you want me. I promise," Elizabeth assured her, as she hugged Georgiana closer. She continued, "And do not worry about your brother and me; we are both very stubborn, but we manage to coexist, even if not always tranquilly."

"Wonderful, now, let us both get ready. Remember, Fitzwilliam is escorting us to the theatre tonight. It will be very exciting. I can hardly wait."

Elizabeth had forgotten. In spite of what she had said to Georgiana, she was furious with Darcy. She did not want to see him again so soon. She had decided she would stay in her room and brood, feigning a headache. Seeing Georgiana's enthusiasm, Elizabeth realised that was no longer a possibility.

It was her job to accompany Georgiana out in public. Georgiana steadfastly refused any invitation that excluded Elizabeth. As there were many amongst the *ton* whose only interest was in the Darcys, Georgiana declined quite a few invitations. Little did it matter. In her eyes, Elizabeth was her friend as well as her equal. She did not intend to engage the society of those who chose to look down upon Elizabeth. Attendance at the theatre, operas, exhibits, private dinner parties with close friends of the Matlocks, and occasional private balls marked their calendar for the Season, along with a surfeit of callers of both genders. Darcy was always in attendance, much to the delight of the young ladies and their mothers, and to the chagrin of the gentlemen.

Fortunately, Elizabeth was not made to think she was hindering Georgiana's prospects. While men found both women charming, only the wealthiest men of the highest circles approached Georgiana. Those gentlemen of more modest means sought out Elizabeth. Mr. Clennan was but one of those men. Luckily for Darcy, Elizabeth was unaware that he had spoken with another gentleman on her behalf to decline his suit.

Richard also planned to accompany them to the theatre that night. He often joined the Darcys, Elizabeth, and often times, Mrs. Annesley for social outings. As Georgiana's co-guardian, he was as excited as was Darcy to participate in her coming out. Elizabeth's opinion of Richard remained unchanged over the course of their acquaintance. She perceived him as an incredible flirt; much like Darcy in physical appearance, but far more amiable. He delighted in entertaining her, but not to the extent of their first meeting when she found him overwhelming in his attentions. Richard was particularly careful not to annoy Darcy in his interactions with Elizabeth. Although Darcy refused to admit it, it was obvious to Richard how Darcy felt about her. He knew his cousin too well. He simply did not believe Darcy's intentions towards her were as innocent as professed.

In due time, Georgiana and Elizabeth joined Darcy and Richard in the drawing room for their departure for the theatre. Darcy did his best to engage Elizabeth and appear contrite. As no real apology was forthcoming, Elizabeth was not inclined to offer her forgiveness. The two were at an impasse.

There was at least one other young woman who looked forward to the night at the theatre as much as Georgiana. When Caroline Bingley learnt that their party would be seated in the Darcy box for the evening, she was ecstatic. Caroline always prided herself on what she perceived as her *special* connection to Darcy. *How many other young ladies of the ton commonly shared his luxurious box?* Indeed, Caroline felt herself to be rather special.

The performance that night was one of Shakespeare's works, not that it mattered. People were there to see and to be seen. Caroline went to considerable lengths preparing for that evening, for at the height of the Season, she was the young lady who would be seen with Mr. Darcy; she planned to make sure of that. All eyes would be trained upon Miss Darcy, being that it was her first Season. By default, those same eyes would be on Caroline. Sure, Darcy's sister would be seen on his arm during the interval and seated next to him in the box, but he had two arms after all, as well as two sides. Caroline believed after that night, there would be no doubt amongst the *ton* that she was Darcy's choice.

Despite her usual tendency to arrive fashionably late to the theatre, that evening Caroline wanted to leave nothing to chance, for instance, that there might be no free seats next to Darcy, or Heaven forbid *that little chit Eliza Bennet* might be seated beside him. Imagine her surprise when the Darcy party arrived at the theatre shortly afterwards and was espied entering the Matlock box. Caroline's indignation was evident. She quickly turned to her brother and demanded an explanation. Charles responded to his irate sister with a smug smile and re-focused his attention to the stage.

If not for the fact that Caroline knew Lady Matlock did not favour her, she would have forced her brother to escort her to the Matlock box to try to finagle an invitation to dinner after the theatre. Rather than all eyes focused upon Caroline as she had intended, it seemed all eyes were honed in on the Matlock box. At least, Caroline's eyes were. To her dismay, Miss Theresa Rupert was also a guest in the Matlock box. Caroline mentally calculated the number of times the young lady had been seen in Darcy's company over the past weeks.

Upon entering the Matlock box, Darcy greeted everyone cordially. He thoughtfully told Miss Theresa that it was a pleasure to see her again; but rather than take the seat next to her, which was clearly intended for him by his aunt's design, he offered the seat to Georgiana.

Thus situated, Darcy viewed the night's performance of *The Taming of the Shrew* with particularly keen interest. Of course, he had seen it before; as a long-standing patron of the theatre, he had seen the performance on at least two other occasions. However, that night it seemed as if he viewed it from an entirely new perspective.

All the occupants of the Matlock box descended upon Matlock House for a light supper after the theatre. It was a pleasant affair for everyone. Though Elizabeth was not seated close enough to Darcy to be bothered with conversing with him, she could observe him discreetly. Darcy was seated beside Miss Theresa. He was not at all discourteous. While he did not start any conversation with her, he always responded to her inquiries with civility. Based upon Elizabeth's observations of the two, it seemed Miss Theresa had risen to the level of Caroline Bingley in Darcy's estimation; that indeed was a significant improvement.

~~~

Days passed. Soon even Georgiana was affected by the undercurrent of tension between Elizabeth and her brother. She surmised Elizabeth had not yet forgiven him for the lapse that caused their quarrel. Elizabeth sought to minimise her presence in Darcy's company when possible. That proved a challenge, in and of itself, for since the start of the Season, Darcy never left the house unless he was escorting Georgiana and, consequently, Elizabeth around town. To the extent Elizabeth could not escape Darcy's presence, she responded to him with feigned civility. Georgiana wanted to speak with Elizabeth and Darcy about their situation, but she did not want to put herself in the
~~~

position of choosing sides, so she remained silent. She hoped the two of them would work out their differences soon.

Before the stand-off between the two of them was allowed to last much longer, Darcy asked Elizabeth into his study to explain his actions. Despite his underlying motive, he knew he was right to speak on her behalf to potential suitors, and Elizabeth knew he was wrong to do so without consulting with her.

Darcy spoke of his role as master of his household and his obligation to receive callers, along with Georgiana, when he was present in the home. He said he would continue to exercise his right to remain in Georgiana's company when a gentleman caller was in his home, even if it meant remaining when the caller was clearly there to see Elizabeth.

Willing to do anything to heal the rift between them, Darcy promised that he would not speak on her behalf again unless she gave him leave to do so, and he offered a sincere apology for his past interference. Lastly, he spoke to Elizabeth of her role as his sister's companion. While he understood that given her personality, she could not help but attract many admirers, her primary responsibility was to Georgiana.

Later that afternoon, as Elizabeth took a stroll in Hyde Park, accompanied by her maid and a footman, she reflected upon Darcy's words. She imagined that if she were to meet someone with whom she wanted to accept a courtship, she would have to quit her job as Georgiana's companion immediately, and move back in with her uncle and aunt. As a young maiden, she would need to be properly chaperoned during the courtship, and other than the Gardiners, who would be able to do so? *Unless it is to be an extremely short courtship, how would I continue to help support my family in Meryton, as well as not be a burden to the Gardiners?*

~~~
~~~

Over the next days, the tension between Darcy and Elizabeth gradually faded, and the two returned to their former level of amity. As much a relief as it was for them, it was equally so for Georgiana. As an outside observer, she could see that neither of them was especially happy during the impasse.

Determined not to interfere in Elizabeth's affairs, Darcy remained a silent spectator when gentlemen callers were received in his home. He noticed that one gentleman, a relatively new comer amongst the *ton*, appeared to visit more regularly than most, and he was not there to see Georgiana.

Darcy also noticed the gentleman always endeavoured to be near Elizabeth at many of the private balls they attended. The last time they had attended the theatre, the gentleman had appeared to watch Elizabeth more than he had watched the play. Darcy began to make inquiries to find out as much as he could about the mysterious man.

The gentleman's name was Mr. Arthur Garrett. He was five and twenty, and wealthy in his own right. Mr. Garrett gained entry into society by the marriage of his younger sister into a prominent family. The Garrett family was among the landed gentry; though, like the Bingleys, their fortune was earned in trade.

One morning, Darcy sat in the drawing room with Georgiana, Elizabeth, and Mrs. Annesley as they received calls from Mrs. Rupert, Miss Theresa, a jovial gentleman named Mr. Long, and Mr. Garrett. Darcy sat just off to the side of the room, his thoughts thousands of miles away, when Mr. Garrett approached him.

"Mr. Darcy, might I have the privilege of a private audience with you this morning?"

Startled, Darcy responded, "What... oh, yes, yes of course, Mr. Garrett. Please join me in my study."

The two gentlemen left the drawing room, barely noticed. Darcy felt as though he was taking the longest walk of his life. Once the gentlemen were in the study and seated at the desk, the two men embarked upon a conversation that could only cause Darcy considerable pain and discomfort. Darcy was so caught up in his own thoughts on the implications of the discussion on his life that he was brought back to the present, most alarmingly, when he thought he heard Mr. Garrett say that he wished for a private interview with Elizabeth.

"Pardon me, Mr. Garrett. What did you just say?"

"Mr. Darcy, I asked if I might have a private interview with Miss Elizabeth."

It was suddenly Darcy's decisive moment, as he vividly recalled Elizabeth's words never to speak on her behalf again and his promise to abide by her wishes. After a minute or two of hesitation, Darcy replied, "Yes, of course. Please excuse me for a moment." Darcy walked to his door and told the footman to ask Miss Elizabeth to see him in his study. Utterly resigned to his fate, he returned to his chair to await Elizabeth's arrival.

Elizabeth was somewhat puzzled. What purpose did Mr. Darcy have that meant calling her into his study while callers were being received? She excused herself and quickly made way to find out the reason for his summons. Upon entering the room, Elizabeth was surprised to find Darcy and Mr. Garrett seated at the desk. The two men immediately stood upon her entrance. Darcy walked over to Elizabeth and asked her to take a seat.

"Thank you for joining us, Miss Elizabeth. Mr. Garrett has requested a private interview with you. Now, if you two will excuse me, I will return to my other guests in the drawing room. Good day, Mr. Garrett." Darcy bowed slightly in Elizabeth's direction and headed towards the door.

Elizabeth beseeched, "Mr. Darcy, please do not feel obligated to leave your own study on my behalf. I am sure Mr. Garrett can have nothing to say of which you should not be privy."

Darcy directed his attention to Mr. Garrett. "As you can see, sir, Miss Elizabeth is very modest." Turning to Elizabeth he said softly, "I shall leave the door open. My footman will remain just outside. Please be assured of your privacy."

Upon Darcy's departure, Mr. Garrett moved to a seat closer to Elizabeth. Without interruption, he spoke endlessly of his deep admiration for her and his abiding devotion. As Elizabeth sat in a state of *déjà vu*, she could not help thinking to herself, *Have I not been here before?* The reality of the gentleman, best described as Mr. Collins's identical twin brother, standing before her with an extended hand, broke her trance-like state.

"Miss Elizabeth, shall we go to Mr. Darcy to inform him that you have accepted my suit?"

"Mr. Garrett, what are you saying? I have agreed to no such thing."

"My dear Miss Elizabeth, you have not disagreed. Let me just say that you have made me the happiest of men."

"Please forgive me, and allow me to make myself perfectly clear. Though I am honoured by your request, I do not accept it, sir."

"My dear, though I never thought so before, I am beginning to comprehend why Mr. Darcy said you were modest. I see that it is your modesty that obliges you to suspend your immediate acceptance of my suit."

"Mr. Garrett, please refrain from referring to me with such terms of endearment. I cannot, and I shall not, accept you."

"Miss Elizabeth, despite your manifold attractions, you can by no means be certain that an offer like mine shall be made to you again."

Thinking to herself once more, *As if I have never heard that before*. Finally, she stood and said, "Mr. Garrett, please believe me when I say I do not accept your offer. I beg your pardon, sir." Elizabeth curtseyed and quickly exited the room, leaving a rather befuddled Mr. Garrett behind.

Elizabeth returned to the drawing room to see a different group of callers being received. She quickly found a seat and attended to the conversations of those around her. Elizabeth refused to look at Darcy.

~ *Chapter 5* ~
Who Is This Man

As the Season drew to a close, Darcy, Georgiana, and Elizabeth prepared to journey to Pemberley where they were to spend the summer months. Mrs. Annesley retired as planned and moved to Lincolnshire to live with her daughter.

Nights on the road were spent in establishments often frequented by the Darcys. Elizabeth had witnessed Darcy's thoughtfulness with respect to members of his staff at Darcy House. It amazed her to see him extend that same level of courtesy to the innkeepers and their staffs. It was a new experience for Elizabeth to travel in a fashion second nature to the Darcys. They were treated as royalty by the proprietors. They dined in private rooms and slept in the finest suites. That in conjunction with the luxurious Darcy coach, made the long journey to Pemberley seem no hardship at all.

The pleasant weather afforded Darcy the occasion to ride on horseback throughout most of the journey. Towards the journey's end, upon entering Pemberley Woods, he had the carriage stop so that he could join Elizabeth and Georgiana inside. He woke Elizabeth with a light touch upon her hand. Darcy placed his finger to his lips to hush her, wishing to avoid stirring Georgiana. Quietly, he handed her out of the carriage and led her along a path to a landing that afforded a picturesque view of Pemberley House.

Enjoying the view of Pemberley from afar, Darcy stood as closely behind Elizabeth as possible without actually touching, closer than propriety dictated. Wanting nothing more than to wrap his arms around her to capture her in his embrace, he fought the temptation by clasping his hands together behind his back. Elizabeth was increasingly conscious of his nearness but too caught up in the magnificence and splendour of Pemberley to be overly concerned. The panoramic view was wonderfully breath-taking. Elizabeth stood entranced. *I have never seen a place for which nature has done more, or where natural beauty has been so little counteracted by an awkward taste. Every disposition of the ground is good.* Equally captured by the moment, Darcy leaned forward and placed his hand along the small of Elizabeth's back while he pointed out another view of Pemberley Woods, but only for a moment before he remembered himself and resumed his former stance. Darcy for so long had dreamed of the occasion when he would bring Elizabeth to that spot. He relished their private moment together. The sweet-smelling scent of her hair intoxicated him. He longed to run his fingers through the soft, luxurious tresses cascading over her shoulders and down her back. Facing away from him, Elizabeth was oblivious to Darcy's increasing discomfort.

Georgiana awakened to find herself all alone in the carriage. Upon drawing the shades back, she immediately recognised her surroundings. Knowing her brother as she did, she quickly surmised where he had taken Elizabeth. She set off upon the path and came upon Darcy and Elizabeth rather hastily. Upon observing Darcy's closeness to Elizabeth, Georgiana suddenly realised that her brother more than just admired her friend. Thinking her brother the most honourable man in the world, she wondered if he had fallen in love with Elizabeth. *Why else would he exhibit such behaviour?* Never before had Darcy been less pleased to see his sister than at that moment. On the other hand, he could not have been more grateful, for he was about to place his hand upon the small of Elizabeth's back once again, to point out another site. As Georgiana approached, Darcy moved away from Elizabeth, to a distance a few steps off, to allow his ardour to subside. Georgiana took hold of Elizabeth's hand and led her to another spot where she began pointing out her own favourite sites. Soon, Darcy escorted the young women back to the carriage. He joined them inside so that he could continue to point out areas of interest to Elizabeth as they resumed the journey to Pemberley.

~~~

The warm reception from the entire Pemberley staff towards Darcy and Georgiana upon their arrival at the manor house was encouraging. It delighted Elizabeth to receive a fair share of that warmth when introduced to Darcy's housekeeper, Mrs. Reynolds. Darcy asked Mrs. Reynolds to see to it personally that Elizabeth was comfortably settled into their home.

As Mrs. Reynolds gave Elizabeth a brief tour of the grand house, she spoke at length of Darcy's admirable qualities. Elizabeth could see that the elderly woman took enormous pleasure in speaking of her young master. She encouraged her by asking questions on things she did not yet know of him and remarking on the things she knew all too well.

This is going pretty far, Elizabeth thought, when Mrs. Reynolds fretted that her master might never marry; her thought being that no one was good enough for him. Still she listened with increasing astonishment. When Mrs. Reynolds spoke of his amiability as a child, and how he was always the sweetest-
~~~

tempered and most generous-hearted boy in the world, Elizabeth thought, *Are we talking about the same person?* Cognizant that Darcy was her employer as well, and not wishing to cause offence, she said, "Pemberley is lucky in having such a master."

Indeed, the housekeeper continued, saying it was no wonder he was so good-natured now that he was all grown up. Elizabeth almost stared at her. *Can this be Mr. Darcy?* Elizabeth listened, wondered, doubted, and was impatient for more. And more commendation of Mr. Darcy is just what Mrs. Reynolds imparted.

Upon completion of her tour of the house, Elizabeth considered all that she had heard. *In what an amiable light does this place him! As a brother, a landlord, and a master, how many people's happiness are in his guardianship! How much of pleasure or pain it is in his power to bestow! How much of good or evil must be done by him! Every idea brought forward by his housekeeper is favourable to his character.* Elizabeth could not help but admit that she too had seen evidence of some of the admirable qualities attributed to Darcy. However, she had seen evidence of his arrogance and disdain towards others as well; though she readily conceded, she also bore witness to his willingness to change.

~~~

During the first week of his return, Darcy was hidden away in his study, often with his steward, Mr. Fletcher, managing Pemberley affairs. He trusted his steward to take care of the estate in his absence, but Darcy was in full command when he returned. As a testament to the housekeeper's strong praise, Darcy worked from sun up to sun down and late into the nights to catch up on things from his prolonged absence. When he was not working in his study pouring over estate accounts, he was
~~~

out among the tenants, attending to various concerns. This came as no surprise to Georgiana as she was all too aware of her brother's propensity to immerse himself in work upon his return to Pemberley. Elizabeth, however, was somewhat bothered. As much as she loved spending time with Georgiana, the longer she went without seeing Darcy, the more she missed his company.

Then again, Elizabeth was enjoying her freedom at Pemberley immensely. She woke early and set off each morning on long, solitary walks. She was careful not to venture too far from the house and restricted her rambles to the paths that Darcy had pointed out to her on her first day. She always returned in time to enjoy mid-morning breakfast with Georgiana, who had not been an early riser in London and tended to arise even later at Pemberley.

One morning, Elizabeth came back from her walk earlier than usual. She did not expect to see Darcy sitting in the breakfast room, reading the paper and drinking coffee. As she entered the room, he stood to greet her with a warm smile.

"Miss Elizabeth, it is a pleasure to see you this morning. I trust you enjoyed your morning stroll."

"Yes, I did, sir. It was very refreshing. I am thoroughly enjoying this freedom," she stated cheerfully. Elizabeth excused the servant as she prepared her own plate. "I am surprised to see you this morning. I was beginning to think you had escaped to town."

"No, I did not. Have I neglected you, Miss Elizabeth?" he teased. Before she could respond to his taunt, he said, "Allow me to make amends immediately. I am about to go for a quick ride. Please join me."

"On horseback?"

"Yes, of course."

"I will have to decline your invitation. I do not ride on horseback. I never learnt to ride. There, I am not so accomplished after all."

"You have never ridden on horseback, Miss Elizabeth?"

"No, never," she answered truthfully.

"Then, we must address that straight away. Georgiana loves to ride, and we spend a great deal of time riding during the summer. I will simply have to teach you."

"As busy as you are, I would hate to keep you from more pressing matters."

"Nothing would give me more pleasure. Let us get started today. Since you may not have a proper riding habit, change into whatever you think is best. This afternoon, the three of us will go into Lambton to shop." Before Elizabeth could protest, Darcy said, "Meet me in my study as soon as you are ready," as he walked out of the room.

A half hour later, Elizabeth and Darcy headed towards the stables. He said, "Thank you for agreeing to this without opposition, Miss Elizabeth."

"You make it rather difficult to say no, but I must confess I do not like horses."

"Why is that?"

"I saw my sister fall from a horse when we were small children. She broke her arm during the fall. While she recovered from the experience and even went on to become an excellent rider, I never got over it."

"Trust me, Miss Elizabeth, you have nothing to fear. I will never let you fall, and I believe you will soon come to love the horse I have chosen for you."

As they approached the stables, a groomsman led a magnificent chestnut mare to them and handed the reins to Darcy. Elizabeth was reluctant to come close to the horse, so disinclined that Darcy handed the reins back over to the groom, walked over to Elizabeth and took her delicate hands into his. Purposely, he spoke very softly. "Please trust me. Georgiana was also afraid of horses initially, but I taught her to ride." As he gently massaged the back of her hands, he said, "Close your eyes."

Elizabeth briefly hesitated, and then willingly went along. Darcy continued, "Now breathe slowly, calmly." Nearly whispering, he said, "You are safe with me. I will protect you. I will always protect you. Do you trust me?"

Elizabeth shook her head in assent. Darcy continued. "Please do not be afraid. This first lesson... all of your lessons will go smoothly." Continuing to stroke the back of her hands with his fingertips, he said softly, "I will take my time with you. We will go as fast or as slowly as you wish. If at any time, you feel we are moving too fast... that I am rushing you... tell me to stop. And I will. I will stop. I want you to enjoy this."

Darcy modulated his tone to one that was even more soothing. "We have plenty of time to do this... all day... all week... all summer, if that is what it takes. This is but the first step." Pausing a moment longer and slowing his cadence, "You feel completely safe and comfortable with me. You trust me." Slowly caressing the back of her hands and each of her fingers, he continued, "I have chosen the gentlest mare in my stables for you. She is beautiful. Her name is Bella."

Darcy instinctively released one of Elizabeth's hands and gently brushed a lock of her hair to the side of her face. "I will stay by your side, I promise. I will not leave you." After a few moments, he sensed that Elizabeth was totally relaxed. He took the reins of the horse (which the groom had brought closer). Darcy continued, "You trust me. I am right here. Open your eyes."

Elizabeth was so mesmerised by Darcy's soft, soothing, yet stimulating voice, that upon opening her eyes, she was not a bit uneasy finding herself within inches of the horse. Looking at the horse and stroking her mane, Darcy said, "See Bella... she is beautiful." Turning towards Elizabeth, he asked, "Would you like to touch her coat to feel its softness?" Elizabeth agreed. She allowed Darcy to place her hand on Bella's neck and gently guide her strokes. Soon, Darcy released his hold upon Elizabeth's hand to allow her to interact with Bella, while he stepped a foot or so away and drank some of the cold water offered to him by the groom.

"She is beautiful, sir," Elizabeth expressed, after a few moments.

"I would like to guide you once around the stable yard. I am going to help you saddle, and I will maintain the reins to lead Bella. Is that acceptable?" he asked as he returned close to her side.

Elizabeth silently consented. Darcy gently lifted her to place her in the saddle. After checking to see that she was properly secured and guiding her into the correct position atop the horse, he said, "I am going to lead Bella, but I will be right here."

Darcy guided Bella into a slow pace as he led her along the boundary of the stable yard. After a couple of laps, Darcy commented, "You are an excellent student, Miss Elizabeth." Seeking a change of pace, he asked, "Are you comfortable with one more lesson this morning?"

"What do you have in mind?" she questioned with some trepidation.

"I am thinking of a slow gallop."

"How will we manage that? I am not ready to do this without you. How do you plan to keep up?"

"Let me show you. Now, close your eyes again... and trust me," he responded. She did as he asked. Darcy climbed atop of Bella, behind Elizabeth.

Elizabeth did not hesitate to open her eyes once she realised she was practically sitting in Darcy's lap. She protested, "Sir, I do not think this is proper."

"Relax. I am the teacher after all. Believe me, this is an acceptable technique. Now close your eyes. I will tell you when to open them. Trust me."

Once Elizabeth closed her eyes, Darcy prompted Bella into a slow gait. After a few circuits around the yard, he set out on a path that led to one of his favourite spots. He brought Bella to a halt and asked Elizabeth to open her eyes to the view of a beautiful Grecian love temple situated beside a rather large pond. The temple was a large circular structure with an open, airy design that boasted six imposing stone pillars and a black domed top, surrounded by a variety of shrubbery bushes and flowers. Inside, there was a purposefully arranged iron seating set. Elizabeth was so delighted that she did not protest Darcy's actions in taking her far beyond the stables. He dismounted and helped Elizabeth to get down. After securing Bella, he offered his arm to Elizabeth, and they walked to the temple.

Elizabeth expressed with utter delight, "This is the most beautiful place!"

"Yes, it is one of my favourite places. I thought you would enjoy seeing it. I often come here when I am overwhelmed and in need of solitude."

"You have granted me access into your private sanctuary. What shall you do if I begin to come here often?"

"I would not worry about that. Your eyes were closed. Besides, you can only get here on horseback."

Darcy spoke at length on the history of the temple. His grandfather had commissioned its building as a tribute to his grandmother. Darcy related some of his childhood memories associated with the spot. Seeing that side of Darcy amazed Elizabeth. She resisted the urge to stare at him. His entire demeanour changed. As she listened to him speak enthusiastically of his love for Pemberley, she considered that he was arresting, engaging, and pleasing. She wondered, *Who is this man, and what has he done with Mr. Darcy?*

Soon, Darcy decided it was time to head back. After assisting Elizabeth onto the saddle and again guiding her into the correct posture while furthering her lesson by explaining his actions, he mounted Bella. He leaned in closely to her ear and whispered, "Close your eyes."

"No, not this time," she responded defiantly.

"Then, prepare yourself for a most thrilling ride."

"But I trust you, sir."

"I promise you will not regret it," Darcy said as he positioned Elizabeth closer to him, much closer than she was before, and urged Bella into a fast gallop. Elizabeth found the excitement of the ride, in combination with the sensations Darcy evoked in her with his hand positioned securely around her waist, as exhilarating as he had suggested it would be.

Still holding her close as they approached the stable, Darcy spoke softly into Elizabeth's ear, "Shall we have another lesson in the morning?"

"I think it will be best if Georgiana joins us for our next lesson, sir," she demurred, somewhat bewildered.

"If you insist. I am at your command," he submitted.

As he reluctantly relinquished his hold, Elizabeth asserted, "I shall remember that the next time I am summoned to your study."

~~~

Elizabeth had come to enjoy Darcy's company immensely. She liked him very much; perhaps a little too much, she thought. As hard as she fought it, she could not stop herself. She trusted
~~~

him. She was certain he would never violate her trust. However, despite his words to the contrary, Elizabeth was sure every rule of propriety had been broken on the morning of her riding lesson. She would not think about that; instead, she would simply enjoy the friendship he seemed willing to offer and not expect more. *As long as he does not expect anything more of me,* she considered. As for her newly discovered regard for Mr. Darcy, that would be her secret. She would not allow him or anyone else any indication of her increased admiration.

Darcy had begun to suspect that Elizabeth's regard for him had improved significantly. He knew it would be difficult to mask his love for her, now that they were at Pemberley. Indeed, his conundrum was great. There was so much that he wanted to share with her. How could he without raising her expectations? He loved her too much to do anything that would hurt her. Darcy concluded it would help if he kept his hands off of her, and rather, focused upon their growing friendship. That was the only way to proceed. He would have to be content to touch her, caress her, and revere her body solely in his dreams.

Darcy spent the following weeks attending to both Georgiana and Elizabeth. The remaining horseback riding lessons were conducted in Georgiana's company. Soon, Elizabeth became accomplished enough to ride on her own and explore the sites of Pemberley on horseback, along with the Darcys.

He also began to share breakfast daily with Elizabeth, after her morning walks. He scheduled his days to spend parts of the afternoons and have dinner with the young women. This meant working late into the nights and often early in the mornings.

In spite of their best intentions to mask their increasing regard, especially from each other, Georgiana soon came to realise that not only did Darcy have strong feelings for Elizabeth, but Elizabeth was beginning to care for him, as well. Georgiana was at once both excited that the two people she loved most in the world might be falling in love with each other, and frustrated that they were too stubborn to admit it. While she refused to do anything to interfere, she decided she would allow the two as much time together as necessary to come to their senses.

As much as Georgiana enjoyed horseback riding, she elected not to take part in many of their planned excursions to allow Darcy and Elizabeth to be alone. In the days leading up to Elizabeth's birthday, she even expended considerable time and effort to organise a celebration picnic, only to feign illness on the day of the event. She had worked, along side of Mrs. Reynolds, to plan an intimate luncheon in an open field of fragrant orchids and wild-flowers. The servants were not to remain once everything was set up.

Therefore, Elizabeth found herself to be relaxing on a blanket, in a beautiful and private setting, alone with Darcy. On that occasion, Darcy removed his jacket and loosened his cravat as he also relaxed on the blanket, but at the opposite end, in an effort to protect Elizabeth's sensibilities, as well as his own. They just finished eating a light fare when Darcy handed Elizabeth a beautifully wrapped gift.

"Happy birthday, Miss Elizabeth."

Elizabeth knew of Darcy's generosity and delight in presenting gifts to Georgiana, so she was not caught off guard by his gesture altogether. She expected a small, insignificant trinket, but upon opening the box, she was stunned to see two lovely pearl bracelets.

"Sir, I cannot accept this gift. It is too much."

Darcy smiled. He reflected upon how it was nothing compared to what he would have preferred to give her. "Of course you can. This is a gift from Georgiana and me, to you. Georgiana selected it."

"But sir, I am your employee."

"You are more than an employee to me, Miss Elizabeth. Let me help with this," Darcy said as he reached for the bracelets. He took his time as he was securing them on her wrist, rousing Elizabeth's sensibilities with his intimacy.

"They are beautiful. Thank you," she said, as she held them up for inspection.

"It is true you know. Yes, you are Georgiana's companion, but you are also her dearest friend. You mean a great deal to me, as well. Other than Georgiana and Richard, there is no one other than you with whom I feel closer."

"Not even Mr. Bingley?" she teased.

"That is different."

"How so?"

"It is just different." He contemplated a moment and then tentatively, yet softly stated, "I hope it is acceptable that all I can offer is friendship, Miss Elizabeth."

"Why Mr. Darcy, are you afraid of *raising my expectations?*" she responded in a haughty voice, aiming to emulate his own.

"Perhaps," he expressed rather cautiously.

"Well, do not worry. I know it is only a matter of time before Lady Matlock finds the perfect match for you," she teased, wishing to lighten the mood.

"Oh, I am not worried about that."

"Why is that? I am certain it is her greatest goal in life."

"It is quite simple. I know my duty to my family, but I will marry someone of my choosing, or I will not marry at all." Wanting to do nothing more than to change the subject, he said, "Let us speak of other things. Shall we discuss books? You and I have not sparred since our arrival at Pemberley."

"I knew it was my impertinence that you found irresistible," she spoke in jest, prompting Darcy to chuckle. She continued, "So which book shall we discuss today?"

The two settled upon a book they had both read recently and a lively debate ensued. Soon afterwards, Darcy and Elizabeth began reading their own books. Darcy appeared more interested in Elizabeth's book than he was in his own. She seemed quite amused, judging by her smiles and quiet laughter.

"Why are you so amused?" he could no longer resist asking.

Elizabeth read the last passage of her book again, out loud. "You find that amusing?" he asked, doubt evident in his voice.

"Here, see for yourself," Elizabeth stated as she pointed to the next humorous passage while handing him her book.

"No, read it to me," Darcy insisted, refusing the book.

Elizabeth proceeded to read several pages. After a few minutes, she observed that Darcy appeared quite relaxed. In fact, he was fully reclined on the blanket with his eyes closed and his arms positioned behind his head in support.

"Excuse me sir, but why am I entertaining you?" she asked brashly.

"Is it my fault that I find your voice wonderfully pleasing? I could listen to you all day."

"I am sure of it. I might say the same of you," Elizabeth responded daringly.

"Fair enough," he said, as he reached for the book. "It is my turn, madam. Sit back, relax, and listen to the master."

The two continued in that fashion for nearly a half hour, as they enjoyed seeing who could best pantomime the book's characters and mimic their voices, before they realised it was time to head back. They arrived back at the house to find Georgiana in the music room practising. She raced over to embrace Elizabeth and admire the bracelets. She apologised profusely for missing the picnic and promised to make it up to her during the special birthday dinner she had planned.

~~~

The arrival of the Bingleys, specifically Miss Caroline Bingley, interrupted the tranquillity of the Pemberley household. She arrived like a storm and immediately assumed a proprietary air as she descended the splendid halls, much to the dismay of the entire staff, including Mrs. Reynolds.

Caroline had her sights set on Darcy. Given her standing as the sister of his close friend and, thereby, her frequent presence in Darcy's beloved home, she felt she had a particular relationship with him. What other potential rival for Darcy's affections had ever graced the halls of Pemberley? That in itself signalled a special place in his esteem, she believed. Imagine her indignation when she learned that Elizabeth resided in the family wing! Caroline herself always resided in the opposite side of the great home in the guest wing, when she visited. At first, she was positive that it was Georgiana's doing. However, after observing the interactions between Darcy and Elizabeth during the first couple of days of her visit, she began to wonder.

The misguided young woman was used to Darcy's focusing upon Georgiana, almost to the exclusion of others. Now, Darcy appeared equally solicitous of Elizabeth, much to Caroline's dismay. She had not come all this way to play a secondary role to the hired help.

It did not take long for Darcy to realise that Caroline was exhibiting the same petty attitude towards Elizabeth as she had in Hertfordshire. Darcy marvelled at Elizabeth's ability to outwit Caroline at every turn. The fact remained that she would always be a gentleman's daughter, even in her position as Georgiana's companion. That trumped Caroline's status as the daughter of a tradesman, regardless of her wealth and connections.
~~~

Darcy also suspected Caroline was jealous of his attentions towards Elizabeth, because she was even more solicitous and possessive of him when Elizabeth was present. Ever willing to sacrifice, he decided the least he could do was to remove himself from Caroline's company to limit their exposure to each other, for Elizabeth's sake. Therefore, Darcy encouraged Bingley, and at times Mr. Hurst, in activities that allowed them to spend as much time apart from the women as possible.

In the absence of the gentlemen's company, it was only a matter of time until Elizabeth, Georgiana, and even Lady Grace grew weary of Caroline's and Louisa's propensity to take pot-shots at Elizabeth. Caroline's comments were also extended to Elizabeth's family, sometimes to the point of being harsh, such was her vitriol towards Elizabeth. When Caroline chose to disparage Jane's working as a governess in Scotland, Elizabeth had endured all she could take, and yet continued to remain civil. Lady Grace was offended deeply on Elizabeth's behalf. She wondered if all the money in the world could compensate for having to endure such a sister.

Elizabeth, Georgiana, and Lady Grace formed a close bond. The three decided upon pastimes that Caroline and Louisa were not inclined to pursue, such as outdoor activities, for the only time Caroline sought to be out-of-doors was when she thought she might encounter Darcy.

One evening after dinner, while awaiting the gentlemen's company, Caroline overheard the new sisterhood discussing plans to spend the following morning horseback riding. Anxious to have her share in the conversation, she promptly moved to the other side of the room where the three ladies sat.

"Why, Miss Eliza, my dear," Caroline condescended, "I did not think you rode horseback. During our time at Hertfordshire, you seemed to take an eager interest in walking throughout the countryside."

Georgiana responded, "Elizabeth rides very well. My brother taught her." Georgiana could not resist exacerbating her guest because of the way Caroline shamelessly flaunted herself in front of Darcy.

"Mr. Darcy taught your companion to ride. When did this happen?" Caroline asked, doubting the veracity of what she had heard.

"I learnt to ride since coming to Pemberley. Both Mr. Darcy and Georgiana have been very instrumental in my training."

The gentlemen chose that moment to join the women, spurring Caroline to seize upon Darcy. She immediately rushed to his side and intertwined her arm with his.

"Mr. Darcy, I understand you taught Miss Eliza to ride. How generous of you... few can boast of having such an attentive master."

"I do what I can," he replied as he tried, unsuccessfully to remove her arm from his.

"Is that so? I think I should like to have a few riding lessons myself, if you are still in the business of providing them, that is," she cajoled, while batting her eyes suggestively.

"Miss Caroline, you are welcome to visit my stables at any time. If you insist upon riding lessons, I will speak with my groom and have him attend you." Before she could respond, Darcy excused himself from his guests and acted as if he were heading out to make such arrangements.

~ ~ ~

Bright and early that next day, Lady Grace, Georgiana, and Elizabeth headed towards the stables as planned. They were not alone. It seemed everyone wished to ride that morning. Darcy,

Bingley, Mr. and Mrs. Hurst, and finally, Caroline rounded out the party.

Darcy's groom expected them. Eight fine horses were properly saddled and lined up in the stable yard. Without much thought, Darcy went to Bella's side, intending to help Elizabeth into her saddle. Caroline immediately lost all interest in the horse she initially favoured. It seemed that Bella was the only choice for her.

"What a beautiful creature, I should be delighted to ride her," she said, as she quickly approached Darcy.

"Then, I am afraid you will be most inconvenienced. Bella is Miss Elizabeth's horse," Darcy responded, with no thought for the implication of his words.

"A paid companion with her own horse, I never heard of such a thing!"

Darcy ignored Caroline's protest and led Bella to Elizabeth. "Miss Elizabeth, your horse eagerly awaits. May I assist you?"

Elizabeth smiled. Given the awkwardness of the moment, what else was there to do? She remained speechless as Darcy lifted her into the saddle, the same as he had done countless times before. Somehow, in front of the Bingleys, the meticulous attention he showed her left her feeling a bit uncomfortable. As usual, he lingered by her side until he was thoroughly convinced of her security.

In the meantime, Caroline grew more and more incensed by the minute. She refused the horse the groom brought forward to her. "This is absurd. I insist upon being satisfied. Since when does the hired help usurp a guest's prerogative? Surely, Miss Eliza can be inconvenienced for a day!"

The last thing Elizabeth wanted or needed was to be the subject of Caroline's diatribe. "Very well, Miss Caroline, you are welcome to ride Bella."

Darcy intervened. "Miss Elizabeth, are you quite certain? You are not obliged to give up riding Bella, simply to appease her."

"Indeed, Mr. Darcy, it is no bother at all. I shall ride one of your other beautiful horses this morning." Darcy would have objected, except he now had an opportunity to aid her once again. Darcy assisted Elizabeth down and led her by the hand to the horse originally selected for Caroline. His attentions went unnoticed by everyone, except Caroline.

"Mr. Darcy," Caroline carped, "I could use a fair bit of your assistance as well."

Without directly acknowledging her, Darcy turned to his groom. "Mr. Jones, will you give help to my guest?"

"Yes Sir, Mr. Darcy," the somewhat reluctant groom stated. That was not the first time he had dealt with the tempestuous young woman.

Darcy quickly returned his attention to Elizabeth, who had freed her hand from his by then. "Miss Elizabeth, though I am confident in your riding ability, I urge you to take your time this morning. Furthermore, I insist upon riding along beside you."

"As much as I fear it will only make matters worse with your guest, I think I should like it if you were to stay close by until I grow comfortable with the horse." Elizabeth smiled. "What is its name?"

Darcy returned her smile. "I will introduce you."

While Darcy acquainted Elizabeth with the other horse, Caroline was causing quite a scene. It seemed that Bella was not of the same mind as Elizabeth. She would not stand still for Caroline's mount. Caroline refused the groom's assistance out of spite, and insisted upon using a mounting block. After several unsuccessful attempts, finally Caroline was saddled and ready to proceed. Suddenly, after only a few steps, in a decidedly uncharacteristic display of unbridled aggression, Bella reared up on her hind legs—a move that rendered poor Caroline faced down upon the ground.

Everyone, including Darcy and Elizabeth, raced towards her. The latter two attempted to calm Bella. As regarded Caroline, fortunately, all that was wounded was her pride. Her brother helped her to her feet, and her sister did her best to brush away the soil from her clothing and remove the straw from her hair. Again, Caroline was vexed by Darcy's inattention. There she was, an honoured guest, and he was tending to the wild beast having just tried to kill her. Caroline brushed her eager attendants away and stormed off to the manor house in a huff, convinced that Darcy might rue the day he had treated her so abominably.

~~~

A couple of weeks after the arrival of the Bingleys, Colonel Richard Fitzwilliam showed up at Pemberley. Darcy had grown tired of Caroline's antics and her disparaging attitude towards Elizabeth. He even counselled Bingley to admonish his sister, but to no avail. Darcy welcomed the excuse to spend time alone with Richard. They were practically inseparable. The two were mindful of joining the guests for meals and after dinner entertainment, but other than that, they enjoyed long horseback excursions and other sporting activities.

One afternoon, whilst in the billiard room, Richard brought up a conversation he had put off for a week. "I say, old fellow, when are you planning to return to town? Very soon, I hope."

"I plan to stay here through Christmas and return to town for Lady Ellen's Twelfth Night Ball."

"So long, you say. You have become quite the domestic, have you not?" Richard asked sarcastically.
~~~

"I must admit, I am quite content when at Pemberley," Darcy stated, as a matter of fact.

"And speaking of contentment, I glimpsed the pleasing Antoinette before I left London. She looked fairly restless, what with so much idle time on her hands."

"Antoinette is not your concern," Darcy voiced quickly. After a long, reflective pause he continued, "Despite the obvious drawbacks, her advantages are not to be disregarded. How many in her place are better compensated? What more might she wish for?"

"Well let us see—perhaps companionship, passion... Look, if you are no longer interested, why do you not let go of her? There are plenty of gentlemen waiting in the wings, including myself."

"I have no intention to 'let go' of her. It is not as if I never plan to return to London."

"Good Heavens, you are a selfish prick! She is a passionate, desirable woman who should not be placed upon a pedestal, waiting for you to return. She is not some vestal virgin; she is a whore. Have some compassion and end your ridiculous arrangement over the poor thing."

"She is the one I prefer. I will not share her!"

"For Heaven's sake, you are simply using her to satiate your lust for Miss Elizabeth!"

"Even if that is true, what of it? I do as I please without answering to anyone, even you. Stay out of my affairs Richard, and do not go near Antoinette."

"Calm down, old man! Look, how about we settle this with a fencing match? If I win, we are off on a quick jaunt to town."

"What makes you think I would agree to that? Everything that I want and need is here."

"Not everything," Richard said with certitude. "How long has it been anyway? I am only looking out for you, my friend."

"Fine, if I win, you will back off on this subject once and for all," Darcy uttered as he threw the pool cue stick down on the billiards table in surrender.

"It is a deal," Richard cheerfully agreed, after inwardly congratulating himself on his ability to disturb the composure of his otherwise calm and collected younger cousin.

After a bruising match, Darcy conceded defeat and agreed to a brief sojourn to London, once the Bingleys departed. There was no way he would leave Georgiana and Elizabeth at the mercy of Caroline Bingley. He wondered if he had let Richard defeat him. Many months had passed since Darcy last had shared Antoinette's bed, not since before the start of the Season when he had stayed out all night and had been "caught" coming home just before dawn. After months of fantasising of making love to Elizabeth, whom he could never have, he was tormented and in desperate need of a passionate release in the arms of a woman.

~~~

Less than a week later, Darcy and Richard returned. Richard remained a few days at Pemberley before going to visit his parents. As Richard made the short journey to his family's home in Matlock, he could not help but reflect upon the changes in his cousin Darcy. The brief sojourn was far from entertaining. Darcy had become quite the killjoy. He decided he would not try again to persuade Darcy to accompany him to town, as he shamelessly had done so. Richard considered that his lovesick cousin was determined to put his life on hold while he decided whether to pursue Miss Elizabeth. Who was he to interfere?
~~~

Feeling guilty for his debauchery during his trip with Richard, Darcy immersed himself in his work upon his return to Pemberley. Much like he did when they first arrived at Pemberley months ago, Darcy isolated himself in his study. Elizabeth and Georgiana rarely saw him. Darcy reckoned that his guilt was not associated with the idea of having betrayed the woman he loved, but rather that he had abandoned the young women to go off to enjoy his carefree bachelor lifestyle in London.

Frustrated by his lack of concentration one morning, Darcy set off on horseback. He rode out to the temple. Elizabeth was there.

"Good morning, Miss Elizabeth, I am surprised to find you here." He dismounted his horse and bowed to her.

"I am quite sorry to have intruded upon your sanctuary, Mr. Darcy. I warned you, though, that it might become a favourite of mine, did I not?"

"I do not mind sharing it with you, Miss Elizabeth."

Darcy walked towards the pond and stared off into the distance, seemingly distracted. His detached demeanour prompted Elizabeth to wonder if she should be there. She cautiously approached him from behind and said, "Perhaps I should leave."

"No, do not leave on my account," he replied, without turning to face her.

"Forgive my saying this, but you seem so distracted. In fact, you have been distant since your return. We hardly see you at all," she expressed tentatively.

"I am sorry for neglecting you," Darcy responded, still somewhat faraway.

"Mr. Darcy, you have not neglected me. If you would like to talk about what is bothering you, I am happy to listen."

At last, Darcy turned towards Elizabeth. He murmured with deep remorse, "I feel as though I have been negligent. I feel that in leaving Georgiana and you here at Pemberley, whilst I gallivanted in town with my cousin, I was being dishonourable. Better that I had remained here with you... two."

"You must stop berating yourself. Georgiana and I missed you, but we hardly felt abandoned."

"I am afraid it is more than that. I should not have gone," he confessed. "If you knew, really knew what I am like," he struggled with the words.

"What, that you are arrogant and self-absorbed? I am not blind, Mr. Darcy. However, you are none of those things when here at Pemberley. You are kind and generous. You work very hard and take your responsibilities seriously. Moreover, if you are truly concerned about your actions, then why do you not change them? What is stopping you? You are your own master. You have everything you should ever want."

"You are wrong. I do not have everything I want. There is one thing I want desperately, yet can never have."

"Then, perhaps you do not want it enough."

"You do not understand. I doubt you ever would."

Not wishing to pry into Darcy's affairs, Elizabeth replied, "Then, let us speak of other things. You must admit, you were glad to see the colonel. You two were joined at the hip from the moment of his arrival. Who would blame you for spending time with your cousin and enjoying male camaraderie?"

"I must admit I was hiding out from the Bingleys. Charles and I have drifted apart since his marriage, and his brother and sisters are not among my favourite people," he frankly conceded. His melancholy slowly faded. After several minutes of continued light banter between the two of them, Darcy said, "I am glad I found you this morning. You are good for my spirits."

"I am glad I could help," she responded, genuinely pleased to see the positive change in his demeanour.

"If you feel up to it, what say you we venture out farther this morning? I know of another incredible spot I wish to show you."

Upon her acceptance, Darcy took Elizabeth's hand and led her to her horse to help her mount. As he lingered by her to correct her sitting posture and to make sure she was secure, she protested, "Mr. Darcy, I know what I am about. I made it here, did I not?"

"So, you have become quite the horsewoman, have you? Perhaps we should select a more challenging mount upon our return to the stables."

"No, thank you. Bella suits me just fine," Elizabeth said while gently stroking Bella's neck.

As Darcy walked over to mount his stallion, he said, "I am concerned about your riding out so far alone. What if something should happen to you?"

"Am I about to be summoned to your study, Mr. Darcy?"

"You might, if I find you so far out alone again. Perhaps I should assign a riding escort for you."

"Please do not go to such lengths on my behalf. I will abide by your admonishment. I promise. Now, lead on, Mr. Darcy."

~~~

Some while later, Darcy and Elizabeth rode along a serpentine path, silently communicating in peculiar harmony.

Earlier, upon reaching their destination, she had playfully chastised him by suggesting his plan was not carefully thought out. She had missed breakfast that morning. Her hunger pangs quietly rumbled.

"Pardon me, madam, for not properly anticipating your appetite," Darcy said. "Of course, I rarely am unprepared for these
~~~

types of excursions. Bear with me just a short while longer, and I will share what sustenance I have with you."

When they came upon the place he intended, Darcy dismounted his horse. He lifted Elizabeth down from Bella. He then handed Elizabeth a blanket.

"Please find an ideal spot for dining, while I secure our horses." She did as he recommended. He joined her rather quickly with a saddlebag slung over his shoulder and helped her spread the covering on the soft patch of grass. Darcy encouraged Elizabeth to sit, as he bent to his knees to produce the contents of his fine leather bag.

She was delighted. Indeed, he was quite prepared with food and drink enough for the two of them. She said, "You surprise me, Mr. Darcy. It is almost as if you planned this."

"I am afraid I did not, as you will soon find. You see, we must share a single flask of ale, for I never travel with glasses. I hope you do not mind roughing it."

"Mr. Darcy, you speak as if I am a prim and delicate blossom. Do you really see me as such?"

He chuckled. "Actually, I do. Are you suggesting otherwise?"

She viewed his sentiments as a challenge. She reached for the flask, and try as she might, she was simply unable to open it. Darcy reached out his hand, "Allow me, my lady."

She had no choice but to hand the flask over to him. Her thirstiness far outweighed her vanity. Darcy easily removed the top and handed it back to her with a look that spurred her to refute any notion of her being fragile. He cautioned, "Mind you take care to sip slowly."

Elizabeth attempted a large swig, so much so that she began coughing, violently. Darcy moved closer to her side to comfort her, but Elizabeth was not having it. She insisted she was just fine. She took another drink—this time much slower, before handing the metal container to Darcy. It was not something that she had ever tasted before. She certainly did not intend to drink it again. She was not about to admit that to him. The rest of the impromptu meal, they consumed in relative silence.

The untroubled silence continued as they rode along the winding path. Occasionally, one would look over at the other in quiet wonderment. Elizabeth was perfectly comfortable with Darcy. Their friendship, though platonic, was unfathomable. She could easily surmise the familiar nature of their relationship would raise eyebrows beyond the confines of Pemberley. They spent far more time alone than a single man and a young maiden ought, but therein existed the trust factor. She trusted him implicitly.

Darcy reflected upon the past few days in town with his cousin, and his incessant innuendos that he was using one woman as a substitute for the other. *Preposterous*, he thought. What he felt for Elizabeth was not mere lust. The feelings she inspired in him were impossible to describe. There was no comparison to what he felt when in her company and what he felt in the company of others. There could be no substitute for Elizabeth.

~ *Chapter 6* ~
In Some Danger

In late September, Darcy took Georgiana and Elizabeth to Matlock for an extended visit. All the Fitzwilliams, as well as two other families, were in residence. In addition to Mr. and Mrs. Rupert and Miss Theresa, there were Lord and Lady Stafford, their eldest son and heir, young Lord Harry and their striking daughter Lady Harriette, who had also come out the past Season, to complete the guest list.

The Staffords were long-time friends of the Matlocks. In fact, Lord Stafford had always harboured the hope that Lord Harry and Georgiana Darcy might form an alliance that would unite the two distinguished families. From Lady Matlock's perspective, the Staffords having an eligible daughter was a mere bonus.

Lady Matlock considered that while Miss Theresa was an ideal choice for Darcy, there might as well be another contender. Like Miss Theresa, Lady Harriette was quite accomplished. However, the two young beauties were decidedly different in physical appearance. Lady Harriette was strikingly tall and voluptuous, with facial features and hair colouring favouring those of Elizabeth. Richard could not help but laugh at the irony. He wondered if his mother had sensed Darcy's preference for Miss Elizabeth. He thought, *let the games begin.*

Richard was profoundly disappointed. Darcy afforded both young ladies an equal share of civility. If not for the fact that young Lord Harry seemed fixated upon Georgiana, Darcy would have avoided the company of the other guests altogether. Whenever he was with Richard, there were always plenty of diversions to enjoy. Despite Richard's many attempts to distract Darcy and engage him in fencing, riding, and hunting, Darcy remained steadfast. As long as Lord Harry was in Georgiana's company, so was Darcy. Darcy had suspected the young man's partiality to Georgiana from his frequent calls during her coming out Season. Now he was certain of it.

Darcy and Elizabeth exercised guarded formality towards each other, now beyond the intimate environs of Pemberley. It would not do for anyone to suspect the increased level of familiarity between the two of them, as it could easily be misinterpreted. Elizabeth was not in any way put-off; she was far more entertained by Lady Matlock's persistent matchmaking. Elizabeth observed that Miss Theresa seemed to have changed her tactic with Darcy. She was no longer solicitous, in fact, she seemed rather disinterested. *Is she a woman scorned?* Elizabeth wondered. She witnessed behaviour in Miss Theresa reminiscent of her own impertinence towards him during their early days in Hertfordshire. Elizabeth thought the young lady might be on to something, as nothing else had worked. She knew Darcy could not resist a challenge. However, Darcy remained entirely unaffected by Miss Theresa. Whenever she attempted to spar verbally with him, he quickly conceded with no effort by saying, "Perhaps you are correct," or words to that effect, before diverting his attention elsewhere.

Lady Harriette surely did not know what to make of Mr. Darcy. Knowing of his reputation, it disconcerted her when he barely acknowledged her upon their introduction. Though, he was cordial, she fully expected to garner far more of his attention than she had elicited. She also knew that Miss Theresa had her heart set upon winning Mr. Darcy and had spent significant time in his company during the past Season, with no better results than what she had observed over the last few days. Lady Harriette was as cunning as she was beautiful. She decided to wait and assess the situation before launching a strategy to capture Darcy's interest.

When Miss Theresa learnt that the Staffords were among the Matlocks' guests, she was far from pleased. She understood she was running out of time. Everyone in the *ton* knew of Lady Matlock's determination to see Darcy well matched. She had worked hard to gain Lady Matlock's good opinion, but now it seemed she preferred Lady Harriette. Miss Theresa soon realised the only reason her family was even there was because they had received the invitation earlier in the year, when Lady Matlock thought that Darcy fancied her.

Miss Theresa had grown quite frustrated in her attempts to win Darcy. Indeed, she needed a different tactic. Upon deliberation of the past months, she considered that nothing she had done to win Mr. Darcy had worked. She was a beautiful young lady and used to having her way. She was much admired by many gentlemen. Only none of them was Darcy. From the night of her introduction to him, when he had wooed her, he had captured her heart. She believed herself to be deeply in love with him, and she would not be easily persuaded to give him up. She determined that she would no longer appear solicitous of him, thinking that was her mistake. Instead, she would seem disinterested. Mr. Darcy was obviously a man who enjoyed a challenge, and she was just the person to give it to him.

However, after the first week, even that strategy failed her. She settled upon the ultimate ploy… to orchestrate a compromising situation with him. Miss Theresa learnt that Darcy was an early riser. She took to the habit of rising early, as well. She often observed him as he headed towards the stables. She also observed Georgiana's impertinent companion set out for early morning strolls, but made no association with Mr. Darcy's habits. She concocted what she thought was the perfect plan.

One morning, aware of when Darcy would be returning, she set out for a ride herself. She planned it so that upon his return, he would spot her lying upon the ground, thrown helplessly from her horse. True to her plan, Darcy soon rode along the path and spotted a young woman lying on the ground just ahead.

Darcy panicked as he raced towards her. He jumped from his horse, thinking it was Elizabeth, for who else would be about at that hour? Realising that it was not Elizabeth, but Miss Theresa, he slowed his approach. He knelt beside her and asked whether she was injured. Seeing the genuine concern in his beautiful eyes, she felt as if her plan had worked. Darcy would have no choice but to carry her back to the house, especially if she had badly injured her ankle. She pretended a terrific deal of pain, and suggested she suffered a sprain. She asked him to help her to the house.

Unbeknownst to Miss Theresa, Richard had joined Darcy on his ride. He approached them at that precise moment. Darcy stood to explain Miss Theresa's predicament. Knowing Darcy as he did, Richard concluded there was no chance of Darcy subjecting himself to a compromising situation with Miss Theresa, even in the act of coming to her aid as a gentleman. Richard took over. He approached Miss Theresa and decided to take a look at her ankle to assess her injury. When she protested that she was sure it was a sprain, as she had suffered the supposed malady as a child, Richard simply picked her up and placed her side-saddled on his stallion. Richard took the reins of his horse and led it along the path to the house, whilst Darcy trailed along slowly on his own horse, relieved to have dodged that bullet. From what he had heard of Miss Theresa's horsemanship abilities, he seriously doubted she had taken a fall. Nevertheless, with her having instigated the subterfuge, he was thankful that it would be a day or two before he would see her again, as she recovered from her *injury*.

Unfortunately, for poor Mr. Darcy, Lady Harriette chose that same day to launch her strategy to win his affections. Like Miss Theresa, she also became an early riser. She too began to note the early morning comings and goings. She was quite amused to see Miss Theresa arriving at the house in the arms of Colonel Fitzwilliam whilst Darcy walked along behind them; she could only imagine the cause of that turn of events. Lady Harriette was much too clever to attempt such a lame ruse. She decided upon a direct assault. However, the first order of business was to pay a courtesy call on Miss Theresa.

Lady Harriette visited Miss Theresa in her room to inquire after her injury. Their conversation began on a light and cordial note, but soon took an unpleasant turn.

"There is another matter I wish to discuss with you. I think it is only fair to let you know I have every intention of pursuing and winning Mr. Darcy's affections. I am telling you this because it is no secret that you have your heart set on winning him for yourself. In fact, you have had the entire Season to do just that, and you have failed miserably. It is time for you to bow out, gracefully or not," Lady Harriette said with a straightforwardness that left Miss Theresa dumbfounded.

Amidst Miss Theresa's fierce protests, Lady Harriette calmly stated, "Please, you had your chance and look at how it ended. Perhaps others might be interested to know whose arms you were in just this morning." As she stood to leave the room, she turned to Miss Theresa and smugly said, "Good day, Miss

Theresa. You have my most sincere wishes for a speedy recovery."

~~~

Lady Harriette was extremely close to her brother growing up. Therefore, she was no stranger to masculine leisurely activities. She thought of herself as a formidable opponent for anyone, male or female. She began to join Darcy on his early morning rides, despite having no invitation. It did not go unnoticed by Darcy that her stallion was large and menacing, like his own. She finagled him into escorting her to dinner each night and invited him to turn the pages for her as she exhibited on the pianoforte, refusing to take no for an answer as she attached herself to his arm. The last straw for Darcy was when she showed up one afternoon, fully suited with foil in hand to interrupt a fencing match between Richard and himself, and challenged the winner. This, after she had barged into the billiard room earlier, to watch them play.

Darcy observed that, for a young woman of nineteen, Lady Harriette was particularly bold. He genuinely believed that he might be in some danger from the young woman, *physical danger*. There was only one thing to do. He made up an excuse to return to Pemberley on urgent business with his steward. He would return to accompany Georgiana and Elizabeth back to Pemberley in one week.

~~~

The evening before Darcy's departure, Richard and he were in Lord Matlock's study engrossed in an intense game of chess. Richard was far from pleased with his cousin. Lady Ellen had obviously doubled her attempts at playing matchmaker. Instead of having a bit of fun, it seemed that Darcy had elected to withdraw from the battlefield.

"Old man, I must say I am quite disappointed in you."

Darcy responded nonchalantly, "I suppose I have no choice but to hear the cause of your disappointment."

"Indeed, you do not. What has gotten into you? It was bad enough, your attitude in town, but now you seem eager to flee the lovely Lady Harriette's presence, rather than give her the famous Darcy treatment."

"It is quite simple. She does not deserve such treatment. It would be adolescent and cruel. It is far better not to encourage her hopes at all."

"That sounds like the voice of the *would-be* mistress of Pemberley," Richard chided. "Just whose companion is she, that she should have such influence over you?"

Darcy ignored Richard's taunt and rather focused upon his next move. He saw no point in either denying or giving credence to his cousin's sentiments. No one knew Darcy better than Richard. By the same token, no one better understood Darcy's sense of obligation to his family. So what if Richard suspected his overwhelming desire and deep longing for Elizabeth? Both men understood that nothing would ever become of it. Darcy decided to let his cousin have his fun, even if at his own expense. Besides, for once he was on the verge of besting his cousin at chess.

Before they parted company that evening, Darcy asked Richard to keep an eye on his sister in his absence, due to the blossoming relationship with Lord Harry. He also cautioned Richard to stay away from Elizabeth. He had noticed his cousin becoming a little too friendly with her.

Undoubtedly, Richard was spending time with Elizabeth to annoy Darcy. With Darcy so obsessed with watching over Georgiana, and avoiding Miss Theresa and Lady Harriette, Richard had an ample opportunity to get to know her better. While Elizabeth remained somewhat distrustful of him, Richard became quite captivated by her. As Darcy's closest friend, he began to understand why Darcy preferred her to all other women of his acquaintance. She was different from anyone else he had ever known.

Upon Darcy's return to Matlock a week later, Lord Harry approached him to ask permission to court Georgiana. Thinking as he did, that Darcy did not look upon him favourably, Lord Harry had already gained Richard as an ally in his quest. Reluctantly, but at Richard's strong encouragement, Darcy granted his permission, but only on the condition that Georgiana be allowed one more Season before becoming attached. Lord Harry and Georgiana had previously discussed Darcy's wish for her to have at least two Seasons. Lord Harry and she had already reached an understanding, it seemed. Darcy did not need to know that just yet.

~ Chapter 7 ~
Much Brighter Hope

Elizabeth received a letter from her sister Mary. Written over three weeks earlier, it had been rerouted from London, to Pemberley, to Matlock, and back to Pemberley. Mary related that Charlotte Collins née Lucas died in labour along with her child. Mary's retelling of that fateful day caused Elizabeth considerable distress. *Poor dear Charlotte, married to my hideous cousin for nearly a year, now tragically departed.* After a bout of sad reflection, she continued to read the letter clutched tightly in her hand.

Mary wrote that whilst she attempted to offer condolences to Mr. Collins during his time of need, he confessed he could not bear to live alone. They had reached an understanding. They planned to marry in three weeks; a full month after Charlotte's passing. *By now my sister is Mr. Collins's wife,* Elizabeth considered. She had always known that Mary held a favourable opinion of their cousin. It came as no great surprise that she should marry him, but the timing… Elizabeth considered the irony of her family's situation and her own rejection of her cousin's proposal. How different things would be had Mr. Collins offered for Mary, instead of herself, in the first place.

Mary stated in her letter that she understood if Elizabeth could not attend the wedding, especially in light of the disaster that was Mr. Collins's proposal less than a year earlier. Mary expressed her fondest wish that the Bennet family would soon be reunited. Mrs. Bennet and Kitty would return to Longbourn on the eve of her wedding to Mr. Collins, thereby reclaiming their rightful place at Longbourn. Nothing would make her happier than to have Elizabeth and Jane return, as well. Elizabeth smiled as she read her sister's sentiments. *Indeed, it truly would be a wonderful blessing if Jane returned from Scotland, but it is impossible that I should consent to live under Mr. Collins's authority.*

Elizabeth was glad for her sister. She immediately set out to write to Mary of her joy for her and the rest of the family. She also wrote a heartfelt letter to the Lucas family to express her condolences.

~~~

Three days later, Darcy summoned Elizabeth to his study. With Georgiana's courtship formally under way, he had reached a decision about her supervision. He needed to discuss it with Elizabeth.

"Miss Elizabeth, I have decided to hire a chaperon for Georgiana."

"A chaperon, sir; as her companion, is that not one of my duties?"

"I never intended you to watch over her, Miss Elizabeth. I imagine Lord Harry will be here often, now that he has permission to court her. I want them supervised carefully at all times. I do not expect that of you."

"Sir, are you dissatisfied with my work? Do you believe I am an unsuitable companion?" Elizabeth asked with uncertainty.
~~~

"You know that it pleases both Georgiana and me to have you here. However, you are a maiden yourself, as well as Georgiana's closest friend," Darcy responded, trying his best to put her at ease.

"Perhaps you think I will allow the couple too much freedom because I am young and inexperienced, myself. If that is the case, let me assure you, I take my responsibilities very seriously," she affirmed.

"Miss Elizabeth, I am aware of how committed you are to Georgiana, and I trust your care over her, implicitly. You must trust me when I say this is for the best. You should continue to spend as much time with Georgiana as you wish, but you should not feel obligated to attend to her when she is with Lord Harry. That will be the job of the chaperon. This is as much for me as it is for you. I cannot spend all my time watching the young couple. I do not expect you to have to either, even if you do think it is your responsibility."

Darcy continued, "I have arranged an interview with an old friend of the family, a middle-aged, recently widowed woman. Her name is Mrs. Pearce. I invite you to take part, should you wish."

"That is not necessary, sir. Am I excused?"

Sensing her apprehension, Darcy approached Elizabeth and gently placed his reassuring hand on her slender arm. Attempting once more to put her at ease, he took her hand. "Please do not worry, Miss Elizabeth. It will be for the best. You trust me, do you not?"

"Yes, of course I trust you, sir. If you will excuse me, I think I will go out for a walk before dinner." Elizabeth curtseyed and quickly left the room. Darcy stood in awe. He wondered what he might have said to make that go smoother. It was disquieting for him, seeing her reaction to his news. *She is completely unaware that I would do anything for her.*

Elizabeth headed outside for her walk and contemplated Darcy's latest act. Based upon her conversations with Georgiana, she knew Georgiana and Lord Harry were in love, and they planned to wed as soon as the upcoming Season was over. Her days with the Darcys were coming to an end. She could not help but be troubled that Darcy planned to hire a chaperon for Georgiana. She trusted it was not an indictment against her—that it was exactly as he presented it. Elizabeth was certain that she would stay with Georgiana until she married. What was to happen after that? Fortunately, she was no longer obligated to send money to Meryton to help her family. All that she earned from then on would be hers alone. Elizabeth had no doubt that Darcy over compensated her for her services as Georgiana's companion. He paid her handsomely, for all intents and purposes, to enjoy the lifestyle of a wealthy maiden.

She thought of her uncle Gardiner as being a very successful businessman. She decided to write to him to seek his financial advice. Once she left the Darcys, she did not intend to seek employment again. With her uncle's help, she would endeavour to build up a small nest egg and live modesty off the interest, without being an added burden to her family.

Once Elizabeth carefully considered her plans, her spirits rose immensely. She soon strolled merrily along the garden path with much brighter hope for her future.

~ ~ ~

The ensuing weeks at Pemberley passed quickly. Lord Harry remained in Matlock to accommodate his courtship with Georgiana. Given the relatively short distance between the two estates, he visited with her almost daily. Elizabeth found Lord Harry very engaging. He was handsome and good-hearted, and he doted on Georgiana. Elizabeth suspected the two would be a truly loving and affectionate couple when they married. Even Darcy quickly warmed to Lord Harry, as he began to spend more and more of the time at Pemberley. As Darcy predicted, Lord Harry visited so often, it was a relief to Elizabeth that Mrs. Pearce was also there to chaperon the young couple.

Darcy made sure that Elizabeth spent much of her free time with him. The two of them spent hours in the library, reading and debating. Horseback riding was a favourite pastime as the weather permitted. Darcy even invited her into his study to seek her opinion on Pemberley household matters, to Elizabeth's bewilderment, because he had come to value her judgements. It seemed Darcy could not get enough of Elizabeth's company, and she delighted in his company, as well.

~~~

In early December, Darcy began to plan for the Christmas season. He hoped to spend Christmas at Pemberley with Elizabeth. As Georgiana's paid companion, it was Elizabeth's job to go wherever she went during all times; however, as both Georgiana and Darcy regarded her as a close friend, neither would demand it, if Elizabeth chose otherwise. When Darcy asked Elizabeth of her plans for Christmas and whether she would visit her family, Elizabeth said she intended to spend only two days with the Gardiners in London. Therefore, Darcy made his plans so. Giving up his hopes to spend Christmas at Pemberley, he arranged to spend it in town to accommodate Elizabeth. He made extensive plans for their entertainment. He was so looking forward to sharing that time with her.

Days later, Elizabeth received a letter from Jane informing her that she was returning to England. She had given her notice to her employer in Scotland. She looked forward to seeing
~~~

Elizabeth at Longbourn, along with the Gardiners. It would be a marvellous family reunion in their beloved home.

Elizabeth did not want to disappoint Darcy and Georgiana. But, of course she would go to Longbourn now that Jane would be there. Elizabeth set out to speak privately with Darcy, to tell him of her change in plans.

"Mr. Darcy, I have wonderful news. My eldest sister, Jane, is returning to England. She will be at Longbourn in time for Christmas."

Darcy's heart sank. That could only mean one thing. He said, "Indeed that is wonderful news. I am happy for her, and for your family. I imagine you will spend Christmas there, as well."

"Oh yes, I am very excited to see her again! Our whole family will be there, including my uncle and aunt from town. I plan to travel by stagecoach, so that I might arrive as soon as possible," Elizabeth enthusiastically responded.

"You plan to travel from Derbyshire to Hertfordshire by stagecoach," Darcy responded. *Are you out of your mind?* He thought to himself. "Surely, you jest. I would never allow that."

"I beg your pardon, sir," she said with a certain degree of astonishment.

"I will not allow you to travel by stagecoach. What are you thinking?"

"How DARE you? You do not decide how I conduct my own personal affairs! Stop trying to control me!" Elizabeth shouted.

"I am not trying to control you. My concern is for your safety. You know that!" Darcy insisted, thinking to himself, *All these months, and she is still as headstrong as ever.*

"What I know is that you enjoy having your own way in all matters, even those that do not concern you!" Elizabeth insisted, thinking to herself, *All these months, and he is still as officious as ever.*

"And I will have my way this time. I will take you to Longbourn myself," he stated firmly, then mumbled, "even if it means exposing my sister to tradesmen."

Instead of focusing upon his effrontery towards her relatives, she argued, "I will not have it, Mr. Darcy! What might everyone think seeing me personally escorted to Meryton by my employer?"

"Then, I shall take you to London, and you can travel with your uncle and aunt. We will leave in two days hence. Now, if you will excuse me, I must speak with my steward. Good day, Miss Elizabeth," he decreed, as he left her fuming in his study.

The fact was that Elizabeth did not want to abide by Darcy's dictate because she did not want to chance increasing her mother's expectation that she was more than a paid companion. Once she returned to her apartment, Elizabeth recalled the many letters she had received from her mother with explicit instructions on how to use her arts and allurements to ensnare Darcy and secure the future of her family. Mrs. Bennet said it was selfish of Elizabeth to have such a lifestyle while her poor family suffered so. She insisted that Elizabeth would be wealthy beyond any of their dreams with a house in town, many splendid carriages, and such pin-money. In addition, she would put her sisters in the way of rich husbands. It mortified Elizabeth even to imagine her mother's outrageous behaviour if Darcy arrived at Longbourn with her. No, she would never allow that.

Needless to say, the return trip to London was not nearly as pleasant as had been the journey to Pemberley. The weather was harsh, cold and rainy. Darcy spent the bulk of the trip in the closed confines of the carriage with Georgiana and Elizabeth. He spoke very little to either of them, preferring instead to focus his attention upon the passing winter scenery. Instead of putting their differences aside, even for Georgiana's sake, he elected to take his meals in his room, when they rested each night.

When Darcy, Georgiana, Elizabeth, and Mrs. Pearce arrived at Darcy House, he immediately arranged to have Elizabeth properly escorted to the Gardiners' home in Cheapside. His spirits remained as low as the day they argued. Irrationally, he felt he had lost her. What would happen if she decided never to return? It broke his heart as he watched her departure from his home after the tearful goodbye with Georgiana. Elizabeth gave her promise to Georgiana that she would return to London in time to prepare for the Matlock's Twelfth Night Ball.

~ Chapter 8 ~
When Did It Happen

Once Jane and Elizabeth retired for bed the first night after Elizabeth's arrival at Longbourn, the two began a long discourse on their lives over the past year. As Jane related her experiences in Scotland, she did so in a way reflective of her serenity and strength of character.

By Jane's account, though she truly felt blessed to have escaped the harshness often associated with the life of a governess, her day-to-day life left much to desire.

"Lizzy, the life of a governess is one I would scarcely recommend. For twelve hours a day and seven days a week, I was always on duty. In addition to caring for the two small children in my charge, various other household duties befell me, as well. It seemed, it would not do to have a governess in one's household with too much idle time on her hands," Jane said in a lighter tone than the situation likely warranted.

"Dearest Jane, it sounds as if your schedule gave you little time to yourself."

"Indeed, what little time I had to myself, I spent alone in my very small quarters." Jane went on to describe the isolation she often felt in being the governess. She was deemed unsuitable to keep company with the master and mistress and far above the status of the other household servants. She suffered an utter lack of personal privilege in the household, and there were virtually no opportunities to take part in society.

Elizabeth remained remarkably silent as she listened to Jane's account of her life as a governess. She compared Jane's story to her own situation as Georgiana's companion; her maid, elegant living quarters, fine clothing, private balls, Pemberley, Bella.

Jane reached for Elizabeth's hand and sighed, "Lizzy, I would not wish to see you live such a life. My greatest comfort during all those months was in knowing that you were with the Darcys."

Elizabeth insisted, "Jane, you must come to town when we return; that way I will be able to visit with you on my days off. London is so diverting."

"Perhaps, then I might finally meet the *accomplished* Miss Darcy," Jane quipped. Elizabeth detected a hint of resentment that was not typical of Jane. She could only attribute it to the past months in Scotland.

"Mr. Darcy is adamant that Georgiana does not visit with our relatives in town, because they are in trade. In fact, it is a matter of great contention between us; but you are welcome to visit at Darcy House. I have spoken of you so often to Georgiana, she feels as if she already knows you. She cannot wait to meet you."

"Well Lizzy, if he feels that strongly, he must believe he has good reasons. I suppose the difference in social classes is not easily overlooked by a gentleman of his status," Jane said, endeavouring to see things from Darcy's point of view.

"Jane, you are too good. You always make an effort to see the best in everyone."

"Lizzy, you cannot still be so harsh on poor Mr. Darcy. He must think rather highly of you."

"He is arrogant and proud, indeed, but I have to say that he does improve upon closer acquaintance," Elizabeth admitted. She continued, "And Pemberley is a wondrous sight to behold. I have considered that, as master of such a vast estate and substitute parent for Georgiana, he has shouldered much responsibility from a very young age; he had to grow up too quickly, I sometimes think. Perhaps that is why he is proud. I cannot imagine who would not be under such circumstances." Elizabeth went on to say, "I have to admit, he is not so very bad. He and I have grown very close. We are dear friends."

Jane detected what might be construed as too much enthusiasm in her sister's voice as she spoke of Mr. Darcy. She hoped Elizabeth was not seduced by the Darcys' lifestyle. "Are you sure that it is merely a friendship? Could there be more to your relationship than that?"

"I would be lying if I said I was not quite fond of Mr. Darcy, but I do not expect there will ever be more between us than friendship."

Jane had always given Darcy the benefit of the doubt when he was in Hertfordshire. She could not be counted among his many critics, but she also suspected he was a man who was used to getting his way.

"Lizzy, please be careful to protect your heart should you ever wish for more than Mr. Darcy is willing to give," she cautioned her younger sister.

"Thank you for your words of wisdom. Do not worry, I will take them to heart," she said as she embraced Jane. Elizabeth continued, "I really hope you will consider returning with us to town. I could use your support, and while I do not presume to speak for our uncle and aunt, I am certain they will welcome you with open arms."

Jane said, "I do not wish to burden any of our relations, but perhaps it is not unbearable here at Longbourn. Both our brother and Mary have made me feel quite welcomed."

"Then you are far better than me, dear Jane, for I cannot imagine living with Mr. Collins." Elizabeth went on to describe her vision of life as *a poor relation* of Mr. Collins and how it must be to live under his authority.

"Then, that settles it; I shall stay at Longbourn, and you shall have a home should you need it, with our uncle and aunt in town."

Jane felt strongly that if only one of them were to consider Longbourn her home, it was far better that it was herself. Elizabeth should not have to endure her mother's wrath and unwarranted accusations.

~~~

The entire family sought to temper Mrs. Bennet's attitude towards Elizabeth during her stay, including Mr. Collins. Even he could not hide his embarrassment when Mrs. Bennet carelessly reminded Elizabeth that had she not been so headstrong and foolish, and accepted his proposal, she might have spared the family the agony and shame of the past year.

She also blamed Elizabeth for Jane's having to work in Scotland. She often fretted over her ill fate. *If only Lizzy had gone off to Scotland. If only Jane worked for the proud Mr. Darcy. With all her beauty, she would have been certain to turn the man's head.*

Mrs. Bennet even disparaged Elizabeth's expensive clothing and accused her of being above her company, which troubled Elizabeth exceedingly. She had made a concerted effort to visit as many of her home-town acquaintances during her stay as possible, including some of the very people who re-
~~~

fused to receive them when the Bennets fell on hard times, a little under a year ago. With the litany of complaints against her by her mother, Elizabeth supposed her mother had indeed gone distracted.

The Gardiners served as witnesses to all the harsh criticisms and verbal abuses Mrs. Bennet directed towards Elizabeth the entire time. They were proud of Elizabeth to have overcome so much strife for such a young woman, yet keeping her spirit, her wit, and playful manner. She had come so far over the past year, since they had taken her in after the violent death of her father. They doubted Elizabeth would ever be able to live at Longbourn again under the current environment. They could not wait for their return to town.

~~~

One morning, Elizabeth stepped inside the library when Mr. Collins was on an errand in Meryton. She simply wanted to experience the sense of closeness that she once had shared with her father. The room was nothing as she remembered it, for Mr. Collins had redecorated to suit his own tastes. It was his right, but for Elizabeth, it only served as a terribly painful reminder. Longbourn was no longer her home.

Her sister Mary sensed the isolation Elizabeth felt at Longbourn and reached out to her. "Lizzy, I apologise for my mother's behaviour since you arrived. Please say you do not hold it as an indictment against all of us. We are very happy to have you here; you must know that."

"Yes, of course I do, Mary. I am afraid I shall always be a disappointment to our mother," Elizabeth confessed.

"You must know how much we all appreciate you. Your financial support to the family when we resided with our Uncle
~~~

and Aunt Phillips was a blessing, indeed. It made such a difference; you will never know how much."

"Thank you, Mary. I only wish I could have done more," she expressed wistfully. "Tell me, are you happy with Mr. Collins? Do you love him?"

"I love my family, Lizzy. I did what I had to do to bring us together as a family again, here at Longbourn. I did what anyone would have done in a similar circumstance, I am sure," Mary affirmed. Noting Elizabeth's uneasiness with her last statement, she said, "And do not think I was simply being mercenary. I respect Mr. Collins, and I will be a good wife to him."

"I know you will be, Mary. You are a very good person; you cannot help but be a good wife," Elizabeth said, as the two sisters embraced.

"Besides, I have determined to make the best of things. I detected a thing or two from the late Mrs. Collins. All in all, I suppose I manage my dear husband quite well."

"I must admit that to be true, and he shows deep admiration and respect for you. I am happy for you."

"Thank you, Lizzy, and please know that you will always have a home here at Longbourn; do not ever forget it."

Elizabeth felt heartened by Mary's words. She could not help but feel some level of resentment towards Mr. Collins when she initially returned to Longbourn. Her recollection of her family's painful eviction was still fresh in her mind. Yes, it was his right to claim Longbourn as his own upon her father's death; but he might have shown a bit more compassion. Elizabeth knew there was no point in holding on to those bitter memories. Mr. Collins was her brother, and her family was together. It was time to let go of the past.

~~~
~~~

Christmas Eve was a solemn occasion for the family. Elizabeth recalled the last time all of her family was together. Everyone was happy—*Mr. Bennet, intellectual and reclusive... Mrs. Bennet, emotional and excitable... Jane, angelic and serene... Elizabeth, charming and witty... Mary, sombre and rational... Kitty, sweet and bubbly... and Lydia, pampered and naïve.* Those times were long gone. Even Mrs. Bennet was pensive and reflective. Mr. Collins was particularly mindful of the family's mood. In a rare display of exemplary oratory skills, he offered a thankful prayer for his new family, along with a touching mention of the late Mr. Bennet and Miss Lydia.

On Christmas Day, Elizabeth escaped the hustle and bustle of Longbourn for a solitary ramble to Oakham Mount, one of her favourite spots in all of Hertfordshire. It was her place to go when she desired solitude and private rumination. She could not resist feeling triumphant at how Darcy would react if he knew she was out and about the countryside without a proper escort. She often thought about Darcy, especially his likely reactions to various situations throughout most of her days... while comparing the sights and sounds of Hertfordshire to those of Derbyshire... while dining and comparing the dish to one of his favourites... while reading a book and wondering what his take would be on a particular verse.

Elizabeth was counting the days until her return to town, and thus Darcy House. She asked herself how it happened. Why did it happen? When did she fall in love with Mr. Darcy? To all these questions, she could not place a specific cause or an exact time, for it came on so gradually. One question weighed heaviest on her mind; the most fundamental question of all. *What am I to do about it?*

~ Chapter 9 ~
Owe It To

Elizabeth sat in the well-appointed carriage, on the way to Matlock House, recalling the contents of a letter she had received from Georgiana, whilst at Longbourn.

Dearest Elizabeth,

I pray this letter finds you in excellent health, as well as in good spirits. I have so missed you during these past weeks. Nevertheless, I take such comfort in knowing your beloved sister and you are together once again.

My days have been rather eventful, especially since my dearest Lord Harry returned to town after spending Christmas in Stafford with his parents. His sister, Lady Harriette, is in town also, and we are making an effort to become better acquainted with each other. She has visited us here at Darcy House quite often.

Unfortunately, my brother does not fare well. He has not seemed to enjoy himself at all. He has been very sad and detached. Despite the many arrangements made for our entertainment these past weeks, he has declined to take part in any of them. I only wish you were here, Elizabeth.

Fitzwilliam recently decided to join one of his old friends for a hunting trip in Oxfordshire. He will be away until the end of January. Upon your return to town, please send a note to Matlock House, where we both will stay until Fitzwilliam returns. I will arrange to have a carriage bring you to my uncle and aunt's home straight away.

May you thoroughly delight in this time with your family. Please tell Miss Bennet how happy I am that she is in her home and that I look forward to meeting her. I eagerly await our reunion in January.

May God bless you. Your dear friend,
Georgiana Darcy

Elizabeth was both disappointed and relieved. Darcy had occupied her thoughts a great deal over the past weeks. In some respects, she looked forward to seeing him, when she returned to town. She missed him. On the other hand, he was the last person she wanted to see, for she had not decided how best to deal with her newly confessed affection for him. With him set to return to town at the end of January, she had plenty of time to put her feelings into the proper perspective. Still, as she recalled Georgiana's words on Darcy's dismay, she wondered if her absence might have been a contributing factor. That made little sense to her. Of course, Darcy and she had grown close during the past months; but was it so much that her absence saddened him? She doubted that she held such sway over his emotions.

Over Christmastime, Darcy's mood left much to desire. He attended to Georgiana most conscientiously as they both attempted to celebrate the season apart from Elizabeth, as well as apart from Lord Harry, to Georgiana's extent. As the days passed, Darcy grew more and more displeased with his own behaviour, as he pondered the power that Elizabeth held over him, although completely unbeknownst to her. Aside from Richard, she was the only person of his acquaintance who dared to question him. His uncle and aunt often attempted to counsel him, to no avail. Richard he could easily ignore, but he was finding it increasingly difficult to deny Elizabeth anything he thought might increase her pleasure. Surely, it was not wise to allow one person so much influence over him. With that thought in mind, Darcy decided it was unreasonable to continue to obsess over her absence. *Of course, she will return. I will do everything in my power to assure it.* The invitation to join his old friend on an extended hunting trip was just the distraction Darcy needed to prevail over his melancholy.

~~~

The upper echelons of society were out in large numbers for the annual Matlock Twelfth Night Masquerade Ball. Dressed in fabulous costumes of famous literary characters with their identities disguised, most everyone took full advantage of their anonymity to relax the strictures of society and throw caution to the wind. The guests imbibed heavily of the steady flowing drinks, and the atmosphere proved quite raucous as they moved about the ballroom trying to discover one another's identities.

Without informing anyone in his family of his plans, Darcy returned to town earlier than expected so that he might attend the ball. Despite the hunting trip, meant to divert his constant thoughts of Elizabeth, he missed her terribly. He simply had to see her. The masquerade theme gave him the perfect opportunity to observe Elizabeth undetected, as well as escape his aunt's matchmaking schemes, as he and all the other gentlemen in attendance sported masks of one kind or another. Darcy knew exactly the nature of Georgiana's costume, so he could recognise her, and thereby Elizabeth, with relative ease. Elizabeth did not seem as jovial as those around her were. Darcy watched as she turned down one dance request after another,
~~~

before whispering to Georgiana and escaping the room. He followed her. He observed her entering the library and did not hesitate to go into the room after her.

Elizabeth was not in the frame of mind to enjoy the festivities that night. Since they were guests at Matlock House and Mrs. Pearce was not there, it was her obligation to accompany Georgiana. She desired to step away for a short time, to take a break from the merriment. She had just removed her mask when Darcy caught her totally by surprise.

"Mr. Darcy! What are you doing here?" Elizabeth blurted out. "I mean to say, I thought you were away."

"No, I decided to return sooner," Darcy said with a slight wave of his hand. "I saw you escape the ballroom. Are you feeling unwell?" he asked as he moved closer to where she stood.

As if uncertain, Elizabeth said, "Yes! I mean, no. I am all right."

"It is good to see you. Did you enjoy Christmas, Miss Elizabeth?" he asked hesitantly, and then inquired, "I trust your family is well."

Still a bit startled by his abrupt appearance, she expressed, "Yes, I had an enjoyable time. It was a wonderful reunion with my sister Jane. I tried to persuade her to return to town with us."

"I am sure that would have brought you great comfort," he replied with a smile.

"Indeed, you are quite right." Elizabeth finally relaxed. "It is good you are back. Georgiana misses you exceedingly. She has been unhappy during your absence."

"She seems all right now," he stated.

"Well, yes, but for the past few days, she has expressed her sadness over your absence many times."

"And you, Miss Elizabeth, have you missed me, as well?" he asked in a low and deeply caring voice.

"Yes, I have, sir. I am so sorry for disappointing your hopes for Christmas," Elizabeth responded genuinely and softly.

"No, I must apologise to you. I was selfish and stubborn," Darcy insisted.

"You are correct. You are selfish," Elizabeth gently teased, "but we are both stubborn, and like to have our own way."

"Let us not argue over who shares the greater blame for what took place. Shall we call a truce?" Darcy offered hopefully.

"That sounds very agreeable," Elizabeth cheerfully acquiesced.

"I have missed you so much," Darcy murmured, now standing right in front of Elizabeth. Having in mind a chaste gesture, he raised her hand to his lips and kissed it gently. He turned her hand over and kissed her palm tenderly. Ingenuously, Darcy placed his hands on her arms and drew her a bit closer to place a light kiss upon her temple.

It was a lingering kiss. Darcy thought to himself that her skin tasted wonderfully sweet. Her hair smelt of summer roses. The faint tones of the finely tuned orchestra and the intimacy of the dimly lit room cast a magical aura. He moved his hand to raise Elizabeth's chin upwards and soon placed a soft kiss on her cheekbone. Both felt their closeness intoxicating.

Elizabeth stood enchantingly captivated by the moment. *He is here with me. I am not at all ready to see him tonight. He is standing so close. His soft, moist lips are divine. What is he doing here? Can this be a dream?*

Darcy gingerly placed a light kiss along the corner of her mouth. He paused momentarily to take in her beautiful face. Her eyes closed, Elizabeth's lush eyelashes and soft features mesmerised him. Her slightly parted lips were his undoing.

He was utterly tempted to brush his lips affectionately against hers, when he remembered himself. He felt as if he were dreaming, being so close to the woman he loved. Beyond question, it was no dream. He adored her. He promised himself to protect her. *I should not hold her in this way.*

Darcy slowly released his hands and spoke softly, "I beg for forgiveness, Miss Elizabeth. I should not have done that. Please say that you forgive me?"

After allowing a moment to gather her thoughts, whilst the pounding of her heart subsided, Elizabeth responded, "Perhaps, the moment caught us both up. It is Twelfth Night after all, and stranger things have been known to happen. I accept my share of any blame."

"No, you must not blame yourself for my lack of control," Darcy pleaded, distressed that she should harbour such a notion for even a second. "I could not bear to have you think you did anything wrong. The fault lies completely with me. I promise it will not happen again."

After allowing time to make sure of Elizabeth's composure, Darcy suggested that she might leave the room before him, while he remained behind. He took her hand and escorted her to the door to allow her to go. He immediately locked it upon her departure. He sat in a comfortable chair next to the fireplace to compose himself and reflect upon his actions. As he shuddered to think what might have happened earlier in that room, he became woefully remorseful. *How could I lose control like that... after so many months? How will I ever make up for what has taken place?*

~~~

Prior to his departure from Matlock House for the evening, Darcy sought out his uncle to tell him that though he had re-
~~~

turned to town earlier than he had planned, he wished to have Georgiana and Elizabeth stay at Matlock House for a while longer whilst he attended to pressing matters. Then he left the ball, without acknowledging his presence to anyone else, even his sister.

Before he allowed Darcy to leave, Lord Matlock cautioned him on his blithe behaviour. He reminded him of his duty to his family. Yet again, he tried to make it clear to Darcy that he expected more of him than he did his own sons. His eldest son, Lord Robert, had proven a colossal disappointment. His younger son, Richard, seemed destined for a similar fate. However, Darcy had more responsibility than did his sons; the expectations of him were greater. Like his wife, Lord Matlock did not subscribe to the notion that Darcy should marry his cousin Anne to unite the two dynasties. He thought that Darcy should choose a bride from among the *ton*, and the sooner the better. None of them was getting any younger.

As Darcy left Matlock House, he was utterly dejected. His uncle's words, his actions earlier that night, and his overwhelming sense of loneliness weighed heavily upon him. Over six months had passed since Darcy had been with a woman, yet he certainly did not intend to visit Madam Adele's establishment that night. Regardless of months of excruciatingly painful abstinence, he could not taint the memory of what would be the only hint of passion with the woman he loved, in the arms of another.

He did not believe that he would ever patronise such a place again.

~ ~ ~

Elizabeth woke up very early the morning after the ball. She barely slept at all, as she recalled her moments in the library with Darcy. She imagined how it might have felt to share her first kiss. She wondered. Owe it to the mystique of Twelfth Night... the costumes, the whimsy. Soon she thought about Darcy's puzzling behaviour. When he chose, he was charming, attentive, caring, and affectionate. At other times, he was haughty and officious. However, he treated her with deference in his home, far better than a paid companion might reasonably expect. She asked herself, *Is his preferential treatment towards me solely to placate his younger sister? Might he have deeper feelings for me than those of friendship? Are those feelings of a long duration?*

Questions in her mind persisted. *What is the point of dwelling on this line of thinking? Is anything beyond our friendship and my role as Georgiana's companion really important?* If just a matter of the disgrace that had befallen her family the year before, perhaps in time that might be forgotten, but the difference in their social classes had always been wide. Now, it was even more so, with her status in his household. Moreover, even if Darcy himself had not expressed his obligation to his family to make an excellent match, certainly her close association with the Matlocks provided a strong affirmation. It was clear to Elizabeth that they would accept nothing else of him.

When she went down for breakfast, Elizabeth did not mention having seen Mr. Darcy to Georgiana. He had obviously left the ball after their encounter without making his presence known. Elizabeth was not at all surprised when she heard from Lord Matlock that they were to stay at Matlock House a while longer. She considered that Darcy was trying to maintain distance between them after what had occurred the night before. She thought that perhaps it was for the best, for even she could not say with certainty how far things might have progressed had he not stopped when he did. One thing was abundantly clear to her… it would never happen again. She would be the one to make certain of that. Regardless of how she may have felt about him, Elizabeth would not let her guard down with Darcy again.

~~~

After nearly a week of self-imposed exile, Darcy finally brought Georgiana and Elizabeth home from Matlock House. He did not know what he might expect in the aftermath of his actions, but he had gotten to the point where he missed Elizabeth terribly and could no longer bear their separation.

Darcy and Elizabeth's strained behaviour towards one another played out with each appearing to the other to go out of their way to avoid close, personal dealings. Their attempts to avoid situations where they might be alone were futile given Georgiana's penchant for leaving the two of them together—even going so far as to close the door when she left.

Elizabeth's warm and pleasant disposition got the better of her one frosty winter afternoon. Darcy and she sat in the library. Before their encounter on Twelfth Night, it was the scene of many lively debates. The new silence was deafening. She knew enough of Darcy and his taciturn nature to recognise that he could likely go months without engaging in conversation. The persistent silence began to dampen her spirits. They had sat there for over an hour. Steady to his purpose, Darcy scarcely spoke a word to her as he adhered, most conscientiously, to his book. He did not even glance at her.

"Mr. Darcy, how much longer are you planning to carry on in this ridiculous manner when in my company?" she asked as the second hour was approaching.

"I beg your pardon, madam."
~~~

"How long are we to share the same room for hours at a time, with no conversation between us?"

"Excuse me, Miss Elizabeth," he said as he sat his book aside to give her his full attention. "You know how disappointed I am with my behaviour at Matlock House. It is obvious that you have not forgiven me, and our relationship has suffered."

"Am I the one who has been unsociable and taciturn these past weeks?"

"I have made every effort to allow you as much breathing room as possible. You do not seem comfortable when the two of us are alone," he said, longing for nothing more than to bridge the gap between them and return to their past level of amity.

"Mr. Darcy, as I have said repeatedly, all is forgiven. What more do you want?" she beseeched, her frustration steadily growing.

"I want what we had."

"What is it that you think we *had*?" Elizabeth implored, further aggravated.

"I want you to feel comfortable with me and know that I will never harm you. I want the friendship we once shared."

"You are hardly being fair. If I say we cannot go back to the level of friendship we had before, you will think I am blaming you for what happened between us, which I am not. I accept my part in what happened. Nevertheless, because it did happen, we cannot go back. Either of us might be tempted to let our defence down again, and then where would we be?"

"I will not allow it. Do not be afraid."

"I am not afraid of you, Mr. Darcy," Elizabeth exclaimed.

"Then, can we still be friends... like before?"

"Mr. Darcy, as always, you want to have your cake and eat it too!" Elizabeth resolutely declared, "Well, not this time! We

ARE friends, but nothing like we were before. Take it or leave it, sir!" Elizabeth slammed her book shut and left the library in haste.

~ Chapter 10 ~
Distinction of Rank

Darcy brought Georgiana and Elizabeth along with Richard and him on their annual visit to Rosings Park for Easter. Elizabeth observed that it was every bit as grand as described by Mr. Collins. As regarded Lady Catherine de Bourgh, Elizabeth was quite surprised to learn that she was a close relative of Mr. Darcy. She thought her Ladyship was perfectly ridiculous. She wondered at how Darcy had, in good conscience, looked down upon the people of Hertfordshire during his stay when such a ninny as Lady Catherine graced his own family tree.

The amount of attention Lady Catherine showered upon her confounded Elizabeth. She hoped that in being relegated off to the side of the drawing room to sit with Mrs. Jenkinson, Miss Anne de Bourgh's companion, thus preserving the distinction of rank, Lady Catherine would ignore her ignoble presence.

Upon reflection, Elizabeth concluded that her birthright as a gentleman's daughter was what held her Ladyship's interest. Lady Catherine inundated her with questions of her family, her former life in Hertfordshire, and her accomplishments. When the Lady condescended to offer her condolences to Elizabeth on the death of her father in attempting to recover her fallen sister, Elizabeth had about reached the limit of her endurance. To make matters even worse, Lady Catherine said it was she who had encouraged Mr. Collins to descend immediately upon Longbourn to assume his rightful place upon the death of her father; but it had been his late wife who had impertinently intervened to allow the Bennet family the full four weeks to leave.

Elizabeth grew so incensed that she stood and walked across the room, seemingly to admire Lady Catherine's caged birds, but in reality, to calm herself before she said something she might regret. Lady Catherine then directed her attention towards Darcy.

"I find it unfathomable that you have engaged such an attractive young lady as Georgiana's companion," she opined, as if Elizabeth had left the room.

"Lady Catherine, Georgiana is very happy to have Miss Elizabeth as her companion. If I might add, she has been an excellent influence upon my sister."

"I find that hard to imagine as she is practically a child herself." Directing her attention towards Elizabeth once again, Lady Catherine asked, "Pray, what is your age?"

Elizabeth answered, a bit of testiness evident in her voice, "With a younger sister already married, your Ladyship can hardly expect me to own it."

Taken aback, Lady Catherine exclaimed, "Why, I never! Darcy, is this what you consider a *good* influence on Georgiana?"

Completely ignoring her question, Darcy rose from his seat and went to refill his drink.

Lady Catherine returned her focus upon Elizabeth. After a moment, she said, "Come, Miss Elizabeth, and play something for us."

"No, your Ladyship, I beg of you," Elizabeth said. She had advised the great Lady earlier that her skills were not quite adequate, but Lady Catherine had cast off her claims by suggesting that she would not play at all amiss if she practised more and could have the advantage of a London master.

"I must have you play. Music is my delight. If I had ever learnt, I should have been a great proficient, as would Anne, had her health have allowed her to apply."

"Your Ladyship, when I say I play poorly, I do not mean to…" Elizabeth continued in vain before being interrupted once again.

"Nonsense, you must play for us at once. I demand it," Lady Catherine insisted, while assuming a regal stance.

Finally, Georgiana stood up and raced to Elizabeth's side, "Come, Elizabeth. I will join you."

The two young women sat down before the pianoforte to begin playing. Georgiana whispered, "Forgive my aunt's rudeness, Elizabeth. Let us sit here and play. With any luck, she will leave us be for the rest of the evening. What say you?"

"Thank you for rescuing me, Georgiana. How shall I ever repay you?" Elizabeth teased.

~~~

Over the next few days, Elizabeth observed Darcy as he interacted with his *presumed* intended. She was not at all impressed. He seemed as indifferent towards Anne as he was towards any other woman of his acquaintance. She rarely saw the exchange of more than one to two sentences between them. As at Pemberley, he tucked himself away in the study throughout each day, attending to Lady Catherine's estate, and he only made himself available during dinner. Elizabeth noted that Lady Catherine spoke at length of Darcy and Anne's pending engagement with complete certainty. Neither the gentleman, nor the young woman said anything to deny her.
~~~

Elizabeth resolved not to think of the temperamental Mr. Darcy. She almost hoped that he would find himself married to Anne de Bourgh. Anne was frosty and dispassionate, not particularly attractive, and she rarely spoke. *It would serve him right.*

Elizabeth wished to enjoy all that she could during her stay at Rosings Park. Despite the unpleasantness of the haughty and domineering Lady Catherine, the grounds of Rosings Park were among the most magnificent she had ever seen. She went out early each morning for a solitary walk along the many paths. After four days of rambling along the paths with not another soul in sight, it caught Elizabeth by surprise when she spotted Darcy just ahead on his horse, seemingly awaiting her approach.

Darcy slid smoothly from his mount and asked Elizabeth to join him. Before she could object, he took her hand. He led her deep into a secluded wooded area.

"Are you sure you know what you are about, sir? What do you suppose your *betrothed,* Miss Anne de Bourgh, might think of this little adventure?" Elizabeth asked impertinently.

"I will pretend you did not just say that, young lady."

"Where are you taking me, sir?" she asked defiantly.

"Do not be uneasy."

Soon they came upon a clear landing, and Elizabeth spotted a magnificent temple, far grander than the one at Pemberley, high up on a hill overlooking splendid gardens. Its beauty was wonderfully breathtaking. She started walking towards the temple of her own volition.

"Sir, it is beautiful. What do you know of its history?"

Darcy secured Maximus and then walked towards Elizabeth to offer her his arm. As he led her to the structure, the skies burst open, prompting the two to race up the steep hill, hand in hand, to avoid the sudden downpour. By the time of their arrival to take shelter, the cold drenching rain had wet Elizabeth through and through. Darcy remained perfectly dry under his greatcoat. He quickly removed his coat and approached Elizabeth, her body shivering, to wrap it around her.

The two stood directly before one another, as close as two people could stand without touching, their eyes captured by one another's. Darcy was fully aware that he was tempting fate, but he could not help it. It was driving him to distraction to be so near to her and yet, unable to touch her since Twelfth Night. He stood so close while clutching the greatcoat around her body, attempting to keep her warm. His eyes moved from her slightly parted lips to her amazingly dark eyes to her lips again. Her eyes darted between his intensely alluring eyes and his enticing lips. He seemed drawn to her, and he could not escape the pull.

The gusty winds whipping through the open spaces of the temple, the steadily pouring rain and the occasional roar of thunder heightened her sense of susceptibility. This man... so captivating... so handsome... so physically attractive... who relentlessly invaded her dreams each night, now stood before her, evoking bewildering, yet splendid, sensations.

His incredibly soft lips are much too close to mine. Refusing to allow her heart to rule her mind, her mind firmly set upon resisting, Elizabeth scarcely allowed a hint of their lips touching before she stepped back from him. Darcy gazed at her intensely whilst seemingly effortlessly removing his cravat. Tenderly, he dabbed the raindrops from her face, slowly, seductively, enticing her to accept him, until Elizabeth broke all contact and reached for his neckcloth, offering to do it herself.

The two moved several feet apart.

Darcy broke the silence. "Forgive me... for bringing you here, Miss Elizabeth. I shall not absolve myself if you become ill."

"Do not worry, Mr. Darcy. As I was out walking before you joined me, I was bound to run into this storm, at any rate.

Besides, I suffered downpours on many other occasions with no ill effects," she said as she continued to wring her hair with his cravat, all the while driving Darcy to distraction. She continued, "I fear this rain will not end soon. Before too long, everyone will miss us."

"Let us wait until it eases up a bit. Then, I will take you back to the manor house on Maximus. If we follow that path, we will be there in no time at all," he said as he pointed it out to her.

"Sir, it would hardly be proper for me to ride with you on your horse," Elizabeth protested.

"We have shared a mount before," he quipped, genuinely amused by her modesty.

"This is hardly the same thing, Mr. Darcy."

"No, at that time, I was teaching you to ride. This time, I am rescuing a damsel in distress."

Elizabeth harrumphed, "Forever the true gentleman."

Darcy shrugged off her impertinence. "I try. Now, come sit with me and allow me to keep you warm while we wait out the storm."

In light of her persistent reluctance, he said, "Come now, Miss Elizabeth. Let me take care of you. You know that you are freezing."

"On the contrary, I am rather warm," she lied, for she was in truth quite chilled.

"I know you will be much warmer here beside me." He softened his tone. "Sit with me, and I will share the history of the temple with you while we wait."

"I am perfectly capable of hearing the tale from over here," she stated as she found a relatively dry spot to sit. She stated, "And now you may begin."

Soon, the rain began to ease up. Without entreaty, Darcy swept Elizabeth effortlessly into his arms.

"Put me down this instance, Mr. Darcy," she weakly protested. What he wanted most was to impart a tender kiss; he did not. Instead, he carried her to his horse and sat her in his saddle. He mounted the horse as well and then placed his hand firmly on Elizabeth's stomach, pulling her tightly into his lap, and they set off on the path towards the manor house.

The ride was brief, though Elizabeth hardly noticed, for her mind was otherwise engaged. *How am I to keep up my resolve and my equanimity if we are to share moments like this? What is it about this ride that elicits such yearnings?* She recalled the first time as being exhilarating, but this time, she simply lacked the words to describe what she felt.

When they entered the manor house, Darcy stealthily guided Elizabeth through the servants' entrance and along a back stairway to her room, arriving completely undetected. He parted with her at her door and made way to his own room.

~~~

Elizabeth did not join the family for breakfast, causing Darcy to become quite concerned. He asked Georgiana to check on her. Upon entering Elizabeth's room and finding her sitting in front of the fireplace, dressed in a warm robe and drinking hot tea, Georgiana rushed to her side to see what was the matter.

"Elizabeth, when you did not come down for breakfast, everyone worried. Are you feeling ill?"

"No, Georgiana, I think I will be just fine." Elizabeth confessed, "I was caught in a huge downpour this morning, and I decided to use that as a perfect excuse to stay here in my room for a few days, thereby avoiding Lady Catherine." She reached for her friend's hand. "Now Georgiana, you must keep my secret," she urged.
~~~

"I will go along with this little scheme only if I may stay with you, to help nurse you back to health."

"I should like that very much," said Elizabeth.

Georgiana continued, "And you must allow me to tell my brother, so that he will not worry."

Elizabeth vehemently protested, "No, absolutely not. Let him worry."

Easily surmising that Elizabeth was reacting to some lapse on her brother's part, Georgiana reluctantly agreed. The two young women enjoyed the next two days apart from the company of Lady Catherine and by default, Darcy, with Georgiana only putting in an appearance during meals.

Had Georgiana known how deeply the thought of Elizabeth's being ill would upset her brother, she likely would not have agreed to Elizabeth's scheme. She could very well understand why Elizabeth would want to limit contact with her aunt. Who among their party did not wish to avoid Lady Catherine? *Even so, why should Fitzwilliam suffer? What did he do this time?*

By then, both Darcy and Elizabeth were enigmas to Georgiana. She first became aware of her brother's love for Elizabeth months ago. Now Elizabeth was similarly affected. However, he did not seem inclined to do anything about it. Georgiana wondered if her brother would allow the disparities in their stations alone to keep him from sharing his life with the woman he loved.

When Elizabeth joined the family for dinner on the evening before their departure from Rosings Park, it relieved Georgiana to witness her brother's enthusiasm. For the first time in days, he cast off his gloom and made a concerted effort to enjoy the evening. She was especially pleased to see Elizabeth and him conversing after the meal. Though she had no inkling of what they were discussing, they seemed rather intense. When her aunt insisted upon having her share in the conversation, Darcy suggested they were speaking of music. Georgiana imperceptibly shook her head. She certainly hoped Elizabeth and her brother had more to discuss than that.

Indeed, they did. Something needed to change.

~ Chapter 11 ~
Purpose and Meaning

The Darcys' participation in Georgiana's second Season began immediately upon their return to London from Rosings Park. Three weeks later, Lord Harry asked for Georgiana's hand in marriage, and Darcy gave the couple his blessing. The wedding was in six weeks. Lady Matlock was delighted. Playing matchmaker for Darcy became the farthest thing from her mind. Her sole focus was on the planning of a June wedding.

The Season progressed quite differently than the last. The news of Georgiana Darcy's engagement to Lord Harry Middleton signalled there would no longer be a steady stream of gentlemen callers at Darcy House. Darcy's obligation to take part in the Season significantly diminished. As Georgiana's intended, Lord Harry undertook the role as her escort among society. They went everywhere together. His sister, Lady Harriette, often accompanied them; therefore, Darcy never did. He would not be seen in Lady Harriette's company and thus give rise to any sort of speculation of an attachment. Darcy only attended those functions hosted by the Matlocks or their closest friends, and always on his own.

After overstepping the bounds of their tenuous friendship at the temple in Kent, Darcy finally came to appreciate what Elizabeth meant when she said they could not go back to the type of friendship they once had shared. He still felt responsible for her bout of illness following their trip. He endeavoured to respect whatever boundaries she chose to impose on their relationship. If she desired his company, he made himself available; otherwise, he focused his attentions on his work. He mostly kept to the privacy of his study when he was at home during the day. When he was out, he focused upon sporting activities, especially fencing. Though Richard and he no longer shared the same proclivity for debauchery, the two continued to enjoy many other gentlemanly pastimes. On occasion, Darcy spent time at his club with Bingley and other old friends, as well.

For the rest of the Season, each day passed much as the day before with Lady Matlock, Georgiana, and Elizabeth focusing upon the upcoming wedding; splitting their time between Darcy House and Matlock House.

As happy as Georgiana was over her upcoming marriage to Lord Harry, she worried over Elizabeth's fate. She loved her very much, and did not want to have to say goodbye to her best friend. Though Elizabeth often attempted to reassure Georgiana that they would always be friends, Georgiana continued to fret. She could not understand what was happening with her brother. It was increasingly clear that he cared deeply for Elizabeth. She feared he might never overlook his pride and his sense of duty to offer for her. With her marriage to Lord Harry and her place in the highest circles secured, she wondered if her brother might forget society's dictates to pursue his own happiness.

The day of Georgiana's wedding was by all definitions, perfect. She was proudly escorted down the aisle by both Darcy and Richard. Though Georgiana insisted upon a small, simple gathering of immediate family and intimate friends for the ceremony, Lady Matlock insisted upon a more lavish wedding breakfast for the nuptials of the niece of the Earl of Matlock and the son and heir of the Earl of Stafford. Many from the highest circles of society attended. After the grand wedding breakfast, hosted by Lady Matlock at Darcy House, Georgiana and her husband promptly set off for their new town home in Mayfair, with a planned departure on their honeymoon tour in three days hence.

As overjoyed as he was for his sister, Darcy, for the most part, went through the motions that day, doing everything expected of him as the surrogate father of the bride, but with an overwhelming sense of unease. Elizabeth had yet to give him an answer to his proposal. She had avoided giving Darcy an answer before Georgiana's wedding, so as not to overshadow the felicity surrounding the occasion.

~ ~ ~

In the last month leading up to Georgiana's wedding, Darcy had fretted over his imminent separation from Elizabeth. With Georgiana married and out of his home, it would not be possible for Elizabeth to remain under his roof. Darcy had decided to provide a modest home near Hanover Square for Elizabeth. He had charged his solicitor with setting up a trust in Elizabeth's name to pay all her household expenses as well as afford a comfortable yearly stipend for the rest of her life. Acting on her behalf as an *anonymous* benefactor, Darcy had wished to offer Elizabeth a secure and independent future. Other than Elizabeth and his solicitor, he had not intended that anyone should know of his bequest.

Two days before the wedding, Darcy had presented the settlements he had made on Elizabeth's behalf to her. *Elizabeth's astonishment was beyond expression. She stared, coloured, doubted, and was silent.* To Elizabeth, and she was sure to everyone else as well, his plan would be perceived as an arrangement for a mistress!

With the departure of the last of the wedding guests, Elizabeth approached Darcy for a long overdue discussion on his plans for her future.

Darcy sat casually on his desk with his eyes fixed on her face, and Elizabeth stood directly in front of him, barely a foot away, her colour heightened and her arms folded. They were in the midst of a heated argument.

"You know that is not what I have suggested!" Darcy stated emphatically. His resounding voice could be heard outside the door of his study.

"What about perceptions?" Elizabeth argued. "Perception is everything among society! What were you thinking, Mr. Darcy? Despite your *honourable* intentions, I would be exposed to the censure of the world for dissipation, as well as its derision... scorned as a kept woman!"

"It would not be like that, Miss Elizabeth. No one would ever know of my part. I want you to be secure and well-provided for. We will not see each other if need be. Your sisters are welcome to come live with you," he stood, prompting her to take a step back to maintain the distance between them. "I intended no disrespect. You must know that. I only wish for your happiness. I do not want you to have to consider being someone's governess," Darcy asserted.

"I would be living in my own establishment, with servants, and a carriage, for Heaven's sake! Clearly, if not yours, I would be perceived as some wealthy gentleman's mistress!" she shouted.

"No... you misunderstand," was all Darcy could say before Elizabeth interrupted.

"And what about after you have married? I imagine your wife might have something to say about such an arrangement."

With stoic resolve, he replied, "I will never marry."

"Then you, sir, are either a coward or a fool!" Elizabeth angrily hissed.

Darcy was taken aback by her scathing insult. "A coward?" he repeated contemptuously.

"Yes, a coward—of the worse kind; for how else might one describe your behaviour? How dare you say you will never marry when your family and your poor cousin Anne fully expect you to marry her, and have done so for years?" Elizabeth demanded.

"Surely, you do not believe that will ever happen. I would sooner marry Richard," he said in a voice of cool indifference.

"Perhaps you should. You two are far better suited to each other... two peas in a pod," she retorted derisively in response to his sarcastic remark.

Instead of dwelling on that particular line of discussion, Darcy answered back, "You presume to accuse me of being a fool!" He spoke in a cold, arrogant tone that could no longer be repressed despite his feelings for her, such was his dismay.

"Only a fool would say that he will never marry, especially someone such as you with so much to offer."

"Then what does that make you, madam?" he asked disparagingly.

"Mr. Darcy, I wish to marry but only for the deepest love. As I am in love with someone I evidently will never have, I guess that makes me a fool as well."

"Then, in that we are equalled, because I am in love with someone whom I can never have."

"It is different, and you know it! You are a wealthy man—your own master; you may marry whomever you choose."

"No, I cannot. I doubt you will ever understand. My sense of duty and loyalty to my family dictate that I choose a wife from the highest circles. Rather than go against those expectations by offering marriage to the only woman I will ever love, I choose to remain single."

"Then, you are a greater fool than I suspect!" She had heard enough. Resolved, she flatly stated, "Good day, Mr. Darcy." Elizabeth stormed out of the room before he could reply. She could not wait another moment to escape his presence.

The tumult in her mind was now painfully great. Elizabeth was so sorely disappointed in Darcy. He expressed absolutely no regret for his actions. He was utterly convinced of his righteousness in the matter; no amount of discourse on her part would convince him otherwise. How could he not see that he had insulted her with his largesse, and in so doing, deeply wounded her?

Elizabeth had already packed in the days leading up to the wedding everything she intended to take with her. She instructed her maid to send her possessions to Gracechurch Street once she had left Darcy House. All that remained was to impart her decision to Darcy, a message best conveyed in a letter. She did not want to set eyes on him, not just then.

Elizabeth paused at the doorway for a moment, to have a last look. Then, she made her way to the street where she took a public carriage to Cheapside, completely oblivious to all the attention she attracted as an unescorted young woman in Grosvenor Square. Her former maid followed her instructions and delivered the letter to Darcy once Elizabeth had gone.

~~~

Darcy was not in the mood to see anyone after his bitter quarrel with Elizabeth. However, upon discovering it was her maid requesting his audience, he agreed to see her. The young maid quickly handed him the letter and left his study without a word.
~~~

Pondering its meaning, he sat down at his desk and braced himself for the worse.

Dear Sir,

Allow me to start by saying that the time I have spent here in your home, with Georgiana and you, has been among the most fortunate times of my life. I thank you for that.

You thought that I would never understand what you meant in saying that you would never marry, because you could not marry the woman you love. I do understand. I know that I am the woman whom you think you love. I know that your pride, your arrogance, and your belief in your duty to your family rule you. I also know that you do not love me enough to overcome any of those perceived obstacles.

Who willingly denies someone they love a chance for true happiness? As regards the arrangement you have offered me, does it allow me the opportunity to meet and fall in love with someone else? Does it allow me a chance at marriage and motherhood? Or does it require that I must be locked away in Mayfair, forever under your protection?

What would possibly tempt me to accept such an arrangement?

You have astounded me with your latest act. From the moment that I accepted the position as Georgiana's companion, you have attempted to direct every aspect of my life, often-times in a manner that can only be described as heavy-handed and officious. Are you so convinced of your own omnipotence that you truly believe it is up to you alone to provide for my future? After all this time, do you know nothing about me?

You say you did all of this because you do not want me to be anyone's governess. What makes you think I ever plan to? Did you even once think to ask me of my plans? Of course, you did not. Given your selfish disdain of the feelings of others, you believe you know what is best for everyone; why bother to seek anyone else's opinion?

You have finally convinced me that you are the most self-absorbed person I have ever had the misfortune of knowing and that you are the last man in the world to whom I would wish to be indebted.

I reject your offer. It is time we say farewell. You see sir, I have my own purpose and meaning for my life. I am ready to take my chance for true happiness.

I release you. I release myself. We both deserve something wonderful.

Elizabeth Bennet

~ Chapter 12 ~
Perception Equals Truth

And this is her opinion of me? This is the estimation in which she holds me. Such were his recurring thoughts, as Darcy absorbed Elizabeth's words, reading the letter repeatedly. *According to her calculations, my faults are heavy indeed! Elizabeth views me as self-absorbed. All I ever do is think of her. Self-absorbed? Me? This is not happening to me.* Darcy was in complete denial.

He continued in that attitude for hours into the night, feeling sorry for himself. *Elizabeth thought so little of me that she would deliberately misconstrue my intention, and throw it back in my face bundled conveniently with a whole slew of unfounded accusations. What was I thinking? I offered her a secure future... financial independence. This is the gratitude I am to receive!* Darcy thought to himself, *She is wilful. She would cut off her nose to spite her face if it meant defying me.* He soon began vividly recounting the many times she wilfully opposed him over the past months. *Why did I even bother? I could do almost nothing to please her.* He was terribly angry with her.

At around midnight, Darcy began to consider his options. *If I could only see her. If she had not left my home so abruptly, I might have made things right. How I wish that she had stayed and given me a chance to explain things from my point of view.*

Given another chance, I will convince her to see things differently. If not, at the very least we might part on amiable terms—if only.

~~~

Darcy remained sequestered at Darcy House for days. He did not eat, he did not drink, and he slept little, if at all. The loss of Elizabeth from his life devastated him, and he felt completely powerless to do anything about it. He lost interest in all things. When Richard called on him, he immediately knew the source of Darcy's despair.

Refusing to pull any punches, Richard exclaimed, "For God's sake man, did you think the false sense of domestic bliss you created for yourself would last forever? Sooner or later, it had to end."

"Richard, I do not wish to discuss this with you. I simply wish that you leave me alone."

"I hate seeing you like this. The only other time I can recall you like this, was after the death of your father."

"I dare say that whatever I feel now, it is not exactly the same as then."

"Then why carry on this way? You are merely feeling sorry for yourself for a situation that you orchestrated and continued to carry through, to the point of obsession."

"For the last time, I do not wish to discuss it. Perhaps you are trying to help, but that is not what I want. Please leave!" Darcy shouted angrily.

"Do you expect me to leave you here like this, wallowing in self-pity?"

"It is all that I ask. I will be fine. Please leave me alone," Darcy beseeched.
~~~

"The family has already journeyed to Matlock for the summer. I plan to join them shortly. Say you will come with me. You ought not to be all alone."

Resigned, Darcy mumbled, "Thank you for the invitation. You go ahead, and I will consider joining you later. You have my promise."

After a week, Darcy was well on his way to having memorised Elizabeth's letter when a different stream of thoughts plagued him. *What was I thinking? Unfortunately, I was not thinking at all. Of course, the arrangement I offered would lead to the wrong conclusion. Elizabeth was correct; regardless of my intentions, perception equals truth. I wanted desperately to keep her in my life, to protect her. Instead, I ended up offending her and deeply hurting her. How she must hate me. She as much as admitted to me that she was in love with someone. She has lived in my home for well over a year; how could I have missed that she was in love with someone?*

Wait a second; is Elizabeth in love with me?

~ ~ ~

Darcy returned to the one place he knew he could find peace and solace, the place that had always provided him with a great sense of comfort when he needed it most—*Pemberley*. It was there that the truth of Elizabeth's words began to take hold. He was a self-absorbed person with a selfish disdain for the feelings of others, just as she had accused. He admitted how selfishly he had behaved towards Elizabeth. As she had observed earlier, he wanted to have his cake and eat it too, regardless of how negatively it affected her. As selfishly as he had behaved towards Elizabeth, the woman he loved, it hardly compared to how he had treated so many others.

Perceived widely as a man of integrity and honesty among the people of Derbyshire, Darcy vowed to live up to that reputation in all aspects of his life and to become a better man. He doubted that Elizabeth would ever want to see him again, but at least he could honour the memory of their friendship by striving to be more worthy. It was time to take decisive steps in his life.

Darcy wrote to his solicitor and granted him authorisation to contact Madame Adele, the proprietor of the brothel he had patronised for so many past years, to end, formally, his exclusive arrangement with Antoinette. For the first time in his life, he paused to consider the circumstances of the women in that establishment. Was it through force or by choice that they had come there? Darcy was familiar with stories of young women among the tenants at Pemberley who fell from grace. They had been forced into marriage by their parents; even worse fates had befallen them when marriage was not an option. Which of life's ill-fated circumstances might have led to Antoinette ending up in a brothel, he wondered? As he continued to ponder what might have led her into that life, he considered her situation might not have been as dire as most. She had likely escaped some of the dreadfulness that many of the other women had been forced to endure. Whether his selfish arrangement ultimately proved to her detriment or not, he considered that it could not be kind to cast her abruptly into the harsh reality of her world. Perhaps she might fare well if given another chance in life—one with more favourable odds.

He reckoned there were establishments of some sort which opened their doors to unfortunate women, broken off from society, seeking a second chance in life. Was it something in which she might be interested? He had no way of knowing. He shuddered to think of the physical intimacy he had shared with this woman he knew nothing about, other than a name, which may or may not have been properly represented. He realised that while there was no doubt that she was a victim of society and wealthy men like himself, and she was likely penitent and redeemable, it would be presumptuous of him to think he knew what was best for her. Part of his instructions to his solicitor was to use his discretion to ease the process of securing a second chance for her, *should she wish it.* He would bear the cost as reparation for his moral duplicity. Albeit not an overly magnanimous gesture, it was a start.

Darcy thought about the events that initially set him upon the path of patronising a brothel. He recalled his father's words to him when he had lost his innocence. *Wealthy young men are responsible to respect the virtue of innocent maidens. Honourable and decent masters do not cavort with servants. It is the only responsible and socially acceptable sexual outlet for a young gentleman of his standing.* Although Darcy sincerely doubted he would ever have a son of his own, given that he had no intention to marry—if by chance he did marry and have a son, he doubted that he would introduce him to that particular rite of passage for privileged young men.

~~~

Darcy found that Pemberley no longer offered the solace he desperately needed. He felt as if its walls were closing in on him; it seemed such a lonely place. He journeyed to Matlock to visit his family. He needed to face up to all that he had put them through, beginning with his cousin Anne.

Lady Catherine de Bourgh and Anne had returned to Matlock with the rest of the family after Georgiana's wedding. The single-most incentive in Lady Catherine's travelling such a distance had been to garner her brother's support. She had been anxious to have Darcy move forward with the matter of marrying Anne, and she had been terribly vexed that her brother did
~~~

not share her sentiments. She had tirelessly laboured each day of her stay to convince him of the benefits of the match, but to no avail. Such was her absolute joy when Darcy arrived that her happiness knew no bounds. She thought that he had finally come to honour his duty to his family. Immediately upon his arrival, Darcy sought Anne's private company. Lady Catherine was beside herself, thinking that at last her fondest wish was on the brink of being fulfilled.

It was the first time in Darcy's adult life he ever recalled spending time alone with Anne. Elizabeth's admonishments in that regard were painfully true. From the time he entered puberty, he knew he did not desire his cousin Anne. It was too easy to ignore his aunt and not actually confess his lack of intention. If he had spoken up sooner, Anne might have met and fallen in love with someone by now. How would he know that? It was not as though he ever spoke with her on the matter. Darcy realised that his silence could easily pass as his tacit consent to the union. It was the most cowardly thing he could have done, and the injured party was his own flesh and blood.

Darcy was all that was kind and gentle as he told his cousin that he never had any intention of honouring his late mother's wish that they marry. He went to extraordinary lengths to express his remorse, so much to the extent that Anne interrupted him.

"I would not be nearly as hard on myself, if I were you. I have attempted to tell my mother for years that there was nothing between us. She simply refused to listen. Soon, it became easy to follow your example and say nothing at all. It will be good to have it all out in the open, for now it will be much simpler when we meet our soul mates."

"I never thought of you as being a romantic," he awkwardly confessed.

"I do not doubt it, Cousin. I am sure you never thought of me at all," she expressed.

Darcy could not decide whether she was nursing a broken heart with that last statement. He said, "I have been unfair to you. I apologise. If I have hurt you as well, then I apologise even more so. I have been a dreadful cousin, but if you will allow me, I promise to behave better from this point on."

"Do I really have a choice?" she teased, prompting Darcy to end his worrying. Anne reassured him that she bore him no ill feelings.

Darcy's conversation with Lady Catherine did not flow nearly as smoothly. She was positively livid! Lord and Lady Matlock rushed to the drawing room to try to temper her wrath.

"Catherine, what is the meaning of this? You were heard from upstairs," demanded Lord Matlock.

"This young man has the audacity to tell me that he will not marry Anne. My beloved sister and I planned this union at his birth. You must persuade him to behave honourably," she insisted, persisting in her attempt to gain her brother's support.

"What do you expect me to say? I have told you time and again that I have never agreed that Darcy and Anne should marry. It is our intention that he marries an eligible lady of the *ton,* someone with the prestige, the wealth, and the beauty befitting the mistress of Pemberley. Anne would never suit him. Why can you not see that?"

Before Lady Catherine could speak, Darcy interrupted, "My lord, I must confess that I have no wish to honour your plans either, as regards my marrying anyone. I have no intention of ever marrying."

"No intention of ever marrying?" Lord Matlock loudly echoed. "Do not be absurd! You are the master of Pemberley. You owe it to your family to marry and produce an heir, if for nothing else, then for the sake of Pemberley. I will not hear of this foolish notion of yours that you will never marry."

"Nor will I!" Lady Catherine chimed in. "You will do your duty and marry Anne. From your infancy, you were intended for each other. It was the favourite wish of your mother, as well as my own." She directed her attention to her brother and continued, "Whilst in their cradles, we planned the union. Now, when the dearest wish of both sisters would be accomplished, you refuse to lend your support and insist upon their marriage."

"Catherine, you speak nonsense! Whomever Darcy marries must bear him children. Even you can see that Anne is fit for no such thing. Besides her poor health, she is long past her prime. Only a young lady of the *ton* will be suitable to bear the heir to Pemberley," countered Lord Matlock.

"This is not to be borne. I insist on being satisfied," cried Lady Catherine.

In the meantime, Lady Matlock stayed on the sidelines of the circular discussion, a silent observer. She wondered what had happened to Darcy. His demeanour was not at all as it had been on the day of the wedding. His physical appearance was lacking. He had lost weight, and he obviously had not taken very good care of himself. She cringed at the pressures placed upon Darcy to marry, though she realised that he needed the impetus. Left to his own devices, she had no doubt he would never marry, at least not someone of whom the family would approve.

She was forced to consider what she had long suspected but could not bear to admit, even to herself. Darcy was in love. It was obvious to anyone who would see. He had fallen in love with someone he knew he could not have. There could be no doubt of the object of his affections. Try as he might in hiding it, his eyes had rested upon *her* when he thought no one was aware. His smiles and his conversations had been reserved for *her*. Lady Matlock shook her head as she considered that Miss Elizabeth Bennet, Georgiana's paid companion, despite her beauty, her charms, and her standing as a gentleman's daughter, could hardly be deemed an acceptable wife for Darcy and mistress of Pemberley. As much as she wished that Darcy might have been able to follow his heart, she understood that such a union would never be tolerated.

~ *Chapter 13* ~
Universally Acknowledged Truth

Elizabeth felt disheartened by the manner of her separation from Darcy and her realisation that he did not love her enough to offer her more than protection. Every time she thought of his preposterous proposal, she recoiled. She comprehended how her scathing words might have hurt him, but she believed strongly that he deserved every last one of them. He had wounded her deeply, and she meant for him to know just how much.

Nevertheless, Elizabeth was not formed for ill-humour. She determined to persevere. She had experienced so much turmoil over the past eighteen months. She clung to the belief that "this too shall pass." As planned, she moved in with the Gardiners in Cheapside. With her savings over the past year and prudent investment by her uncle, she had amassed a small amount of money which provided a return that allowed her to pay her own personal expenses. At least she would not burden her family in that sense.

One week after her return to the Gardiners' home, Elizabeth was out shopping with her aunt near a fashionable part of London. She was startled to happen upon Mrs. Pearce, Georgiana's former chaperon. After introducing the two women to one another, Elizabeth said, "Mrs. Pearce, it surprises me to see you in town. I thought you had returned to your home in Derbyshire."

"Oh no, my dear, I now live here. Mr. Darcy has made it possible for me to live in a very modest residence near Hanover Square, at no extra cost to myself, as recompense for my service as Lady Georgiana's chaperon. It was always part of our agreement. He knew that I wished to live in town, which is one of the reasons he hired me in the first place. We both expected the job to last a short duration. Things worked out well for all parties concerned." Mrs. Pearce went on to explain that, with the combination of her inheritance from her late husband's estate and Mr. Darcy's generosity, she would manage to live quite comfortably.

Elizabeth smiled at the elderly woman as she continued to prattle on, extolling Darcy's virtues. She said, "He is such a fine young gentleman, and I have known him all his life. He is so kind and generous to a fault. He is widely known for providing for those in his service as well as he can. He is just as his father was in that respect, the very best of masters."

Elizabeth cautiously asked, "How is Mr. Darcy?"

"He is no longer in town. He returned to Pemberley. I dare say for the best, for he did not fare well during those last days here. He appears to have suffered a great loss beyond having given his dear sister away. I do hope his spirits recover now that he has returned to his beloved home. It broke my heart seeing him that way."

Once Elizabeth parted ways with Mrs. Pearce, she was anxious to return with her aunt to Gracechurch Street. She pondered the meaning of Mrs. Pearce's words. *Is Mr. Darcy as generous as she seems to suggest? Is it possible that his inherent generosity blinded him to his offence against me?*

Elizabeth filled her days with activities of one sort or another. She enjoyed spending time with her four younger cousins, and she eagerly attended the park each day with them, along with their nanny. Though the Gardiners' style of living was comfortable, it was not affluent. Elizabeth did all she could in helping her aunt with the day-to-day activities of the household. She had no time to sit around idly and dwell on the past. It was only at night, when the warm embrace of sleep always managed to elude her, that she allowed herself to think of Darcy. As disenchanted as she felt during those moments, she knew she would never forget him.

She often recalled their time together—a recollection fraught with conflicting emotions. The night in the library at Matlock House... captured in his tender embrace and the magic of their near-kiss. The day she stood much too close to him under the protective cover of the temple in Kent, their lips eager to unite... her mind telling her heart to beware. The feelings his nearness invoked throughout her entire being, mind, body, and soul. Would she ever experience such powerful feelings again? Therein existed the conflict. Had they kissed, where might it have led? Would they now be together? No doubt he had no intentions to let her go; would she have had the power to leave? More questions than answers, she confessed, and always with a single tear that travelled softly down her cheek.

Such were her nights. She woke each morning with a sense of clarity. Elizabeth did not intend to suffer Darcy's absence. She reckoned not only were their stations in life different, something that could be overcome should he manage to quash his pride, but it was also painfully obvious their goals in life differed. In fact, their goals were entirely contrary to one another's, for she dearly wanted to marry someday and raise a family, and he vowed he would never marry. Elizabeth did not fully accept Darcy's excuse for not marrying because he did not want to go against his family's expectations. She figured she had spent enough time with the self-absorbed Mr. Darcy, to know better than that. Elizabeth suspected he was just using that as an excuse to do exactly as he pleased, that being to avoid marriage at all costs. Of course, she allowed that she could be wrong, but all the evidence before her supported her opinion. Such was her belief, and she would stick to it until proven otherwise.

She often recalled, with a healthy dose of cynicism, the universally acknowledged truth that *a single man in possession of a good fortune must be in want of a wife.* Though quite distressing to admit, the tenet clearly did not apply to that particular man.

~ ~ ~

After the first few weeks with the Gardiners, Elizabeth returned to Hertfordshire for an extended visit. Mary's marriage to Mr. Collins and the family's return to Longbourn had restored a modicum of their status in Hertfordshire. The neighbourhood's righteous indignation over the hasty marriage finally subsided, and the good people of Meryton received her family once again.

Happy news abounded for the Bennets as regarded both Jane and Kitty. Jane had agreed to marry a Mr. Thomas Eliot. Kitty planned to wed Mr. John Lovett, a clerk in her Uncle Phillips's practice, the week after Jane's nuptials.

Jane's wedding was two weeks hence. Her intended, a local gentleman, was a widower with two young children. He owned a comfortable estate not ten miles from Longbourn. He had long admired Jane from the time they were both young, but had failed to make her an offer because his family forbade the match. Instead, he had married his family's choice. He had never forgotten Jane. His young bride had died in a carriage accident just two years earlier. When Jane had returned home from Scotland, he had sought her out, courted her, and offered her his hand in marriage.

Elizabeth and Jane shared a heartfelt *tête-à-tête* soon after Elizabeth's arrival. While Elizabeth had concerns about Jane's plans for her life, Jane was equally concerned about Elizabeth's situation. She felt compelled to tell Jane everything that had happened upon her return to town in January. When she related Darcy's offensive proposal, Jane was very sympathetic.

"Clearly, he was not thinking rationally. If he believes himself to be in love, then his acts were a sign of his great desperation to keep you in his life. It is obvious his pride will not allow him to consider the honourable path. You did the right thing in refusing him. Perchance your letter will help him face the consequences of what he has done and encourage him to mend his ways."

"At the very least, I would wish that he understood the pain I felt in receiving such an offer," Elizabeth confided.

"Do you think you will ever be able to forgive his offences against you?" Jane asked as she lovingly placed her hand atop Elizabeth's.

"It is hard to say. I could more easily forgive him for his thoughtlessness and his pride, had he not wounded my sensibilities so wretchedly. As it stands, it is his abominable pride that will likely hamper any further association."

"But Lizzy, I know you plan to continue your friendship with Lady Georgiana. How shall you react when you see Mr. Darcy? You are aware it is only a matter of time. Will you be friends or indifferent acquaintances?"

"Whatever we are to become, we could never be indifferent. I imagine that I will simply tolerate him, for everyone's sake. And while we might put forth some efforts towards amiability with one another, I shall never truly esteem him as a friend without strong evidence of his contrition and willingness to amend his arrogant and selfish ways."

Endeavouring to end the conversation on Mr. Darcy, Elizabeth spoke to Jane about her betrothed. Elizabeth discerned the transformation wrought in Jane's persona by their reduced circumstances, and it saddened her. Jane and she had vowed to marry for love. Now, she feared Jane might be settling for something far less. Elizabeth wondered if her life would soon come to that. She knew that if she were to move back to Hertfordshire to live with her family, her chances of meeting anyone would be appreciably diminished.

"Lizzy, I believe I will be very happy with Mr. Eliot. I have always held him in high esteem, and he has offered me a beautiful home as well as a secure future. I have great affection for his two wonderful children, and he and I both look forward to adding to our family. Lizzy, we would like nothing more than for you to come to stay with us once we settle. Please say you will consider it."

"Jane, I promise I will visit you often. Moreover, I thank you for your kind offer, but I believe my life is in town. Who knows? Perhaps, I shall soon meet a nice, respectable man to share my life. Living in town will increase my prospects considerably, do you not agree?" Elizabeth responded part mockingly but with a smidgen of sincerity.

~~~

Despite the joys of being reunited with her family, Elizabeth suffered a great deal of distress. When Mrs. Bennet was not busy undermining Mary's place as the new mistress of Longbourn, she was criticising Elizabeth. Mrs. Bennet found it unforgivable that after living in Mr. Darcy's home for over a year, Elizabeth had failed to use her feminine wiles to snatch
~~~

him. Mrs. Bennet insisted that true to her predictions, Elizabeth, with all of her impertinence, had ended up an old maid and a burden to them all.

What hurt Elizabeth the most about her mother's passionate and demonstrative wailing was that despite her hatred of Darcy, it vexed her exceedingly that Elizabeth had not ensnared him. It was widely known that Mrs. Bennet had despised Darcy when he had resided at Netherfield. She had not hesitated to let her feelings be known. There was hardly a person in Hertfordshire who had been unaware of her indignation towards the proud, despicable man, as she had made plainly clear when she had boasted aloud of her Jane's forthcoming nuptials with Mr. Bingley at the Netherfield ball. What did it matter that she hated the man, if he should have married Elizabeth and raised all of their lots in life? To Elizabeth's mortification, her mother continued to that day to spill her vitriol against Darcy to anyone who cared to listen.

Upon their arrival at Longbourn for the weddings of their nieces, it did not take long for the Gardiners to recognise Elizabeth's anguish. Both grew disgusted with Mrs. Bennet's constant badgering of Elizabeth over her perceived inadequacies and disappointment as a daughter. Conveniently forgetting the turmoil brought upon the family as a result of the behaviour of her youngest daughter, Lydia, Mrs. Bennet claimed that except for Elizabeth, all of her daughters had made her exceedingly proud by procuring such fine husbands.

Both Mr. and Mrs. Gardiner believed strongly that they had to get Elizabeth away from Longbourn—the sooner, the better.

~~~

Darcy did not need anyone to tell him that having Elizabeth in
~~~

his life was meant to be temporary. Deep inside, he knew it as the truth. What he never truly had considered was how it would be once she was gone. He could not have imagined it would be completely miserable. When she left his home in London, he felt as though he had lost everything.

Upon his return to Pemberley from the bedlam at Matlock, Darcy once again isolated himself. He cut himself off from everything and yet, he was utterly besieged, for all he did was think of Elizabeth. Every room was now linked implicitly to her. The breakfast room where most mornings, it was just the two of them. The drawing room where they spent evenings after dinner, the library where they sparred and debated for hours at a time, and the music room where Georgiana and she enjoyed performing a duet that they had practised all day for his delight. Once, he ventured into her apartment where many of her effects remained as she had left them before Christmas. He had never entered that room before, even as a child. Therein was the sheer essence of Elizabeth.

He could no longer enter his stables without espying Bella and being drawn back to pleasant memories of Elizabeth. He had shown her all of his favourite spots around Pemberley. Now they all held precious memories. He had lost count of the many times he had come across her after she had ridden off to one of those spots on her own, despite his admonishment against her riding alone. *Elizabeth,* Darcy reflected, *fearless, headstrong, independent, witty, intellectual, good-humoured, and kind-hearted... the best thing to have ever happened to me.*

To Darcy, Elizabeth was now a part of Pemberley; it meant nothing to him without her.

One day he stood at the spot offering the panoramic view of his ancestral lands, the same spot he had shown Elizabeth when he initially brought her to his home. He recalled how marvellous it had felt when he shared it with her that first day.

With the weight of Pemberley's legacy upon his shoulders, he reflected upon his family's past. *How many marriages of convenience had taken place? How many were marriages of love? Surely, in the expanse of years gone by, from generation to generation, there were many courageous ancestors who defied the dictates of society... married outside their sphere... married for love. The walls of Pemberley had not come crashing down. Its legacy endured.*

He had been such a fool. He, who professed not to care for society. He, who was his own master, had foolishly lost the only woman he knew he would ever love, had loved for nearly two years. He had lost her adhering to the dictates of a society he scorned.

Darcy realised that had he not been so prideful, he would not be so utterly and completely alone, with misery as his only company. Invariably, the thoughts in his mind kept returning to the same questions. *Could Elizabeth have been in love with me? If so, have my actions destroyed that love? If she loved me once, might she love me again? Might I find her, court her, and win her heart once more?*

Having ascended from the depths of despair that emanated from his own self-imposed strictures, Darcy determined to start anew. He had enough of self-pitying and self-denial. He vowed to pursue the woman he loved, to ask for her forgiveness, and to seek a second chance.

Georgiana was returning from her wedding tour soon. After a brief stay at Pemberley, Lord Harry and she would journey to their own home. Darcy surmised that given the close friendship between Georgiana and Elizabeth, it would only be a short amount of time before Elizabeth would be invited to Stafford for a visit. He would be there, as well. He prayed it would not be too late.

~ *Chapter 14* ~
His Greatest Wish

The Gardiners had long-planned a trip for that summer. Their original plan was for a tour of the Lakes, but business concerns dictated an abbreviated trip, one that would take them only so far as Derbyshire. They intended to spend a week in Lambton, where Mrs. Gardiner had passed some of her youth. At first, they were to leave their young children in Mary's care and collect them along with Elizabeth from Longbourn, upon their return to London. Thinking it was the best thing to take her away from her current environment, they invited Elizabeth to go with them, to separate her from the caustic put downs by Mrs. Bennet.

Elizabeth was perplexed over what to do; stay at Longbourn and suffer her mother's verbal abuse, or travel with her aunt and uncle to Derbyshire, where she would spend a week within a few miles of Mr. Darcy's home. There was no doubt that if Jane still lived there, Elizabeth would have stayed at Longbourn. Alas, Jane was gone. Now, Longbourn seemed such a lonely place. Elizabeth decided it was better by far that she accompany her uncle and aunt on their trip.

Inevitably, it happened that the Gardiners wished to see Pemberley. For one, it was a place that Mrs. Gardiner had heard so much about as a child. More importantly to them, it was the former residence of their beloved niece for over six months. Knowing absolutely nothing of the specific nature of the relationship of their niece with the young master, and only that she was a dear friend of his sister, they had no reason not to visit. Of course, Elizabeth felt that she had plenty of reasons not to assent to a day trip to Pemberley, none of which she wished to share. What was she to say? That Mr. Darcy and she had not parted on good terms, she was furious with him, and she had no wish to see him, not even to chance it. Elizabeth guarded her privacy too well. Jane was the only person on earth in whom she had ever confided.

Elizabeth mentally calculated the odds that she might meet Darcy on their tour of his home. First, she knew he spent only half his time at Pemberley. There were many places he might be —in Matlock, in Kent, at Rosings Park. With Georgiana away on her honeymoon, she thought it was more likely that he would be in town cavorting with Richard. Second, in all her time there, though she was knowledgeable that the home was open to public tours, the family had neither been inconvenienced, nor in direct contact with the visitors. Mrs. Reynolds was diligent in guarding the family's privacy. Elizabeth figured that as long as she remained on the formal tour, her chances of encountering Darcy were minuscule.

Her dread soon gave way to excitement, for she longed to see Pemberley again... one last time. When she had left in December, she had not thought she would not be returning. Perhaps the visit would serve to bring her much-needed closure of that chapter of her life.

~~~

If Elizabeth could but describe the mixture of emotions that flooded her mind as they approached Pemberley, she would ad-
~~~

mit to a feeling of coming home. Until that moment, she never realised how much she missed the sights, sounds, and the rejuvenating air of Pemberley Woods.

Mrs. Reynolds and the staff delighted in seeing Elizabeth again. She had brought such liveliness to the great halls of Pemberley when she had resided there.

"Miss Elizabeth, my dear," the housekeeper expressed, "it is such a pleasure to see you." And indeed it was, for Mrs. Reynolds had never known the master to be as happy as he was when she was last there. When he returned over six weeks ago, he was totally dejected. She suspected the reason now stood before her. She continued, "How disappointed Mr. Darcy will be to know that you were here and that he missed you. You see, he is at Matlock and is only expected to return tomorrow." Mrs. Reynolds studied Elizabeth carefully to gauge her reaction to the news but was unable to discern its impact.

"Actually, I am travelling with my uncle and aunt. We are staying in Lambton. They wish very much to apply to see the house and the grounds," Elizabeth said enthusiastically, once having made the proper introductions.

"Why, it is my pleasure to give your relations a tour of Pemberley. However, you my dear, should not feel obliged to join us. I imagine you wish to revisit at your own leisure. You go right ahead while I attend to your relatives," she insisted.

With Darcy far away in Matlock, Elizabeth inwardly breathed a deep sigh of relief that she would not see him. Elizabeth gladly conceded to Mrs. Reynolds's directive and quickly made her way out of the house to one of her favourite paths. She lost track of time as she ambled about the grounds, nostalgically. Though she was not dressed to ride, she longed to see Bella once again. On her way to the stables to visit with Bella, Elizabeth caught sight of Darcy.

The two of them stood frozen in their steps. Surprised beyond measure, they simply stared at each other. Darcy wondered if Elizabeth could be merely a figment of his imagination, a product of his desire. Elizabeth wondered if her luck could be any worse. Realising that it was truly Elizabeth, Darcy wanted to run to her and sweep her into his arms. Elizabeth wanted to run away. Instead, she awaited Darcy's approach.

"I thought you were away. Mrs. Reynolds said you were in Matlock," she awkwardly declared.

"No... no, I am not. Actually, I arrived at Pemberley a short while ago without informing Mrs. Reynolds of my return."

"I am so sorry for intruding upon you like this. I wanted to see Pemberley again, one last time. You must believe me, I had planned to stay on the tour to avoid any chances of seeing you," cried Elizabeth, by now overly embarrassed.

"Please do not say that, Eliz... Miss Elizabeth. You honour me by your presence. I have missed you terribly these past weeks." Darcy took her hand in his and raised it to his lips to impart a light kiss. He asked, "Where are you staying?"

"I am staying at the inn in Lambton. I am here with my aunt and uncle."

"So, are you enjoying your trip? How long do you intend to visit?"

"A little under a week—my aunt has more friends in Lambton whom she plans to see."

"Let us find them at once. I wish to invite you all to stay here at Pemberley during your visit."

"I assure you that is not necessary."

"Please, I insist. Besides, Georgiana will return from her wedding trip in a few days, and she will want to spend as much time with you as possible before she leaves Pemberley for her new home in Stafford."

"Then, perhaps I shall return when she arrives."

"Please do not leave, Miss Elizabeth," he urged. "At least let us see if your uncle and aunt will accept my invitation."

Elizabeth knew not what to think of Mr. Darcy's rather improbable plea. Before she could protest further, he had already engaged her arm in his, and they were on their way to the house in search of her relatives.

Upon locating the Gardiners on the tour of his home, Elizabeth made the introductions. Darcy greeted them most cordially and welcomed them to Pemberley. He further astonished Elizabeth by offering to conduct the rest of the tour himself, thereby relieving Mrs. Reynolds of the task.

Elizabeth marvelled at the extent of Darcy's graciousness towards her relatives. Of course, she had seen Darcy put a pleasing persona forth before. He was adept at masking his true sentiments by charming people when it suited his purposes. Scarcely knowing what to make of his present demeanour, she thought to herself... *he seems truly genuine.*

Darcy provided an extensive tour of the grounds. All throughout, Mrs. Gardiner reflected upon the many letters from her niece, each expounding upon the majesty of Pemberley; she appreciated Elizabeth's overwhelming praise. Upon pointing out his well-stocked lake, Darcy invited Mr. Gardiner to take advantage of all that Pemberley offered by accepting his invitation to stay at Pemberley for the rest of their trip.

As surprised as Mr. Gardiner was to receive such an invitation, he was not of a mind to say no. He was extremely curious about the enigmatic Mr. Darcy. He understood from Elizabeth that Mr. Darcy was class conscious, haughty, and taciturn. Her description hardly fit the man who had extended the warm invitation. The matter that enticed him the most was that it might be his only chance to know more of the man who had been responsible for his niece's welfare for so long. Whenever Elizabeth had visited with them while she was in the Darcys' service, she had spoken enthusiastically of the former Miss Darcy, but she rarely had spoken of Mr. Darcy. Mr. Gardiner did not intend to pass on the opportunity to learn more about the young man.

Having received Mr. Gardiner's acceptance, Darcy led the party to the drawing room. He parted from them briefly to make his staff available to arrange for their move from the inn at Lambton to his home, post-haste.

Once Darcy made off to attend to his guests, it delighted Mrs. Reynolds to see that his spirits had lifted appreciably. Without giving it any thought, Mrs. Reynolds had the staff prepare Elizabeth's apartment for her stay. Upon the master's instructions, it had remained undisturbed since her departure last December. The staff readied apartments for the Gardiners in the guest wing.

Darcy's guests settled in their respective apartments in time to prepare for dinner. When a maid showed the Gardiners to their apartments, they expressed concern that they were not accompanied by their niece. The maid explained that Miss Elizabeth had gone to her own apartment in the family wing. Expressing their concern to one another, they concluded that since Elizabeth had lived safely under Mr. Darcy's protection for well over a year, they would not question her. It was obvious that the staff deferred to her. They treated her like a member of the household. They trusted Elizabeth. They hoped Elizabeth knew what she was about.

Dinner was an intimate and enjoyable affair. They dined in the small, informal dining room. While Darcy sat at the head of the table, he was sure to have the Gardiners seated on either side of him, with Elizabeth seated next to her aunt. Darcy and Mrs. Gardiner discussed, at length, their common knowledge of the town of Lambton. He also spoke enthusiastically with Mr. Gardiner on sporting topics. Elizabeth watched the scene before her with great contemplation. After dinner, Darcy invited Mr. Gardiner into his study to enjoy a glass of port before rejoining the ladies in the drawing room.

Once alone with Elizabeth, Mrs. Gardiner remarked on the general splendours of Pemberley and eventually on its young master.

"Lizzy, why were you worried about coming here? I know we did not expect to see the great man himself, but it has turned out quite pleasantly. He is so kind and considerate, not at all as you described him." Mrs. Gardiner went on to comment on the very pleasing aspects of his mouth when Darcy spoke, as well as the air of dignity of his countenance, which gave a favourable idea of his heart.

Elizabeth demurred. "I can hardly imagine what has brought about this transformation."

"Can you not, my dear?" her aunt asked sceptically.

"Indeed, I cannot. Though I can admit to having seen evidence of his willingness to change when confronted with..." Elizabeth paused, "oh never mind what I was about to say." She was not about to confess that the only time she had known him to change was when she rebuked him. She asked herself, *Have my reproofs affected a change in him to such a vast extent as his behaviour suggests?*

Upon the gentlemen's return, Darcy mentioned to the Gardiners how much he had enjoyed it when Georgiana and Elizabeth had played duets on the pianoforte after dinner, thereby prompting Mr. Gardiner to insist that Elizabeth play for them. Darcy eagerly offered to turn the pages. Though Darcy was overcome by her nearness, he did his best to follow along with her performance and turn the pages at the right time. The uneasy tension they both had felt earlier in the afternoon was slowly fading. It seemed the two of them had tacitly agreed to put their differences aside for one evening.

Elizabeth had not a clue what to make of the day's events. That Darcy was extremely considerate, at times even solicitous, of her relatives was one thing. It was another that her relatives were thoroughly approving of him. She wondered what had brought about such a change in the man she thought she knew so well.

The fact was that the Gardiners' views on the distinctions between rank and privilege were never so naïve as their niece's. They lived with it every day. It was a surprise for both Gardiners finally to meet Mr. Darcy and witness no such pretensions on his part, to say the least, especially as Elizabeth had spoken otherwise of his character.

As for Darcy, himself, with so much to contemplate, he knew he would find no sleep that night. Elizabeth was in his home again and just down the hall. He vowed he would do everything in his power to keep her in his life. He had been granted the second chance he had prayed for.

~~~

The next morning, Elizabeth came down to the breakfast room dressed in her finely tailored blue riding habit. She begged her uncle and aunt's forgiveness that she would not join them on the morning calls on their friends in Lambton. She simply wanted to spend the day riding Bella and rambling about the grounds of Pemberley. When Darcy offered to assign a riding escort to her, she assured him she would be fine and promised not to venture too far. Darcy knew better, but he did not protest. Besides, he had the perfect escort in mind. After grabbing a roll, Elizabeth wished her uncle and aunt a pleasant day and headed for the stables.

Darcy headed out immediately upon the Gardiners' departure for the morning. He rode urgently, directly to the temple.
~~~

He spotted Elizabeth standing near the pond, seemingly miles away. She startled slightly when she first became aware of his presence there. Securing his horse, Darcy spoke out, "How did I know I would find you here?"

"I warned you, sir. This has become my favourite spot in all of Pemberley," she said. Elizabeth was not surprised completely that Darcy had followed her. Despite the pleasantness of the previous evening, there remained between them many things that needed saying.

Darcy tentatively approached Elizabeth and said, "It gives me great pleasure to share it with you." Taking her hand, he continued, "I have missed you more than you know. I am so sorry for all the pain that I caused you.

"You must believe me, I never intended to hurt you or offend you with my offer. I was so afraid of losing you in my life; I was grasping at straws. I now can see how insulting it must have been."

Elizabeth attempted to withdraw her hand. Darcy refused to let go. He continued, "One part of your letter remains with me and gives me reason to hope." Darcy lifted his eyes to hers. "Were you in love with me? Do you love me? Because, I must confess, you were correct about my feelings. I do love you, most ardently. I have always loved you."

"Sir," Elizabeth wanted very much to speak.

Darcy drew her closer and placed his hand on her cheek, "Please, let me continue. I love you. These past weeks have been a torment, not knowing how you were or even where you were. I love you. I never wish to part from you from this day forward. Please end my agony by doing me the honour of accepting my hand."

Elizabeth's eyes glistened with unshed tears as she listened to Darcy speak the words she had longed to hear. He looked into her eyes and whispered. "Please do not cry. Please say you will be mine, Elizabeth. I want you, and I need you. I can no longer bear to live without you."

Elizabeth remained silent. She gradually broke away from Darcy's grasp and turned to face the pond. "Please do not turn away. This is our chance. You are here, and I cannot bear to see us part ever again." Darcy pulled her back into his arms and touched her cheek lovingly. "I am ready to love you the way you should be loved, the way you need to be loved, and the way you want to be loved."

Darcy felt even if Elizabeth loved him, her reluctance was understandable. He had been selfish and prideful his entire life and especially towards her. How was she to know he had changed? Holding Elizabeth loosely within his caring embrace, in between placing light kisses on her temple and her cheeks, he murmured, "Say yes... please, say yes. I have changed. I am no longer the self-absorbed person you once knew. You are the one who is most important to me... only you. I adore you. I beg of you, let me be the one to give you something— *wonderful*."

"You hurt me," Elizabeth spoke poignantly, pulling away slightly to study his face.

Darcy nodded his head in acknowledgement of the veracity of her sentiments. "I know. I am so sorry."

"Do not do it again."

"Never again, not if I can help it." He touched her face. "Does that mean you forgive me, and you will accept my hand?"

"Yes."

"Yes?"

"Yes, I love you." Elizabeth professed. Overcome with delight, Darcy swept her up and spun her around before gently placing her back on her feet and imparting a tender kiss on her brow.

"Elizabeth, thank you, I feel as though I am the luckiest man on earth," he said. "I plan to spend each day of the rest of my life endeavouring to be a man truly worthy of your love and affection," he murmured as the two stood, their foreheads pressed together while Darcy clutched both of her hands to his chest. Darcy moved one of his hands to cup Elizabeth's face, tilting it upwards to admire her beauty. Irresistibly drawn to one another, both closed their eyes as their eager lips touched for the first time, allowing a taste of what they both felt they had missed all of their lives. Increasingly, their kisses grew more passionate. "Do not move," he said as he released her. He walked over to his stallion and retrieved a blanket.

He spread the blanket on the ground before her. After removing both of their riding jackets, Darcy helped Elizabeth settle into a comfortable position. He then sat behind her, encircling her in his arms. The two sat in that fashion for a while, delighting in the splendour of the spot that would forever hold a memorable place in their hearts, silently relishing in the intimacy of the moment.

Brushing her hair aside, he placed a kiss behind her ear and whispered, "This feels so right to have you here. You belong here."

Feeling at home in his comforting embrace, Elizabeth nestled a bit closer and turned to face Darcy, her eyes sparkling with joyousness. She smiled and said, "It is a pleasure being here with you like this. I have missed our closeness."

"Indeed, we have grown very close this past year. I am so thankful that I did not shatter it all with my foolish proposal."

"Please, think no more of all that. I believe you will have to learn some of my philosophy."

"And what is that?" he asked with his head resting upon her soft shoulder, breathing in the sweet fragrance of her delicate skin.

"To think only of the past as its remembrance gives you pleasure," she said, prompting Darcy to chuckle.

He kissed the back of her slender neck again. "Are you comfortable?" Elizabeth nodded affirmatively. "Are you sure? Is there nothing I can do to make you more comfortable?" he asked as he continued gratifying her senses with soft kisses along her neck.

"What do you propose?" she inquired, endearingly.

Darcy demonstrated his desire by stretching out on the blanket and persuading her to relax beside him. He had waited his entire life for a moment such as this—to lie next to the woman of his dreams, the only woman he ever had loved.

"This is more comfortable," he spoke softly. He placed his hand on her face and kissed her tenderly. "Do you agree?"

Darcy ceased his attentions to Elizabeth's pleasing lips as he sought to capture the essence of her beauty in his mind forever. He studied her face, her amazing eyes, and her slightly swollen lips with a temperance that soothed her. Any lingering concerns that Elizabeth might have felt about the depth of his love and devotion vanished.

Elizabeth stroked the side of his face, rousing Darcy to resume their kisses. Between kisses, he moaned, "I have waited for this moment forever. You are so very beautiful. I can hardly wait to make you mine." He kissed her again and whispered, "All mine."

Elizabeth opened her eyes to gaze into his, uncertain of his intentions. Darcy placed his fingers lightly upon her lips to ease her concern. He uttered sensuously, "Trust me. I will not make you mine just yet... not now, certainly not here, not before our wedding night. I simply wish to hold you, to feel your body next to mine, and allow you to experience the depth of my affections," all the while enticing her with kisses.

Darcy trailed kisses along her delicate neckline, until ultimately forestalled by her habit shirt. That was an inducement enough to take things more slowly. He softly caressed and tenderly massaged her bust through the smooth, thin cloth of her shirt. He yearned to explore more of her body, but reminded himself that there would be plenty of time for that. In that moment, his aim was in giving pleasure to his bride-to-be, and in acclimating her to his titillating touches, his sensual caresses, and his arousing kisses.

Elizabeth's soft moans were symphonic, urging Darcy to heighten her pleasure even more by deftly positioning himself and pressing against her in satisfying rhythm. At length, his own aching desire served as a reminder that he was reaching the confines of his endurance. He gradually ceased his amorous attentions and sought Elizabeth's eyes.

Though not quite certain of what had just occurred, she knew she did not want it to end. Elizabeth beheld a look in Darcy's alluring eyes innately recognisable to her, smouldering passion. In that moment, she knew she would never get enough of him.

Filled with glee, Darcy laughed quietly and pulled Elizabeth into his lap as he sat upright. He said, "Let us marry within a week, here at Pemberley. I find it unbearable to think of your leaving me ever again."

"So soon sir; how will we ever explain such an impulsiveness?" she questioned, at last regaining her composure.

Darcy and Elizabeth spent the next half hour or so discussing their impending nuptials and how best to explain their sudden decision to their families. Elizabeth was as eager as Darcy to remain by his side and, therefore, agreeable to whatever explanations he put forth.

Walking along holding hands, once they had handed the horses off to the stable boy, Elizabeth often looked up to admire

Darcy's strikingly handsome profile. She sought to discuss the changes she perceived in his character. When she questioned him on the change in attitude towards her relatives and even towards her, for that matter, in offering his hand, he explained, "I have attended to your reproofs, and I am endeavouring to be a better man."

"Why?"

"Surely, you must know. I am heartily ashamed I let my pride overrule my heart for so long, thereby denying us both a chance at happiness.

"I have been a selfish being all my life, in practice, and sometimes, in principle. As a child, I was given good principles, but left to follow them in pride and conceit. Unfortunately, as an only son... for many years an only child, I was spoilt by my parents, who allowed, encouraged, almost taught me to be selfish and overbearing, to care for none beyond my own family circle, to think meanly of all the rest of the world, and their sense and worth compared with my own. Such I was, and might still have been, but for you, dearest, loveliest Elizabeth," he expounded, before bringing her hand to his lips for a lingering kiss.

"I am pleased you finally thought to give us a chance. I have missed you very much, almost as much as I missed Pemberley," she teased. "Now sincerely, what about your family—how do you suppose they will take the news? I know enough of them to know they barely tolerate anyone outside the highest circles."

"You are the only woman for me, and there is nothing I would not do for you. All of this means nothing to me without you in my life.

"Elizabeth, I cannot promise you that everyone will accept our marriage. We will have Georgiana and Richard's support. As for Lady Catherine, I have no hope. However, there is some hope with Lady Ellen... perhaps even my uncle. I will travel to Matlock tomorrow to tell them personally." In response to the uneasy concern shown on Elizabeth's face, he continued, "But you, my love, are not to worry. We all know how *self-absorbed* I can be," he expressed with a contrite smile. "Either they will respect my choice, or they will risk losing me."

"Sir, I know that my letter to you was rather harsh," she said, reminded of her parting words to him as being the most self-absorbed person she had ever had the misfortune of knowing.

"What did you say that was not true?"

"Still, I would feel better if you told me you destroyed the letter."

"I consider it your first love letter to me. I shall cherish it always. In fact, it is safely locked away with the rest of the family treasures," he teased. He kissed her, and they continued along. Silently, Darcy debated the hastiness of their plans to marry. He said, "Elizabeth, you would tell me if you thought I was rushing you into marriage, would you not?"

"Of course I would. Why do you ask?" she inquired.

"I know how close you are to your family, especially your eldest sister. I am willing to wait if you want your entire family with you for our wedding. We will marry in Hertfordshire should you wish it, my love."

"It would be nice to have my dear sister Jane with me, as I was with her. She is such an inspiration to me. I feel she suffered the most from our family's downfall. The loss of Mr. Bingley only compounded her pain. I think that hurt her more than even she was ever willing to admit."

"Bingley? I am afraid I do not understand. Are you saying your sister felt a strong attachment to him, that she suffered his departure? I did not think she was very affected by him," he confided, somewhat startled by Elizabeth's revelation.

"Jane rarely shows her true feelings to anyone, but let me assure you, she liked him very much. She was very hurt by his abrupt departure. I am afraid she was the object of all the people of Hertfordshire's derision for disappointed hopes, for a time. Of course, all that changed when my sister Lydia ran away."

"I am very sorry to hear that. I fear that what I am about to say will only distress you further. I hope you will understand."

"What is it?" She started to worry.

"I was instrumental in persuading Bingley to depart from Netherfield after the ball," he pleaded guiltily.

"You convinced Mr. Bingley to abandon my sister? How could you?" Elizabeth demanded angrily, halting them in their tracks.

Darcy took Elizabeth's hand and led her to a nearby bench. He encouraged her to sit, while he disclosed his part in the scheme. Begging her to hear him out before she reacted excess-ively, he began to recount the events of his time in Hertfordshire, and most importantly, the night of the Nether-field ball. He spoke of Bingley's unguarded attentions to Miss Bennet having given rise to a general expectation of their mar-riage. He confessed that he observed the young woman most attentively during the ball and detected no particular regard for his friend on her part.

To his surprise, Elizabeth sat patiently and listened to all that he said. He waited for her to say something. She said noth-ing.

Darcy reiterated, "I felt Bingley was getting in over his head with your sister, and that his attachment was deeper than hers. I surmised that her heart was not easily touched. I did not want to see him rush into something he might soon regret. However, by your own account of your sister's feelings, I confess my misapprehensions, and I apologise for my interference."

Finally, she spoke in a tone that could bring him no pleasure at all. "And what of my family's lack of fortune, our want of connections? I suppose that had something to do with your reasoning, as well," Elizabeth replied accusingly.

"No, but as much as I hate to admit it, there was the matter of the lack of propriety shown time and again by your family. Of course, I excused you and your eldest sister. The fact of the matter is that I had no right to judge. I am very sorry for that."

Elizabeth stood and walked away, trying to absorb all that she had just heard. Darcy approached her from behind and placed his hand lightly along the small of her back. Elizabeth flinched and brusquely turned to face him. Somewhat despondent, she said, "I was of the belief it was my family's misfortunes that caused Mr. Bingley to stay away—only to learn he had married another so soon after returning to town. I began to accept that perhaps he never loved my sister at all... and now you tell me this, Mr. Darcy."

~ *Chapter 15* ~
Absence of Malice

"Tell me, what is to be done? How can I make amends?" That was the burning question put forth by Darcy; still, he had yet to entertain a reply. Elizabeth was lost in her reverie, ostensibly miles away. Elizabeth thought of the past, when she first had realised her eldest sister's feelings for Mr. Bingley. She had surmised, even if no one else had, that her sister had delighted in Bingley's attentions and had been well on her way to falling in love with him, despite the short duration of their acquaintance. She had known her sister well, and had supposed that everyone else must. Indeed, she called to mind the response of her dear friend, the late Charlotte Collins née Lucas, to her shared assessment. She remembered Charlotte's exact words.

It may perhaps be pleasant to be able to impose on the public in such a case; but it is sometimes a disadvantage to be so very guarded. If a woman conceals her affection with the same skill from the object of it, she may lose the opportunity of fixing him; and it will then be but poor consolation to believe the world equally in the dark. There is so much of gratitude or vanity in almost every attachment, that it is not safe to leave any to itself. We can all begin freely—a slight preference is natural enough; but there are very few of us who have heart enough to be really in love without encouragement. In nine cases out of ten, a woman had better show more affection than she feels. Bingley likes your sister undoubtedly; but he may never do more than like her, if she does not help him on...

Back then, Elizabeth had argued that Bingley would have to be a simpleton not to perceive Jane's regard for him. Nonetheless, Charlotte's words had rung truest.

Elizabeth considered her own family's possible role, which Darcy had mentioned in terms of such a mortifying, yet merited reproach. Even she had been deeply embarrassed by their antics at the Netherfield ball. How could she deny that credit to his assertions in one instance, which she was obliged to give in the other? He declared himself to have been totally unsuspecting of her sister's attachment. There was confirmation in Charlotte's opinion, the undeniable justice of his description of Jane, and her own opinion that Jane's feelings, though fervent, were well-concealed. *In light of all the evidence that lent credence to his argument, perhaps he indeed acted in the kindness of his friend and completely in the absence of malice.*

Recalling herself to the present, Elizabeth realised that Darcy had asked her a question.

"Tell me, what is to be done—how can I make amends?" he beseeched.

"I shall not lay the blame at your feet in its entirety. Mr. Bingley surely is culpable for his own actions, and he did marry someone else within weeks of his departure. Perhaps it is for the best. What is done, is done. Both have married elsewhere. My brother Mr. Eliot is a kind man. He is sure to make Jane very happy. His feelings for her are of a long duration. I will not hold this against you, Mr. Darcy, but I have to say, I am not entirely reconciled to your absurd and impertinent interference in the affair. You sir, are not completely absolved," she conceded.

"As long as you will be my wife, I will suffer whatever punishment you see fit," he confessed as he placed a loving kiss on the inside of her palm.

Withdrawing her hand, Elizabeth asked, "Before we go further, are there other dark secrets you wish to confide in me?"

No... not if we are to have our happily ever after any time soon, he thought to himself, but upon second thought, Darcy said, "I am not a perfect man, and I have not lived a perfect life, as you have known well. In every aspect of my past, for better or worse, I have conducted myself in a manner consistent with gentlemen of my standing." Darcy claimed Elizabeth's hand and continued, "Trust me, if there were something in my past that would affect our felicity in marriage, I would tell you so. As regards our future, I vow that I will be a deeply devoted husband, a generous lover, and a most loyal friend." Darcy kissed the inside of her palm once more and said, "Let me assure you, you are the most important person in the world to me."

Darcy pulled Elizabeth into his embrace and kissed her on her temple. Wanting to make her happy, he offered, "Perhaps we can persuade your sister and her new family to join us here at Pemberley for an extended holiday, or if you wish, we will travel to Hertfordshire for a lengthy visit."

"Let us marry here at Pemberley as we planned by the week's end, go on the romantic wedding journey that you promised, and extend an invitation to my family to visit Pemberley upon our return," Elizabeth replied.

"We shall do whatever is your heart's desire."

"Oh, Mr. Darcy, I am just getting started. You may want to reconsider ceding so much power before the wedding," she said.

"I have always been in your power, my love," he moaned as he kissed her lips.

~~~

They parted upon reaching the house. Darcy sought out Mrs. Reynolds to share his happy news and to ask her to meet with Elizabeth to discuss the wedding details. He wanted Mrs. Reynolds to handle everything because he did not want to overwhelm his intended, though they agreed that Mrs. Reynolds should seek her opinions. He also asked Mrs. Reynolds to have the mistress's apartment readied and to assign an appropriate lady's maid for his new bride.

Darcy went to his study to write to his solicitors to prepare the settlement agreement, and he summoned an express rider to carry the letter to town. He asked to have Mr. Gardiner meet him upon his return from Lambton.

As Mr. Gardiner entered the room, Darcy set the papers he was reading aside to attend to him. "Mr. Gardiner, I requested your presence to tell you that I have asked Miss Elizabeth to be my wife, and she has agreed. We plan to marry within a week. We ask for your blessings."

Astounded by Darcy's straightforwardness, Mr. Gardiner responded, "Of course, Elizabeth is free to make such a decision, and I am happy for her; but I have to say that this is a complete surprise. What has happened to bring about this sudden proposal, and might I ask prompts such haste?"

"With all due respect, Mr. Gardiner, I must confess this is not at all sudden. Miss Elizabeth and I have grown close as friends over the past year; neither of us would allow to the other that our feelings were stronger than that. However, our separation has led us to consider that we mean far more to one another than we had previously admitted. We are deeply in love. We have missed each other terribly, and we do not plan to part again."
~~~

Slowly digesting Mr. Darcy's assertions, Mr. Gardiner offered, "You have my blessing, but what of the rest of her family? Surely, they should be in attendance for the wedding."

"We hope Mrs. Gardiner and you will stay here to witness the ceremony. We will invite the rest of the family for a visit to Pemberley after the honeymoon period."

"How do you intend to get a license? To travel to London and back within the week, surely cannot be done."

"I plan to travel to Matlock and acquire a special license from the bishop. He is a close friend of the family. I do not expect any delays. However, if I must travel to London, so be it. Miss Elizabeth will remain at Pemberley until I return."

While Darcy met with Mr. Gardiner, Elizabeth shared the joyful news with her aunt. Mrs. Gardiner was happy but rather pensive. Despite the fact that Elizabeth had never shared her sentiments towards Mr. Darcy with her aunt, she suspected that Elizabeth was fonder of him than she allowed, and had been for a while. Of course, Mrs. Gardiner never suspected the extent of her niece's sentiments.

"This is completely surprising. Do you truly love him, Lizzy?"

"While I admit I did not always love him as I do now, I must say yes, I love him very much."

"You certainly have done a good job of hiding that fact. You have always hinted of him as being such a proud, disagreeable sort. However, that means nothing if you really love him."

"I really do. I have loved him for months now," she replied, her eyes beaming with joy.

"I am glad to hear that. It should go a long way in ensuring your felicity in this marriage. It is clear how much he admires you, Lizzy. And that he has chosen you as mistress of all this, indeed, is a testament to the strength of his love. He has had to shoulder so much for a very long time, and now he will have you by his side. Please do not forget, he needs your strength and your support, as well as your love. Be kind to him, my dear."

Mrs. Gardiner encouraged Elizabeth to open up to her about her sentiments on the journey upon which she was about to embark. It meant the world to Elizabeth. As fiercely independent as she believed herself to be, she greatly needed a caring, maternal figure to help her understand the swell of emotions she was experiencing.

After the heartfelt talk with her aunt, Elizabeth went off to write to her family to tell them of the impending nuptials, along with promising to invite them all to Pemberley after the honeymoon period. Elizabeth could only imagine how her mother would react to the news. She thanked God that she did not have to bear witness to the display.

~~~

Mrs. Reynolds arranged a special dinner for the engaged couple that night. Afterwards, the party spent time in the music room listening to Elizabeth play the pianoforte and enjoying light conversation. Darcy was totally enthralled by Elizabeth, and for the first time, he did not try to mask his affection for her before others. As they parted for the evening, he discreetly asked Elizabeth if he could come to her that night, to which she quietly agreed.

Despite the lateness of the hour, when Elizabeth answered the door to her apartment, she was fully dressed in the gown she had worn to dinner. Although he was more casually attired, having removed his dinner jacket and cravat, Darcy was far from disappointed. After their amorous interlude earlier at the temple, he doubted he could have remained steady to his purpose of increasing their intimacy gradually before the wedding night had she been less formally attired, as well.
~~~

Elizabeth's eyes were drawn to his neckline. The sight of him *sans* cravat had always elicited an innate response in her. She wondered if this might finally be her chance to reach out and touch his chest hair. *It looks so soft,* she thought, as she willed her hands to stay by her side. The two found their physical attraction to one another overwhelming. Darcy walked into her sitting room and drew her into his embrace for a deep kiss that left her breathless. At the end of the kiss, Darcy studied her face to read her reaction to his being in her apartment. Wanting to make sure of her comfort, Darcy guided Elizabeth over to the sofa and drew her into his lap.

"Have I told you how beautiful you look tonight?"

"No, sir, I am afraid you have not."

"You look beautiful tonight," he moaned, as he softly kissed her shoulder and lightly massaged her neck.

He whispered, "Have I told you how delectable you taste tonight?"

With indescribable sensations pulsing up and down her spine, Elizabeth voiced, "Hardly."

"You taste delectable," Darcy whispered, his warm breath caressing her ear.

Darcy and Elizabeth carried on in that fashion for a while, their intimate whispers of sweet nothings interspersed with light kisses and caresses. Darcy soon eased Elizabeth astride his lap, allowing him to pay homage to her bosom. He trailed soft kisses along her neckline, reaching the enticing décolletage of her gown. He cupped her breasts with both hands as he gently massaged them and trailed moist kisses along her delicate skin, kissing down between her breasts as he worked his way between them both. By the time he commenced sucking her through her gown, Elizabeth had intertwined her fingers in his incredibly soft hair. Instinctively, she pressed herself up and down his expanse.

Darcy was exceedingly pleased to see that Elizabeth was as passionate as he had always dreamt. He could barely wait to make her his. He aimed to heighten her pleasure more and more over the days leading to the wedding. He enjoyed the process immensely, in spite of his pressing physical needs. Reluctantly, he kissed Elizabeth goodnight to depart for his own bedchamber. Before leaving her, he obtained Elizabeth's promise to meet him at the temple the next morning before he set off for Matlock.

~~~

Elizabeth awakened to the fragrant scent of roses. She opened her eyes to the breathtaking vision of magnificent bouquets, dozens and dozens placed throughout her room. She sat up in bed and selected one of the flowers from the vase on the bedside table. She smiled as she inhaled its sweet petals, only one thought uppermost in her mind— *Mr. Darcy.*

Darcy was there when Elizabeth arrived at the temple. He personally had arranged an intimate breakfast for the two of them. He quickly approached her and helped her dismount Bella. After securing the mare, he took Elizabeth's hand and led her to the elegantly set table. Darcy lingered a bit to trail soft kisses to the back of her neck and along her shoulder as he helped Elizabeth settle into her seat. Upon taking his own seat, he began finger feeding her the various assortment of fresh fruits he had ordered to be prepared.

"Did you sleep well, my love?" he asked as he kissed her cheek.

"I hardly slept at all, sir."

"Nor did I. I was far too engaged in thinking of you and envisioning the pleasures that await us as man and wife."

"I thought of our wedding also."
~~~

"Did you? Tell me your thoughts," he murmured. He seriously doubted that their thoughts tended along the same lines.

"I hesitate to admit, but I am somewhat fretful about what is expected of me."

"Do not worry. You will be an extraordinary mistress of Pemberley. You are everything I wish for." He smiled with delight. "You are charming, witty, intelligent, beautiful... and passionate."

"Passionate, do you really think so?"

"I do. Where is this uncertainty coming from, my love? It is not like you to be unsure of yourself."

"I do not want to disappoint you... I mean to say… on our wedding night."

"You could never disappoint me. I adore you. Please do not be concerned. I am eager to make you mine, but I am willing to wait until you are ready, I promise. All I ask is this, *please* do not make me wait too long," he said with a gentle kiss upon her temple.

"Whoever said anything about waiting? I simply do not want to disappoint you. We have already waited far too long just to admit our love for one…" she managed before Darcy's lips were upon hers.

"Good," he eventually replied, "because, when I say I never wish to be parted from you ever again, I mean it. I want us to be together, always. I want you to spend every night for the rest of our lives, sharing my bed."

"I think that will scarcely be necessary in a home the size of Pemberley, sir," she playfully teased.

"Oh, believe me, it will be necessary."

"Sincerely, sir, I want our wedding night to be perfect and…"

Darcy interrupted with a kiss, "It will be. Have you spoken with your aunt? Has she told you anything of what you might expect?"

"Yes, but I am not comfortable sharing that with you," she awkwardly confessed.

"Come now, Elizabeth. Let us not be shy with one another. I want us to discuss everything, especially matters such as that. What did she say?"

"Mr. Darcy, I will only tell you that my aunt said I must trust you."

Darcy smiled and kissed Elizabeth's cheek. "And do you trust me… I mean to say, really trust me, in spite of everything?"

Elizabeth did not answer immediately, so speaking soft and low, Darcy said, "You must trust me, Elizabeth. I love you above all else." He took Elizabeth's hand and said, "I love you." He kissed her palm and said, "I will always love you." He kissed her fingertips and said, "Trust me." He kissed Elizabeth passionately before murmuring, "Do you trust me?"

Elizabeth smiled warmly. She affirmed her trust in Darcy by initiating an affectionate kiss.

Darcy reached into his pocket and retrieved a beautiful ring. He told Elizabeth that the ring once had belonged to his grandmother; that his grandfather had presented it to her at that exact spot. Now it belonged to Elizabeth. After placing the ring upon Elizabeth's finger, he stood and helped her from her seat. Taking her hand, he said, "Come with me."

He led Elizabeth to a blanket he had placed upon the ground, close to the pond. Darcy reclined on the blanket and welcomed Elizabeth on top of him, as he encouraged her legs open, positioning her astride his body. Kissing her and cupping her bottom, he slowly swayed the softness of her body against the hardness of his. Having long since removed both of their riding jackets, he untied and removed her habit shirt to caress her bosom. His slow, rhythmic thrusts were in arousing harmony with his ardent attentions to her lips.

Desiring more of her, he slowly lowered her chemise to expose her bosom. He gasped at her splendour and began gently kissing around her breasts. Gradually moving towards her nipples, he lightly circled each with the tip of his tongue. Amidst Elizabeth's sighs and moans, he tasted her for what seemed like an eternity, whispering, "Elizabeth, I want you."

Elizabeth savoured the sensations piercing through her body and sought to meet Darcy's passions. The thought raced through her mind that she should not allow him such liberties, but her mind was not nearly as engaged as her body. When kissing her lips, his lips were fiery... when suckling her, his lips were soft, gentle, and rousing. She seemed mesmerised.

Relishing in the pleasures he bestowed, Elizabeth experienced ecstasy. Darcy ceased his adulation bit by bit and allowed her body to calm gradually. He then guided Elizabeth to relax beside him. He faced her and stroked her cheeks. Elizabeth asked, "Mr. Darcy... will it always be this incredible?"

"My dearest Elizabeth, that was but a small taste of what we will experience once you become my wife."

Her heart still beating rapidly, she asked, "How shall I ever survive?"

After a moment or two of looking intently into her amazing eyes, Darcy said, "I love you so much. I hate that I have to leave you while I go off to Matlock. I promise to return as soon as possible." Darcy kissed her again before continuing, "In my absence, you are effectively mistress of Pemberley. I leave you to attend to our guests. However, do not worry. Mrs. Reynolds is very fond of you. She will help in any way she can. All you need do is ask."

"I shall not worry. Nevertheless, please hurry back. I can hardly wait for your return," Elizabeth said, as she initiated a kiss.

Eventually, Darcy responded with a gorgeous smile. "With much more of your kisses like that, I shall never leave," he murmured as he returned her kindness.

In due course, Darcy rearranged Elizabeth's chemise and riding shirt and assisted her with her jacket. With one last kiss, he led her to Bella to help her mount, and then watched as she rode away.

~ *Chapter 16* ~
Shades of Pemberley

Darcy's next order of business was to visit his uncle and aunt, after obtaining the special license. Lady Catherine and Anne had returned to Rosings Park weeks earlier. That meant one less battle, at least for the time being. When Darcy initially met with Richard, he was somewhat shocked by the news of Darcy's impending nuptials, much to Darcy's dismay.

"My God, Richard, if I am to receive such a response from you, what should I expect from the rest of the family? My sole dependence in coming here today was on you."

"Do not get me wrong, old friend. I am very happy for you. I guess after all this time, I never thought you would actually ask for Miss Elizabeth's hand in marriage."

"Yet, I speak nothing but the truth. She loves me, and we will marry in a matter of days. Do I have your support?"

"Of course, you do. Moreover, yes, I will be your groomsman. However, Heaven help you with that group of *aristocrats* we call our family."

"I realise they may not accept it. I have told Miss Elizabeth as much. However, I am my own master, and I do not need their approval or their acceptance. Though, for the sake of family unity, I would like to have it."

"Well, let us go and speak with them. I will be by your side," Richard assured Darcy with a firm slap on his back.

"Thank you, I think," Darcy jested.

The conversation with Lord and Lady Matlock began on a very rough note, to say the least. Lord Matlock blasted away. "First, you come before us with a foolish notion that you will never marry. Now, you stand here with an even more preposterous notion that you intend to marry a young woman who is so inferior to you in consequence, that it is laughable. She was Georgiana's paid companion, for Christ's sake!

"Why, such an unfeeling, selfish girl, that she should not consider that marriage to her must disgrace you in the eyes of everybody.

"And then, there is the matter of her family—no fortune, no connections. Not to mention that she has relatives in trade! Are the shades of Pemberley to be thus polluted?" he demanded.

"That is the last derogatory remark I will hear from you in reference to my future bride," Darcy threatened.

"What your uncle has said is nothing compared to what you should expect to hear amongst society. Heaven and earth! Of what are you thinking, Fitzwilliam?" His aunt implored, greatly disheartened by Darcy's choice for his life.

"I resolve to act in that manner which will, in my opinion, constitute my happiness, even without reference to you, and more especially without reference to persons of society so wholly unconnected with me."

"In other words, you resolve to ruin yourself in the opinion of all your friends, and make yourself the contempt of the world," Lord Matlock lamented.

"With regard to the indignation of the world, if the two of you were excited by my marriage, the world in general would have too much sense to join in the scorn.

"I ask that you accept my choice. Anything less than total acceptance, kindness, and consideration on the part of either of you towards my future bride, and I will cut off all ties with both of you," Darcy stated resolutely.

"How dare you threaten me, Fitzwilliam? Why, you are like a son to me, and Georgiana, a daughter. It has always been so," Lady Matlock adamantly declared.

"I do not dare to speak for Georgiana, except that I know this is what she would want for me. I am not asking for your blessing. I only ask for your acceptance. I do not want to lose either of you, but if you refuse, we shall never see each other again."

Lord Matlock shouted, "Fitzwilliam Darcy, you have always been spoilt, selfish, and wilful. I will NOT be intimidated!"

"I have said all I have to say. Goodbye, Lord Matlock, Lady Matlock." He turned to leave the room. Richard, despite remaining silent throughout, followed close upon his heels.

Lady Matlock cried out, "Fitzwilliam, please do not leave like this. I love you. I do not want to lose you. I promise I will do my best. We will accept your decision to marry the young woman and afford her all due respect as your wife and mistress of Pemberley."

She walked across the room and embraced Darcy. "Thank you, Lady Ellen. I trust you will come to the wedding."

"Of course, Fitzwilliam, we are your closest family members. We will come to the wedding. I imagine you will be married after several months. Do you intend to remain at Pemberley or will you travel to Hertfordshire with Miss Bennet?"

"We plan to marry at Pemberley by the end of this week."

"Why, that is only a few days from now!" Lord Matlock yelled, still not quite reconciled to the union, despite his wife's edict; thinking instead that he would have time enough to put an end to Darcy's absurdity. "For Heaven's sake, what is the rush? First, you announce that you plan to marry the young woman, whose family is marred by scandal, and then you assert that you plan to give rise to yet another scandal by rushing into an injudiciously ill-timed wedding."

Lady Matlock reiterated her husband's stance, "Think of her reputation. Has the Bennet family not suffered enough disgrace? Why undo any benefit they might derive from this union with an added scandal?"

Darcy argued, "It is hardly scandalous. It is not as if we are eloping, for Heaven's sake! I have waited too long as it is, in declaring myself to Miss Elizabeth. Now that she has accepted me, I do not intend to wait a minute longer than is necessary. I plan to take my bride on an extended wedding tour. By the time we return, any idle gossip should have died down. If not, no matter, it is not as though we are overly fond of *society*."

~ ~ ~

After Darcy's departure for Pemberley, Lady Matlock recalled her many attempts to promote a suitable match for Darcy. She reckoned that she was only doing her duty. If she had to do it all again, she would not change a thing; but there was one thing she should have done. Would that she could have done something to remove Miss Elizabeth Bennet as Georgiana's companion as soon as she had suspected Darcy's attraction to her. She did not consider that he would ever act upon it, not even for a moment. Still, it devastated her when he said he would never marry. She would rather he married someone below their circle than marry no one at all. Thus resolved, she would accept the union and welcome his bride-to-be into the family with open arms.

In Darcy's absence from Pemberley, the Gardiners accompanied Elizabeth to Lambton to buy a few items for her wedding trousseau. They shopped at Lambton's finest shops. Many of the proprietors were already familiar with Elizabeth, on account of her previous connection to the Darcys. Upon learning that she was Mr. Darcy's betrothed, they afforded her the epitome of courtesy and the highest priority of service. The Gardiners spared no cost in the purchases they made on Elizabeth's behalf. They were exceedingly proud of her, overjoyed that she had found such happiness with Mr. Darcy, and as surprised as they were by the extent of the young couple's attachment, gratified that they, by bringing her to Derbyshire, had been the means of uniting them.

Darcy returned to Pemberley later than he had hoped, having taken longer to get the license than he had envisioned. He found that Elizabeth and the Gardiners, all fully exhausted from an entire day of shopping, had already retired. He went directly to his rooms to bathe and prepare for his visit with his bride-to-be in her apartment.

A half an hour later, Elizabeth answered his light knock at her door. She was wordless to see Darcy so casually attired, wearing only a nightshirt and breeches.

As he slipped inside, he placed his hand upon her cheek and kissed her fervently. Moments later he murmured, "You are still dressed from dinner."

"Yes sir, I was not sure of your intentions. After your long journey, I thought you might wish to relax in my sitting room and read," she said teasingly.

"That is not my intention. Have you dismissed your maid for the evening?" he asked suggestively.

"Yes, sir, I have," she expressed.

"Excellent, then I shall have to attend to you tonight," he said as he pulled her nearer and started letting her hair down.

"But, sir," she weakly protested, for by then, she was fairly certain she would go wherever he might lead.

"Stop calling me *sir*, especially when we are alone like this," he said as he guided her beyond the sitting room.

"But I shan't call you *Fitzwilliam*. It makes me think of your cousin."

"You will not think of him once I have made you mine," he whispered softly in her ear.

"Is that your intention... tonight?" she asked, with deep uncertainly reflected in her tone.

"No, Elizabeth, tonight... tomorrow night, if you will allow it... I plan to make love to you, as I did this morning. I will make you completely mine on the night of our wedding, my love," he said as he led her to the vanity. Taking her brush in hand, he sat beside her and stroked her long dark hair. Placing a gentle kiss on her neck, he spoke softly, "You are never to cut this."

"Sir," she whispered. To her way of thinking, his kisses along her neckline and his words of his intention were entirely out of concord.

"Not 'sir'… Darcy, William, Highness," he playfully insisted.

"I think I will choose *William.*"

"You shall be the only one to do so, Elizabeth."

"Will you not call me *Lizzy*?"

"I think not. Have you not noticed how I adore your name? I feel as though I am caressing you every time I say *Elizabeth*."

"If you insist," she faintly expressed.

"I do," he said. He looked to see her nightgown placed on the bed. "Is that what you intend to wear tonight?"

"Yes, it is, William."

"Then, let us get you into it."

"No, I do not think so," Elizabeth responded hesitantly.

"Trust me, Elizabeth, and allow me to do this for you," he said as he slowly began removing her clothes, adeptly, piece by piece, from head to toe. As she stood naked before him, her courage rising by the moment, Darcy sat down at the vanity to admire her beauty.

Pulling her into the space of his legs, he traced her body with his long fingers. Darcy was about to taste her hardened nipples when, impulsively, she said, "This is hardly fair. You are fully dressed... well, almost."

"What would you have me remove, my love?" he asked as he stood to remove his nightshirt without awaiting her response.

Elizabeth reached out and touched the soft hair that covered his torso. Finally, having caught the slightest of glimpses during the past, when he was *sans* cravat, and wondering how it might feel, she now indulged herself. *It is magnificent.*

Her actions caught him completely off guard. As she moved her hands to explore his chest, he caught them in his and asked, "Shall I remove anything else?"

Elizabeth's lips trailed her wandering hands. She whispered, "That will do for now." Darcy could not believe his sweet seductress. Deciding that if he did not put a stop to things, he might make her his, completely, that very night, he led her to the bed, picked up her nightgown, pulled it over her head, and gently guided her arms inside the sleeves. He then watched as the gown cascaded to the floor.

"Is there anything else this evening, madam?"

"Well, my hair is not done. I normally wear it plaited, when I sleep at night."

"Perhaps if you teach me, I can better accommodate your needs in the future," he said, trailing his fingers through her long tresses.

She sat on the bed and said, “It will be my pleasure.” She slowly moved through the steps of plaiting her long hair, while looking seductively at Darcy the entire time. Once she had completed her mission, she leaned forward to retrieve a ribbon from the bedside table to secure her braid, thereby affording Darcy an enticing view of her bosom as her gown slid down from her shoulder.

Darcy quickly joined her on the bed and pulled her gown from both shoulders down to her waist. Upon completing an intimate inspection of her bosom with his soft, moist lips and his tongue, unselfishly giving his full attention to each breast, Darcy gradually moved towards her nipples. His warm breath sent chills through Elizabeth’s body. The more cherished he made her feel, the more she sensed what she wanted—nay, needed. With his body pressed against hers, she suspected his need.

Daringly, she uttered, “Take off your breeches. I want to see all of you.”

“Not tonight, my love,” he groaned, unwilling to cease his tender adulations.

“Do you not trust me?”

“I no longer trust myself. You know not what you do to me.”

“I trust you,” she whispered.

Darcy halted his actions. He looked into her eyes. After gauging her intentions to decide whether she was truly ready to see him in all his glory, he rolled on to his back. Encouraging her to sit up, he reached for her hand.

Darcy took Elizabeth’s small hand into his own and brought it to his lips to impart a light kiss, before studying it and intertwining her fingers with his. Then, spreading her delicate fingers apart against his larger ones, he ultimately drew her hand to his lips again and kissed her fingertips. All the while gazing intently into her eyes, he gently guided her hand along the desired path, very gingerly, for he had never experienced her soft touch in that fashion.

Their eyes locked as the effect of her gentle touch became increasingly evident. Elizabeth startled initially. Her bright eyes widened. She attempted to pull her hand away. He would not release it, and he continued to guide her touch in a most pleasing manner. Once she mimicked his actions by her own accord, he hurriedly unbuttoned the fall of his breeches and guided her hand inside to continue her strokes.

"I love this, Elizabeth, please do not stop." He slowly lowered his breeches to his knees and showed Elizabeth how to increase his pleasure even more.

Elizabeth's eyes honed in. Her body reacted in a manner that her mind could not fathom. Her heart palpitating, her small hand hypnotically stroking, she wondered how her body would ever accommodate her intended.

After some time, amidst his moans of ecstasy, Darcy kicked off his remaining garment altogether. Adjusting their positions thus so, he began kissing her, suckling her, and thrusting himself against her smooth silk nightgown. At length, Elizabeth initiated a passionate kiss that nearly proved his undoing.

Darcy beckoned all his strength to master his domain in the wake of Elizabeth's passionate responses. Steadily, and unhurriedly, he persisted until they both succumbed.

The two lovers spent hours talking after he had assisted her into a fresh nightgown, and he had donned his breeches. They finally fell asleep in one another's arms and slept until the wee hours of the morning. He woke her gently with soft kisses and more, and then, reluctantly departed in return to his own room.

~ Chapter 17 ~
Linger Too Long

Darcy rose as bright and early as he ever did, despite having slept in his own bed for a matter of minutes. Elizabeth and he had agreed that with his family arriving that day, there might be precious little alone time. He thereby secured her promise to meet him at the temple early that morning, before their guests began to arrive. Darcy even provided Elizabeth with a taste of what she might expect, as he persisted in gradually acclimating her to their marriage bed.

Lowering her nightgown beyond her waist, he took his time as he trailed his tongue from her lips, along her neckline, down between her breasts to her navel. Lingering there, Darcy lavished his attentions on her, arousing her overwhelmingly as enticing, exhilarating sensations reverberated throughout her nether regions, stimulating her so much so, that she arched her body repeatedly against his. He stopped. Smiling at her mischievously for her ardent response, he looked deep into Elizabeth's eyes, ran his fingers through her loosened hair, down across her cheeks, and kissed her lips softly. He whispered, "Do not linger in bed too long this morning, my love."

~~~
~~~

Elizabeth woke with a start. She could tell by the brightness of her room that she had overslept. When Darcy had left her room earlier that morning, she was unable to return to her peaceful slumber. She thought of all the liberties she had allowed her betrothed over the past few days. That led to thoughts of just how much more she might be willing to grant. She hardly believed that she had initiated the intimacy of last night that led to Mr. Darcy's passionate release. Heretofore, he had always maintained such control during their amorous interludes. Though she was innocent, she had read a romance novel or two, but nothing she had ever read had prepared her for the joys she was experiencing with Darcy. She was somewhat peeved, and yet ultimately curious, that he had aroused her thoroughly earlier, and then he had left her yearning for more. The devilishly delicious grin he wore on his incredibly handsome face as he left her side suggested not only was it his intention to render her thus, but he enjoyed it immensely. Finally, she fell asleep to the most pleasantly arousing and contented dream.

Now, she was late for a promising rendezvous with the very object of her dream. She jumped out of bed and rang for her maid.

Meanwhile, as Elizabeth was running to and from, rushing to get dressed to meet Darcy at the temple, he was downstairs welcoming his sister and her husband to Pemberley. They had arrived hours earlier than expected, such was Georgiana's eagerness to see her brother. She knew from her letter from Richard that Darcy had not been himself since her wedding. She could only attribute it to his anguish over Elizabeth's departure from Darcy House in June. Lord and Lady Matlock also arrived earlier than expected, leaving Darcy with no opportunity to steal away to the temple.

When Darcy told his sister that, not only were Elizabeth and he engaged to be married, but that she was at Pemberley, Georgiana headed straight for Elizabeth's apartment.

At such an early hour, the light knocks on the door startled Elizabeth initially. She could not imagine it to have been Darcy. Understandably, seeing Georgiana standing there caught Elizabeth by surprise. The younger woman entered the room excitedly and embraced Elizabeth.

"Congratulations! Fitzwilliam shared your happy news with me, that the two of you are to be married, tomorrow, here at Pemberley. It is all so exciting! It is the best news in the world. I never imagined that something as wonderful as all this awaited me upon my return!"

"Georgiana, thank you so much for your kind words. I too am very excited, and I am glad for your return. I wish for you to stand beside me, as a 'matron' of honour of sorts."

"Of course, I will. It will be my pleasure. Oh Elizabeth, we only have today and so much to do. However, do not worry; I shall stay by your side all day."

"Actually, Georgiana, I was just on my way out for a…" Elizabeth paused abruptly. She was not about to admit that Darcy and she had made clandestine meeting plans. Instead, she asked, "So, does your brother remain with Lord Harry, or did he perhaps go out?"

"He is with my uncle and aunt, as they arrived shortly after Harry and me. I understand that your Uncle and Aunt Gardiner are here, as well. I so look forward to meeting them. Let us hurry down to join the family for breakfast. Then, you and I will spend the entire day together. I imagine there are hundreds of things to do today, and as your 'matron' of honour, I want to share every moment of it with you."

"It seems a fine plan to me, but I do not know what your brother might say to such a scheme," Elizabeth said in jest.

"I have missed you terribly these past weeks and starting tomorrow, Fitzwilliam will have the rest of his life with you. Besides, Richard will be here shortly. I suppose he can keep my brother occupied most of the day."

Elizabeth and Georgiana arrived downstairs in the breakfast room to find that Lord and Lady Matlock, Mr. and Mrs. Gardiner, Lord Harry, Richard, and Darcy had assembled and were waiting for them. The Fitzwilliams were prompt in offering their felicitations to Elizabeth that she was to become Mrs. Darcy. Darcy introduced Georgiana to the Gardiners, whom she delighted in meeting after many months of hearing of them. The atmosphere was quite amiable as Georgiana spoke enthusiastically of her wedding journey and her excitement over her brother's impending nuptials.

At the end of breakfast, Georgiana announced that, as Elizabeth's "matron" of honour, she would be attending to her all day. She encouraged Richard that he might spend the day with her brother, although that would normally go without saying as the two were always inseparable when in each other's company. Somehow, Georgiana sensed that her brother might have other plans for his last day of bachelorhood. The Gardiners planned to spend the early part of the day in Lambton, calling on old acquaintances, and the afternoon, touring the various sights of Derbyshire.

Georgiana and Elizabeth strolled along, with the former regaling the latter with details of the many adventures of her wedding journey. Georgiana and Elizabeth headed for the idyllic spot of Elizabeth's birthday picnic the year before, there to gather wild-flowers and catch up on girlish talk. It was a glorious midsummer's day, as it had been all week. Elizabeth was positive her wedding day would be just as beautiful. Little over an hour had passed, when the young women caught sight of

Darcy, Richard, and Lord Harry approaching their lovely refuge on horseback.

Georgiana barely waited for her husband to dismount before hurrying to his side to greet him. She led him over to the spot where she sat with Elizabeth. Darcy wasted precious few seconds in joining Elizabeth at her side, as well. Richard reluctantly followed. He was exceedingly annoyed, as it had been Darcy's idea that they go out riding in the first place, and in that particular direction, no less. Though the conversation started out well enough, Darcy and Elizabeth soon became lost in their own intimate repartee, as did Lord Harry and Georgiana, much to Richard's exclusion.

Richard attempted to interrupt the love festival. "Gentlemen, are we to ride out for a spell to enjoy the Derbyshire countryside, or not?"

Receiving no response, a very put out Richard declared, "Fine! I know when I am no longer needed. Lord Harry and Georgiana, I leave it to you to chaperon these two. I am off!"

Lord Harry and Georgiana proved poor chaperones indeed, for not long after Richard raced off, they set upon a secluded path that led away from the field of wild flowers, leaving their charges completely unattended. Darcy released a deep sigh as he pulled Elizabeth into his arms as soon as they were alone.

"I am sorry we were unable to meet at the temple this morning. I had a very special treat in mind."

"I so love treats. Perhaps, you can present it to me now."

"I fear not. What I had in mind requires far more time," he kissed her brow, "and privacy," he added with a kiss to her cheek, "than this spot allows. Not to mention that Lord Harry and Georgiana might return any moment."

"Then, perhaps a tiny sample might suffice. I too am distressed at not seeing you this morning, as we had planned,"

Elizabeth said as she pressed a kiss to the lapel of his riding jacket.

Darcy stood and took a step back to gauge Elizabeth's attire. A light and pleasing muslin, *hardly restrictive*, he thought. In fact, her gown was quite conducive to what he had in mind. He assisted her to her feet and then led her by the hand to a spot where the flowers grew even more untamed, offering some degree of privacy, as well as an advantageous view of the path taken by his sister and brother should they return. Darcy pulled Elizabeth down to sit in his lap, in the midst of the relatively high grass.

Darcy started out slowly, spreading kisses along her neckline and tasting her earlobes. Tentatively, he trailed his fingers from her mouth (which she impetuously sucked), along her neckline, her bosom, and ultimately to the hem of her gown. Beguiling her with deep probing kisses, he slowly inched his hand up her slender legs, caressing her firm thighs, pausing just before reaching his true destination. Elizabeth had requested a tiny sample, and he intended just that. Brushing his hand near her sensuous folds without actually touching her, softly massaging her hips, her small waist, and her belly, and teasing her relentlessly, he slowly began gently massaging and stroking her. The moment he felt her harden and heard her soft moans, he ceased his actions completely, removed his hand to her face, and kissed her.

"A sample, my love," he whispered. "Did you like that?"

"Exceedingly so, perhaps another sample is in order," she beseeched.

"I promise you that and more... but not just now. Tonight, after everyone has retired for the evening, I will come to you."

"By all means, please do."

In the meantime, Lord Harry and Georgiana were enjoying the many splendours of the path that they had chosen. Harry assured her she needed not be concerned that Darcy and his intended would happen along any time soon.

~~~

The couples arrived back at the manor house to find that Lord Robert and Lady Elise had just arrived. Lady Matlock was busy organising things for that evening's dinner party. Ever the consummate hostess, Lady Matlock set out to meet Mrs. Reynolds, immediately upon her arrival, to commandeer the planning and arrangements for the wedding festivities.

For the rest of the day, Elizabeth and Darcy could find no time alone. Georgiana knew she was monopolising Elizabeth's attention at the expense of her brother. The longing looks that he bestowed upon his intended when their paths crossed, left little doubt. It did not bother her one bit.

Of course, Elizabeth was mindful that Darcy had ignited her passions twice that day and both times, purposely left her longing—first at dawn in her apartment and then again, in the field of wild flowers. She decided that two could play at that game. She teasingly enjoyed arousing him with every opportunity presented.

Fortunately, the two lovers sat next to each other at dinner. Elizabeth stepped up her teasing antics by resting her hand on Darcy's thigh throughout the initial courses of the meal. He did all that he could in removing her hand from his leg due to its devastating impact on his composure. Finally, he gave up trying to dislodge her hand from his person. He placed his hand on hers and moved it directly upon a different point... a point which seemed to have a mind of its own. Suddenly flustered, it was now Elizabeth who was the one trying to remove her hand. Once Darcy released her hand, she quickly returned it to her own lap.
~~~

Thankfully, the entire interaction was completely undetected by the other members of the party. In between conversations, each of the guests seemed largely in tune with his or her own thoughts. Lord Matlock, in particular, reflected upon the engaged couple. He thought, *I should have seen this coming. Fitzwilliam never had looked twice at a young woman, and yet with Miss Bennet, he rarely took his eyes off her.* Like his wife, Lord Matlock never once had thought that his nephew, undeniably one of the most highly sought gentlemen of the *ton*, would defy the dictates of society and marry someone who had been in servitude. He had thought it more likely that Fitzwilliam would make the young woman his mistress, but even that scenario was absurd. He had placed so much pressure on his nephew to honour his family and his duty by marrying well. He wondered at his failure. Still, he considered that despite all of her obvious failings and the resulting inclusion of common tradesmen into his family, the new mistress of Pemberley undoubtedly was beautiful, intelligent, charming, and likely to comport herself exceptionally well. Lord Matlock fretted over how in the world he would ever deal with Lady Catherine. Surely, she would blame him for not supporting the match with Anne. He was certain he would never hear the end of it.

Elizabeth observed that while Lady Matlock treated her cordially, and even requested that she be called Lady Ellen, she only tolerated her uncle and aunt. The Gardiners were not unfamiliar with the attitudes of some members of the *ton* towards people in trade, and so, were not put off by the cool condescension of Darcy's family. They conducted themselves with poise and grace. Elizabeth was glad it was the Gardiners that represented her family. She was unsettled at the thought of how Lady Matlock would receive her mother if she acted that way towards the Gardiners. That was until she recalled

Lady Catherine. Elizabeth thought, *If I am to suffer Lady Catherine, the Fitzwilliams should be able to put up with anything.*

The women adjourned to the drawing room after dinner, and the men moved to Darcy's study for their enjoyment of cigars and port. Though Darcy wanted nothing more than to return to Elizabeth's side, Richard took his time as he amused the men with various accounts of Darcy and his less risqué escapades over the past years.

Upon the gentlemen's rejoining the women, the room took on a decidedly festive tone as everyone loosened up a bit towards one another. Lord Matlock finally had deigned to speak with Mr. Gardiner in Darcy's study whilst commenting on the fine port. The two soon had found quite a few topics to discuss, to such an extent that they remained embroiled in robust conversation even whilst in the drawing room.

The ladies also got along well, as Lady Matlock spoke with Elizabeth of her plans to introduce her to London society as Mrs. Fitzwilliam Darcy during the upcoming Season, starting with a grand dinner party after the Twelfth Night Ball, as well as her presentation at court. Though Elizabeth realised that she was only trying to appease her nephew, she expressed her appreciation for Lady Matlock's pledge of support just the same.

Despite the overall success of the evening, Darcy was anxious to have his guests retire. Much to his dismay, his long-winded cousin Richard, when he was not dominating the conversation, insisted upon prolonging the evening by repeatedly appealing to Elizabeth, Georgiana, and Lady Elise to perform on the pianoforte. It was late into the night when everyone finally retired to their respective apartments.

As much as he loved his younger sister and was glad to have her back at Pemberley, if only for a short while longer,

Darcy was not impressed that Georgiana had effectively monopolised Elizabeth from the moment of her arrival. With the household finally retired, he was mere minutes away from joining his bride-to-be in her apartment. She had teased him mercilessly with subtle arts and allurements throughout the entire evening. He could no longer vouch for his ability to wait until after the wedding.

Imagine Darcy's surprise when he tapped at the door to Elizabeth's apartment.

"What are you doing here at this hour? It is after midnight. Do you not know it is bad luck to see the bride on the day of the wedding, before she is escorted down the aisle?"

"I am hardly superstitious, so no, I know no such thing. Besides, it is very late, and I saw the light. I simply wanted to make certain everything is all right."

"Oh, everything is fine. Elizabeth and I were just chatting. I am sorry to have inconvenienced you."

"Now that I am here, I thought I might have a few words with my intended."

"I will be happy to pass on any message. What is it?"

"I simply wanted to wish her a goodnight, in private."

"Unless I am mistaken, you and she said goodnight earlier this evening."

Aggravated, Darcy warned, "Young lady." Georgiana looked at him impertinently in response to his patronising tone and daunting stance, the same tactics that had been effective in reproaching her throughout her youth.

Darcy immediately changed tactics. "Lady Georgiana, do you not have someone else that you might attend to at this hour?"

"Oh no, not tonight! As Elizabeth's 'matron' of honour, it is my duty to be here with her tonight." Standing on her tiptoes, she kissed him on his cheek and said, "Goodnight, brother. We will see you at the chapel bright and early in the morning," and then politely closed the door. Darcy stood there immobilised with a saddened puppy dog face, reminiscent of a young boy denied his favourite treat.

Utterly forlorn, he slowly retreated to his room. Darcy cursed his luck, and that he had not grown closer to Lord Harry during his courtship with Georgiana. *Surely, HE would have been able to remove his wife from Elizabeth's room.*

Settled comfortably on the sofa in her sitting room and having overheard the entire exchange, Elizabeth light-heartedly chided, "Georgiana, you were awfully cruel to your brother."

"It serves him right. Had he not been so stubbornly obtuse, you two might have married months ago," she laughed.

Georgiana retrieved the box that she had set aside upon entering the room. "Elizabeth, I have something special for you. I know you have not had time to shop for a proper wedding trousseau. I have no doubt that you did not bring anything like this along with you. Though you may have purchased something in Lambton, it means so much to me as your sister to present you with this."

Georgiana handed Elizabeth the beautifully wrapped box, which they both eagerly unwrapped to behold an elegant negligée. Georgiana explained it was one of the dozens purchased on her behalf, but she had saved that one especially for Elizabeth, for she was certain it was only a matter of time.

Elizabeth blushed as Georgiana professed, "Though I shudder to think of my brother being amorous, I believe I must put that aside for now and ask you if there is anything you would like me to tell you of what to expect on your wedding night?"

"Oh, so you are a wise old married woman, are you?"

"Lord Harry has been very... shall we say, instructive," Georgiana confessed.

"Actually, and do not dare to repeat a word of this to another living soul, William has been an eager tutor himself," Elizabeth confided.

They both blushed as Georgiana simply mouthed, "O."

Elizabeth insisted, "Of course, a young maiden such as myself can always benefit from the wise counsel of an experienced woman. So, please go ahead and enlighten me."

~ Chapter 18 ~
Sense and Education

The day that the last Bennet daughter married was quite picturesque. The neighbours, even the very prosperous, stood outside with the tenants of Pemberley to witness the joyful couple as they emerged from the chapel after the wedding ceremony and ascended to their carriage. Hearty cheers and enthusiastic shouts of felicitations all added to the tremendous excitement that the young master of Pemberley had chosen a bride.

The prominent families from among the landed gentry in the area attended the wedding breakfast. The early afternoon event was quite festive as family and guests partook in a fabulous full-course meal. Darcy proudly introduced his bride to the neighbours with promises to call on them upon their return from the wedding journey. Georgiana and Lord Harry drew their share of attention as well, as none of the neighbours had ever met him before, what with their wedding in town and his family's residence in Stafford.

All of the traditions consistent with estates as grand as Pemberley were upheld as servants and tenants alike benefited from Mr. Darcy's largess on the day of his wedding. Mrs. Reynolds arranged a festive celebration for the tenants that included food, drink, music, and dancing. The servants were to be treated to a fine meal, punch, and cake later in the evening. Given the scale of the celebrations, one would have thought Mrs. Reynolds had been planning Mr. Darcy's wedding for months. In some respects, she indeed had, for she was sure that she had met the young woman who held Mr. Darcy's heart almost from the beginning of her acquaintance with Elizabeth.

It was with a mixture of sadness and joy that the Gardiners bid their beloved niece adieu. Thinking of the uplifting of her spirits in the two weeks since their departure from Longbourn, they felt that such happiness was well deserved by Elizabeth, and a long time in coming.

Lord Harry and Georgiana gladly changed their plans for the visit. They had originally intended to stay at Pemberley for two to three weeks before returning to London, and ultimately their home in Stafford. They decided to journey to Matlock for a week to allow the newly-weds some privacy. Thereafter, they planned to return to Pemberley for at least a week in order to spend time with Darcy and Elizabeth.

Though the prospect of losing the close camaraderie with his cousin and best friend in the world saddened Richard, one might never have known it based upon his demeanour. He was there for Darcy, every step of the way. He even offered words of encouragement, as well as his best wishes for a long and happy marriage with the woman of his dreams. Darcy tried to assure Richard that, in reality, nothing had changed, and they should stay as close as ever. Of course, Richard certainly knew better. He had witnessed such a transformation in his cousin over the past year, as one by one, Darcy let go of his carefree bachelor attitudes. Darcy had changed. Perhaps, Richard thought, it was time that he did the same.

As Lady Matlock observed how contented Darcy was with Elizabeth, she relinquished any lingering doubts over the union. She was truly happy for her nephew, and she told him so before leaving for her home. She also took Elizabeth aside for a brief *tête-à-tête* and a warm welcome into the family.

Finally, Lord Matlock took Darcy aside and assured him of his respect for his decision to follow his heart. He also spoke of his firm belief that Darcy's parents would be mightily proud of their son on that special day.

~~~

Alone, at last—within minutes of the departure of their last guest, Darcy escorted his bride upstairs to show her into the mistress's apartment. It was open, elegant, and decidedly feminine, the most beautiful room in the entire house, in Elizabeth's view. After the briefest of tours, and with his insistence that she should decorate the room to her own taste, Darcy pulled Elizabeth into his lap as he sat on the sofa.

He traced kisses down from her face, to her throat, and ended near the centre of her chest directly over her heart, lingering, invoking incredibly powerful and soothing feelings in his new bride. He said, "I believe that you, my love, are wearing too much clothing."

"Perhaps you should leave to allow me to change into something more comfortable for dinner. I will meet you downstairs in the drawing room in an hour. Perhaps I shall play something for you on the pianoforte to while the hours away."

"Heaven forbid that we are apart for so long on our wedding day," he said. He kissed her passionately. "I do not want to wait any longer to make you mine. Rather than I leave you to prepare for dinner, might I just leave you to prepare for our bed?" he whispered. Pressing light kisses behind her ear, "Dinner can wait. Do you not agree? Is a half an hour time enough?"
~~~

Thirty minutes later, Darcy stood before Elizabeth in her sitting room. "This is quite lovely," he said, fingering the delicate silk of her negligée.

"Thank you, kind sir. It is a gift from your sister."

"My sister?" He startled, quickly removing his hands. "Georgiana?"

"The one and only," Elizabeth ventured. "Oh, do not look so traumatised. She also shared some advice for our wedding night."

"Please spare me," he prayed, mortified by the very thought. He walked away to pour two glasses of wine. Handing one to Elizabeth, he said, "Come sit with me, Mrs. Darcy."

Elizabeth joined him on the sofa, and he immediately pulled her close into his embrace and lightly kissed her hair.

She repeated her new appellation, "Mrs. Darcy—I love it. I love you."

"And I love you, my dearest."

"Of course, you did not always feel that way. I recall that I was, at one time, not handsome enough to tempt you."

Darcy coloured. "You were not supposed to hear that, my love. I apologise; clearly, I was delusional. For as long as I can recollect, I have considered you as one of the handsomest women of my acquaintance."

"One of many, I suspect." She sipped from her wine glass.

"Hardly," he confessed. "I have never adored, nor loved anyone as I do you. You are by far the most beautiful woman I know."

Elizabeth's spirits soon rising to playfulness, she wanted her husband to account for his having ever fallen in love with her. "How could you begin?" asked she. "I can comprehend your going on charmingly, when you had once made a beginning; but what could set you off in the first place?"

"I cannot fix on the hour, or the spot, or the look, or the words, which laid the foundation. It is too long ago. I was in the middle before I knew that I had begun."

"My beauty you withstood, and as for my behaviour, we butted heads more often than not. Now be sincere; did you admire me for my impertinence?"

"For the liveliness of your mind, I did."

"You may as well call it impertinence at once. It was very little less. The fact is that you were sick of civility, of deference, of officious attention from the Caroline Bingleys and Theresa Ruperts of the *ton*. I roused and interested you, because I was so unlike them. There—I have saved you the trouble of accounting for it; and really, all things considered, I begin to think it perfectly reasonable."

"I dare not argue your point, my love." He paused to kiss her. "Now tell me, when did you realise that you had fallen in love with me?"

"Let me see," she started and as playful as ever, acted as if she considered her next words carefully, "It came on so gradually that I hardly know when it began. However, I believe I must date it from my first seeing the beautiful grounds at Pemberley."

"Oh, you will pay dearly for those sentiments, Mrs. Darcy," he uttered, as he took her glass and placed it on a side table with his. He pulled her into his arms and pressed light kisses all over her face and neckline.

"Come with me," Darcy said as he took Elizabeth's hand and led her to the adjoining door of his apartment. Stepping aside to allow her to enter before him, he stood back to watch her as she viewed his room for the first time.

Elizabeth walked around the room admiring his taste. It was just as she had imagined… expansive, stately, and very masculine. Recalling his words that he wished to have her in his bed every night, she stood directly beside it. It was impressive. Elizabeth had never seen a bed as large as that before. She thought, *So, this is where he sleeps.*

Darcy stood behind her with his hands lightly pressed to her waist, favouring her neckline with pleasing kisses. Placing himself between Elizabeth and the bed, he leaned against its side and pulled her into a tight embrace. He kissed her deeply. Slowly, he removed her negligée and allowed it to fall to the floor. As much as she thought herself ready for that moment, she trembled at the intense excitement of it all. Darcy looked at her intently.

In no clear rush, Darcy trailed soft kisses from her head to her breasts, giving each one its due. Lowering himself to his knees, he massaged her hips whilst his tongue explored her silken belly. Continuing his path lower and at length breathing in her sweet essence, he pleasured her as he had never done before. If not for Darcy's strong hands firmly grasping and massaging her hips, Elizabeth would have been unable to stand. She quivered all over when, at length, he stood to lift her into his arms and lowered her onto his bed.

Entranced, Elizabeth watched as Darcy removed his clothing, piece by piece, and as with her negligée, dropped them to the floor. The taste of her upon his lips left him with no doubt that she was ready for him.

He quickly joined her on their marriage bed. Sensing some uncertainty on her part over what was to come, Darcy patiently enticed her with teasing kisses. He softly kissed her from below her ears, along her neckline and her shoulders, sending glorious sensations throughout her body. Elizabeth entwined her fingers in his soft hair as he cupped her breasts, lavished them with massaging kisses, and sucked her taut nipples. Perceiving a complete surrender of any remaining apprehensions and taking immense pleasure in her passionate reciprocation of his ardent attentions, he commenced slow rhythmic thrusts between her thighs, slightly brushing against her overly moist, sensitive lips. Elizabeth climaxed once more.

As she calmed, he entered her, slowly progressing inch by inch, only pausing when he pierced her maidenhood to acclimate her body to his presence, while urging her to stay just as still. Upon her body's welcoming acceptance of him, he guided her to wrap her legs tightly about him and commenced an easy rhythm to which Elizabeth quickly attuned. They maintained their harmony for some time, as she matched him in pace and intensity until she cried out in rapture, a cry so utterly pleasing to Darcy that he soon moaned in ecstasy amidst the most magnificent release he had ever experienced.

Darcy rolled over unto his back, holding her firmly and positioning her astride his body while remaining deep inside of her. He was insatiable as he engulfed her with impassioned kisses, ardent caresses and sensuous teasing until he was soon as erect as before. He guided her up and down his length, favouring her in just the right spot for what seemed a gloriously infinite passage of time, until she exploded inside. Darcy hushed her endless ecstatic cries of bliss with impassioned kisses and soon released his seed deep inside her once more.

~~~

Darcy awakened an hour or so later, happy indeed to find his bride nestled closely in his embrace, her head resting on his chest. The last thing he wanted to do was awaken her from her slumber. She was the most beautiful thing he had ever beheld. The passion they had shared was beyond belief, in his estimation. He never had dreamed it would be so.

Reluctantly, he left her side to make arrangements for their meal. He returned to his room with a tray he had ordered for
~~~

their evening repast. He had no intention for either of them to leave their rooms for terribly long, not even to dine. Placing the tray on a table, he went to his bed to stir his sleeping beauty. He feathered light kisses along her face and nibbled at her earlobes until she roused.

"Come, my love. Let us have some dinner."

"Dinner? Is it that time already?"

"Actually, it is long past dinner time. You have slept for hours… not that I object. You will need your rest, for I plan to keep you busy all night," he said, as he kissed her moist lips.

"That sounds promising," she responded.

"Indeed, now come, let me nourish you before I ravish you repeatedly," he seductively teased.

"I like the sound of that, Mr. Darcy. Hand me my gown please, so that I might join you."

"If you insist," he said as he handed her the gown. She slipped the gown on while remaining under the bed covers. Darcy could not help but smile at her newly found modesty.

After partaking of a light dinner, followed by a short repose in her sitting room to allow the staff some time to tidy his room, Darcy took Elizabeth back to his bed. They embarked upon a lovemaking excursion that extended late into the night. Hours passed, or so it seemed, as he sought successfully to bring her endless and repeated pleasures while managing to temper his own. When at last, he succumbed, it was wonderful.

~~~

The early morning sun beckoning, Elizabeth wakened in Darcy's arms, her head resting comfortably on his chest, his hand resting on hers. She snuggled closer and released a deep, contented sigh.
~~~

Elizabeth glanced up to study his face. He was quite beautiful. *Who would have imagined that a man of sense and education with much knowledge of the world could seem so youthful and innocent while he slept?*

Innocent, she thought with a smile as she recalled their wedding night. She had been all nerves and anticipation as any new bride should be—for despite all of their amorous endeavours in the days leading up to the wedding, absolutely nothing could have prepared her for becoming his wife. She had been told to expect some degree of pain. *Was there any pain?* She wondered. Whether or not she experienced pain, she could hardly recall, such was her need for fulfilment as he gently pushed inside her inch by inch, tantalisingly in tune with his slow, probing kisses. She seemed to remember his pausing, telling her to relax as he filled her completely. Amidst slow thrusts, urgent thrusts, time ceased to have meaning. At length, she experienced an incredibly powerful crest. She screamed out as euphoric sensation upon sensation flooded through her. With his lips engulfing hers, she felt a thunderous explosion ensued by a wonderfully soothing warmth.

~ *Chapter 19* ~
Again and Again

The Darcys stayed tucked away at Pemberley for the entirety of the following week. They rarely left their rooms during the first couple of days. Both gained a greater appreciation of their love as they began to confide intimate details of their lives, Elizabeth more so than her husband. For after living in his homes for over a year and a half, Elizabeth was all too familiar with Darcy's closest relations, their idiosyncrasies, and their expectations of him. Darcy, however, had not been in the company of her family since their earlier acquaintance in Hertfordshire. He was completely oblivious to the trials she had suffered at Longbourn. Elizabeth had grown so accustomed to confiding her innermost hopes and fears in no one other than Jane, and so it had been all her life. It profoundly touched Elizabeth when Darcy confessed to her that his greatest wish was that she would let him be the one she turned to. She was eager to share everything with him. Now, it seemed, her husband held that coveted role of friend and confidant in her life. Darcy understood as Elizabeth expressed her deepest concern to him.

"I did not miss the fact that your mother thought very little of me, but then again, I did nothing to court her good opinion. I promise you that I will attempt to make up for that when she visits with us," he said, when Elizabeth spoke of her mother's abhorrence towards him.

"I am afraid you do not know my mama. It is not that she merely dislikes you. She is not easily swayed."

"You underestimate my charms, I see. I believe I can be quite persuasive."

"Careful, sir," she expressed, "too much of the famous Darcy charm and Mama might insist upon residing here at Pemberley with us."

"I understand. Nonetheless, I want you to be certain that your family, all of your relations, are welcome here at Pemberley for as long as they wish to stay. The dowager house has remained undisturbed for far too long."

"I appreciate that, more than you know, but I sometimes think that one can actually be settled too near one's family. In such cases as this, no cause is better served by good roads. Where there is a fortune which makes the travelling cost unimportant, distance becomes no evil. What with your fortune, I should imagine the long journey to Hertfordshire is a trifling pursuit at best," she spoke with a smile.

"Then, that settles it. We will do all that we can in assuring that your mother lives comfortably, but she must continue to live far, far away in Hertfordshire," he teased.

"Thank you. I love you, Mr. Darcy." She was glad that he understood her apprehensions as regarded her mother and would not let that affect his esteem.

"Mr. Darcy?" he echoed.

"William... I love you, William."

~~~

Soon Darcy found it necessary to work with his steward in preparation for his planned absence from Pemberley for the rest of
~~~

the summer into early fall, as well as finish the arrangements for the wedding journey. This left Elizabeth with much time on her hands. Having resided at Pemberley for months, Elizabeth was no stranger to the overall workings of the great estate. She began to meet with Mrs. Reynolds daily to become familiar with the details of the household administration. She enjoyed an excellent relationship with Mrs. Reynolds, one that she was eager to keep up, for she recognised the value of having her as a strong ally. Elizabeth also recognised the importance of maintaining a strict routine in the household management. She was impressed with Mrs. Reynolds's seemingly effortless rule. Elizabeth accepted that for the foreseeable future, what with the extended honeymoon they were about to take, Mrs. Reynolds would continue to manage the household. Still she was eager to learn all that she could, so that she might take over her responsibilities as mistress immediately upon her return.

The next several days were spent thus. Darcy and Elizabeth generally slept late, as newly-weds ought and separated for a few hours during the day to attend to estate and household matters. They promptly reunited to enjoy leisurely afternoons in each other's company, followed by intimate dinners.

They spent each night agreeably, in the arms of one another.

Georgiana returned during the second week to spend her last days at Pemberley before moving to her husband's home in Stafford. Elizabeth endeavoured to keep to her schedule of daily meetings with Mrs. Reynolds, as well as to spend time with Georgiana during her stay. The Darcys also received a few callers during that week—a very few, as they were anxious to spend as much time alone as possible without appearing inhospitable. Sometimes, it could not be helped.

~~~
~~~

Lady Catherine and Anne were away from Rosings Park when the letter from Darcy arrived, in which he had stated his intention to marry Miss Elizabeth Bennet. Lady Catherine was distraught by Darcy's revelation at Matlock that he did not intend to marry Anne. The resulting getaway to Brighton had provided a much-needed period of convalescence. Somehow, Lady Catherine's housekeeper had failed to forward Darcy's letter to her during her sojourn. Having read the letter in haste and without properly ascertaining the all the details, she immediately arranged to travel to Pemberley to put a stop to such nonsense, completely unaware that the happy event had occurred over a fortnight ago.

Upon her arrival at Pemberley to make her opinion on the marriage known, she was extremely vexed—first of all, to learn that the marriage had indeed occurred, and second, to find that the couple had departed for their wedding journey. Lady Catherine allowed little time to pass before travelling to Matlock to chastise her brother and sister for allowing and even participating in the travesty.

"I always suspected that little upstart had Darcy in her sights from the moment of my acquaintance with her at Rosings Park. She practically had him sniffing at her heels and bowing to her whims. Imagine Darcy treating her, a paid companion, as Georgiana's equal. I thought it merely a passing fancy. Never did I believe he would abandon the principles of a lifetime, only to succumb to her arts and allurements. Alas, I was mistaken. Nevertheless, fear not, I will carry my point. I will see to it that they are censured, slighted, and despised by everyone connected with us. Their alliance will be deemed a disgrace, their names will not be mentioned, and no one of decency will receive them. This is not to be borne," Lady Catherine warned her brother and sister.

Coming to Elizabeth's defence, Lord and Lady Matlock both defended the union and spoke of the joy they had witnessed on the day of the wedding.

"I am shocked and astonished. I expected to find both of you reasonable. However, do not deceive yourself into a belief that I will ever recede," Lady Catherine persisted.

"Then, it will be you who are perceived as a fool, for we will do all that is within our power in support of Fitzwilliam's marriage. You would be wise to do the same, if for nothing else than for the sake of appearances and family harmony.

"I will host a dinner party for the two of them immediately after the Twelfth Night Ball in January. Mrs. Fitzwilliam Darcy will be officially presented," declared Lady Matlock.

"Why, that obstinate, headstrong girl! Unrefined, a gentleman's daughter indeed," Lady Catherine spat, sarcastically. "One of five sisters, reared with no governess or benefit of the masters. She will prove an embarrassment to the Fitzwilliam family name. This marriage is a travesty. I came here with the determined resolution of carrying my purpose. I will not be dissuaded from it! I have not been used to submit to any person's whims. I have not been in the habit of brooking disappointment."

"Leave it, Catherine! It is done! It is time to make the best of it. Fitzwilliam appears as happy as we have ever known him to be," Lord Matlock stated adamantly.

Her Ladyship was highly incensed. "And this is your real opinion! This is your final resolve! Very well, I shall now know how to act. Do not imagine I will be silenced on this, or that your desires for the new Mrs. Darcy will be gratified. I came to try you. I hoped to find you reasonable; but depend upon it, I will carry my point."

Lady Catherine ranted on, in that way, until she was at the door of the house. Turning hastily around, she added, "I take no leave of you, brother. You deserve no such attention. I am most seriously displeased. You have not heard the last of me," Lady Catherine threatened.

~ ~ ~

At the same time, those at Longbourn engaged in the art of persuasion, as well. Mrs. Bennet was determined to set off for Pemberley, or London, or wherever the Darcys were, to teach Elizabeth all she needed to know to be a great mistress.

When Elizabeth's family received the news of her engagement to Darcy, Mrs. Bennet acclaimed to anyone who would listen how she knew it would be. She was sure Elizabeth was so clever for something. She would not even allow that Elizabeth was in love with the proud man and practically implied that her daughter simply was mercenary. She thanked God that her prayers had been answered and that their lot in life had been raised immensely. Now, her greatest concern was that Elizabeth would somehow ruin it all by failing to be a good mistress of Pemberley, thereby incurring Mr. Darcy's wrath and stemming his benevolence towards the family.

"But Mama, Lizzy has promised to invite the entire family to Pemberley for an extended holiday in December. Everyone is invited, including the Gardiners and my Uncle and Aunt Phillips. Surely, we should honour their wishes. It would be unmannerly to visit them sooner," Mary insisted.

Poor Mary... with Jane comfortably settled ten miles away and Kitty similarly situated with her husband, she alone bore the responsibility to sit with her mother and placate her nerves.

"Oh never you mind all that!" Mrs. Bennet wailed. "Have you no compassion for what your sister must surely be suffering? I am her mother. Pray, why should I stand on ceremony?

What does Lizzy know about being the mistress of such a grand estate? She needs me!"

"Begging your pardon, but I shall not advance a single shilling to assist you in imposing upon Mr. and Mrs. Darcy." Mrs. Bennet spun around and stared at her son-in-law with her mouth gaped open. "I demand that you desist at once and look forward to visiting with them in December, along with the rest of the family." Mr. Collins spoke with such authority as to silence Mrs. Bennet from any further speech on the matter.

~~~

Charles Bingley was delighted to hear that his old friend had finally chosen a wife. He was sure that they might reconnect now that Darcy had relinquished his bachelor status and joined the ranks of marriage. The fact that Lady Grace and Elizabeth got along swimmingly, he deemed favourable, as well. Bingley was positive that he and his family would always be graciously received at Pemberley.

Miss Caroline Bingley was deeply mortified by the news of Darcy's marriage, but as she thought it advisable to retain the right of visiting at Pemberley, decided it best to drop all her resentment. Once presented with the opportunity, she would be almost as attentive to Darcy as ever and would make an effort to pay off every arrear of civility to Elizabeth.

News of Mr. Darcy's wedding equally astounded Miss Theresa Rupert. She pondered long and hard as she considered his choice of a bride. Elizabeth Darcy née Bennet... *Elizabeth Bennet*, she thought, *where have I heard that name before?*

Lady Harriette was beside herself with the news. Now that they were family, she felt that the elusive Mr. Darcy was firmly within her grasp. *No matter*, she thought, *he is married, not dead.* Of course, she would marry as well, un-
~~~

doubtedly to someone of high rank and birth. As regards Darcy, she would simply bide her time.

~~~

The Darcys spent a glorious honeymoon in the beautiful spa towns of Bath and Cheltenham, as well as in Weymouth, the highly fashionable seaside resort. Darcy let the finest lodgings available in each town.

Among the most exciting adventures during their stay in Bath were frequent outings to the theatre, assembly rooms, and concerts. Elizabeth's favourite outing was a visit to Sydney Gardens. Darcy found that he enjoyed the concerts and the dazzling illuminations and fireworks displays as much as his dear wife.

Though it rivalled Bath in its various forms of amusement, it was the semi-rural charms of Cheltenham that most delighted Elizabeth. The private lodging secured by Darcy for their stay was a spacious and airy villa with its own garden and staffed with a full complement of servants. Darcy and Elizabeth were contented with early morning walks before breakfast, leisurely afternoons in the seclusion of their holiday home, and nightly entertainment in the Assembly Room and the Royal Theatre.

The final destination of the wedding journey was the picturesque coastal town of Weymouth. There, they lodged in a beautiful villa, situated by the sea. Elizabeth and Darcy enjoyed easy access to the beach, and took complete advantage to enjoy frequent sea bathing excursions.

On one balmy afternoon, an attractive young lady and an older woman approached Darcy and Elizabeth whilst they were out for a leisurely stroll.

"Mr. Darcy, imagine seeing you here in Weymouth, of all places!"
~~~

"Lady Calder," Darcy bowed.

"I heard of your dear sister Georgiana's, or rather Lady Georgiana's, marriage to Lord Harry Middleton. Pray, how does she get along?"

"She does quite well, thank you," Darcy replied curtly.

"And you sir, what brings you to Weymouth, of all places?" she asked, without acknowledging Elizabeth.

"Pardon me, Mrs. Elizabeth Darcy, this is Lady Gwendolyn Calder. Lady Calder, allow me to introduce my wife."

"Did you say your wife?" she retorted. "Surely, you jest. I have not heard a word of your marrying. Can this be true?"

"Would I say so if it were otherwise?"

"Of course, if you say it, then it must be so," she replied, sensing his annoyance. Still, she was curious. She asked, "When did this come about?"

"Lady Calder, it is a pleasure to meet you. Mr. Darcy and I married nine weeks ago. We are here on our honeymoon," Elizabeth intervened.

"The pleasure is all mine, I am sure, Mrs. Darcy," she condescended. "Mr. Darcy, I am here with my parents. They would be honoured to receive you. Oh, and you must bring your lovely wife along as well."

"Lady Calder, please be assured that should I decide to call upon your parents, it would only be in the company of Mrs. Darcy. Now, I beg you, please pardon us, we must be on our way. Goodbye, Madam," Darcy said, as he bowed and resumed his walk with Elizabeth on his arm.

Some moments later, Darcy said, "I hope you were not offended by Lady Calder just then, my love."

"Certainly not... she is much like most of the ladies I have met since my acquaintance with you, sir; although, I wonder at her attitude towards you. Is she another Miss Theresa Rupert?"

"I am afraid so, my love."

"She seemed particularly familiar. Did you fancy her at all?"

"No, that is to say, no more or no less than any of the other young ladies thrown in my path by my aunt over the years."

"I imagine I shall have to get used to meeting old rivals."

"No, not rivals, simply old acquaintances. No one from the past should ever concern you. My heart belongs to you alone. It has always been so, as it will remain forever more," he whispered in her ear in an openly public display of affection that might have been frowned upon had it been witnessed. Of course, the entire display was completely unobserved.

How advantageous for the Darcys that their beach-front house boasted a covered veranda off the side facing the water. With nothing separating the house and the water except for a long sandy, secluded beach, that night, as well as every other night, the private veranda was the spot of clandestine intimacies most appropriate for a young newly-wed husband and his bride.

~~~

Sunlight streaming in, Elizabeth awakened in Darcy's arms. At last, they had returned to Pemberley a fortnight ago. Her early morning rambles had indeed become a thing of the past. She thought nothing of lying awake thus, admiring her husband's beautiful face. Upon that particular morning, while watching him as he slept, she recalled the night before.

He had made love to her through the night, evoking sensations that kindled her passions like fire, yet soothed her body like a gentle rain. Filling her completely with deep rhythmic thrusts again and again, his only purpose, it had seemed, was to give her pleasure. Darcy had engaged in a soft, familiar calling of her name at his moment of completion that had left her enthralled.
~~~

He was an extraordinary lover, she surmised, as generous as he had pledged he would be on the day of their engagement. Despite the independent spirit that defined her, night after night, Elizabeth gave in to the overwhelming sense of impassioned surrender. On the day of their engagement, he had told her that he wanted her, and he needed her. She realised now that she wanted him and needed him just as much. Her husband, her lover, her friend, and confidant… he was everything to her.

Thinking back to the beginning of their marriage, Elizabeth reminisced on the many ways he loved to explore every aspect of her body with his long fingers; sometimes one, more often times two, massaging, gauging—determining whether she was ready. She was always ready. She marvelled at the many parts of her body that he explored with his tongue, light and flickering when she wanted it to be, hard and firm when she needed it to be. Recalling how much he seemed to enjoy it when she paid homage to his broad chest, she wondered if there might be any other part of him that would revel in such treatment. As her fingers traced down along the rippled path of his torso, she considered… he certainly liked it enough when she touched him there.

Darcy thought he was dreaming, but unlike times before, the dream was more vivid, more real. His hands were deeply entwined in long flowing tresses. The sound of soft moans, an exquisite trailing silkiness, and a warm, moist cradling accompanied his own urgent thrusting... *most undoubtedly—not a dream.*

Some hours later that same morning, it was Darcy's turn to awaken and admire his wife's beauty. He caressed her and gently nibbled on her earlobes to rouse her while she feigned sleep to savour the quiet intimacy of the moment as long as possible. Her soft moans gave her away when she could no longer restrain her responses to his ardent attentions.

"Good morning, my beautiful bride, I was beginning to think you might never stir.

"Is it my fault you insist upon interrupting my sleep each night?"

"Indeed, it is entirely your own doing. As passionate as you are, how am I to resist?"

"Far be it from me to argue your point, sir."

Continuing his tender adulation, he asked, "Then, what shall we do today?"

"To linger here, by your side, and make love all day is my only wish," she decreed.

"Your wish is my command," he murmured, eager to fulfil her every desire. Spooned behind her, he flooded sensual kisses to the back of her neck. Once buried inside her, he engaged in a cadence of deep thrusts, altering from gentle and unhurried to powerful and swift, glorious and intense.

Words could not describe this new experience. He was bringing her to the edge repeatedly, easing and then resuming his passionate onslaught. She could take no more. Elizabeth unceremoniously straddled him and took her own pleasure. Satisfied, she affectionately repaid him the same kindness that he had rendered her.

~~~

The two lovers were on the balcony outside of the master apartment under the moon and the stars, enjoying the warm night air. Darcy wrapped Elizabeth in his loving embrace as he stood behind her, sprinkling light kisses behind her ear and along the back of her neck.

"How are you feeling this evening, Mrs. Darcy?" he murmured affectionately.
~~~

"I feel wonderful. I could not wish for a more perfect evening," she said, as she looked heavenly in admiration of the bright, full moon casting a romantic glow over the pond.

"Surely, there is something I can do to make the evening even more perfect," he softly spoke, suggestively. "My greatest wish is to please you."

"Say you love me," she said blissfully, as she cradled herself closer into his arms.

"You know I do, dearest."

"Yes, but I want you to say it to me again and again, every day for the rest of our lives."

Darcy guided his lovely wife around to face him. He lifted her chin to gaze into the eyes of the woman who meant more to him than life itself. He lightly kissed her right cheek and seductively whispered into her ear, ever so subtly, "I love you."

Darcy returned his gaze into her eyes before lightly kissing her left cheek, and whispered, ever so softly, "I love you."

He looked into his wife's eyes once more, placed a light kiss upon the tip of her nose, and whispered, ever so tenderly, "I love you."

Capturing her amazing eyes once more, he lightly brushed her lips with his fingertips. Before bringing his lips to hers and kissing her passionately, he whispered, ever so ardently, "I love you."

Acknowledgements and Credits

- Jane Austen, *"Pride and Prejudice"*
- William Shakespeare, *"The Taming of the Shrew"*
- Percy Bysshe Shelley, *"Laon and Cythna"* and *"The Masque of Anarchy"*
- The JAFF Community

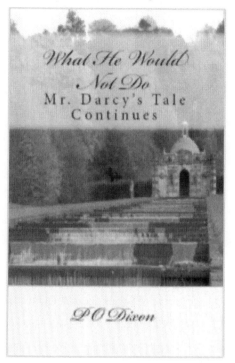

11947561R0014

Made in the USA
Lexington, KY
12 November 2011